TOP KNO

TOP KNOCKER

John Fitzmaurice Mills

WOLFHOUND PRESS

Wolfhound Press receives financial assistance from
The Arts Council (An Chomhairle Ealaíon), Dublin, Ireland.

First published 1990 by
WOLFHOUND PRESS
68 Mountjoy Square, Dublin 1.

British Library Cataloguing in Publication Data
    Mills, John FitzMaurice, 1917–
    Top knocker
    I. Title
    823.914 [F]

    ISBN 0-86327-280-0

Cover design: Jan de Fouw
Typesetting: Seton Music Graphics Ltd., Bantry
Printed by: The Guernsey Press Ltd., Guernsey

Contents

Cast of characters

Aideen Uniacke	*About to become a Top Knocker*
Louise Uniacke	*Her mother*
Neptune Blood	*Family retainer to the Uniackes*
Katty Blood	*His mother*
Mary Dancy	*The last of the inside staff*
Batsy, The Hon. Beatrice Croker	*Eccentric cousin of the Uniackes*
Sean and his wife	*Butler and housekeeper to Batsy*
René Culhane	*A painter of the French school*
Lord and Lady Kilbandan	*Relations of René's*
Tim and Nell Sinclair	*International Art Dealers, with a way of their own*
Angélique	*Director of the Ateliers,where nothing is impossible*
Igor	*Her bodyguard*
Comte Michel de Pollenard	*Once owner of the Château Bienheureux*
Chief Superintendent Con Murphy	*Sergeant of the Garda Siochána (Police)*
Sergeant Bridget Kelly	*Ban Garda (female police)*
Percival Mangon	*Auctioneer, with an eye for himself*
Alfie Brigg	*His clerk, bodyguard and hitman*
Rachel Hollow	*Assistant to Mangon*
Myles Fyrken	*Uniacke's family solicitor*
Herta Poll	*An Austrian, well known across Europe in salesrooms and salons*
Warren B. Westonhofer	*American Art Assessor*
Hiram K. Frack	*American Collector*
Greg Blenney	*Ready for anything truck driver*
Gladys Pilch and Rutty Evans	*End of the line antique traders.*

One

Clare is the odd one out in Ireland. A large chunk of the top half is the wild bald Burren. At the bottom is Bunratty Castle for the instant Medievalists. In the centre is a tiny cathedral that claims as Bishop none less than the Pope. Scattered over the unique landscape are hundreds of stone-forts, stone-circles, cairns and souterrains overshadowed in part by the formidable uprights and capstone of the great Poulnabrone Portal Domen, almost four thousand years old.

But none of this meant anything to Gladys Pilch as she stood beside the ancient Ford Transit parked in the main street of Corrofin. This vehicle served as office, showroom, store and living quarters for both herself and her business partner Rutty Evans.

She looked in dismay at the knuckles of her right hand:

'I've had enough for today — must have knocked up a hundred houses or more.'

Rutty put his arm round her shoulder:

'But look what we've got, Glad.'

'What we've got! Half a dozen donkey brasses, an old scales with weights that don't match, a box of chipped china, a cracked hand-bell, and those two old prints in frames with broken glass...'

Rutty broke in:

'Watch it — don't stare — look nice and casual.'

A dark green Peugeot saloon was approaching down the road that came from Ennis. It slowed and stopped by the little grocery and a tall, slender, dark-haired girl got out and disappeared into the dark interior after threading her way past barrels of dog biscuits, coils of rope and a dilapidated newspaper stand. A few minutes later she came out with a carrier of shopping and got

7

back into the Peugeot. Without a glance at the Ford Transit the girl drove off in the direction of Kilfenora.

'What's so interesting about her then?'

'That, Gladys, was Aideen Uniacke,' answered Rutty.

'The one from the house for tomorrow.'

'Not quite what you'd expect, is she? I caught a glimpse of her when I was helping Percy with the arrangements last time I was over.'

'Bit on the tall side I'd have thought for you, Rutty.'

'Now, now', countered Rutty, 'let's get this stuff sorted out and get back to the Pub. Where did you say it was — somewhere near Feakle? What a name!'

Gladys and Rutty belonged to that order of the antique trade that went under the collective title of 'knockers'. Their base, if it could be called that, was a small 'put-together' bungalow on the north western side of London's green-belt; about a quarter of an acre went with it that was secured behind pig-netting heavily stitched with barbed wire. When they were away hunting, all was left in the charge of Rutty's nephew Doug and Pilot, an eccentric and savage Staffordshire bull terrier.

* * * * * *

Aideen drove through Kilfenora and took the road to Lisdoon-varna and then branched left for Liscannor. A few more miles and she came to the narrow entrance of the car park she sought. Out here one could find a solitude of a special kind. Even if there were other people, she could find that seclusion that comes when one is suddenly confronted with something in nature which is so fine, so immense, so beautiful that a mere mortal shrinks almost out of sight.

The Cliffs of Moher had long ago married something in her consciousness; it was proving to be a bond for life. At their highest point they towered to seven hundred feet, coming up almost vertically from the foaming Atlantic. The cliffs were layered as some gargantuan gâteau, with broad stripes of near-black, deep warm brown, dark dusty yellow and pink-white. They got their name from an ancient caher or stone-fort called *Moher Ui Ruaidhin* which had once stood above Hag's Head to the south of the main heights.

Aideen parked the car and got out taking the rug from the back seat. She passed the local commerce: the man with the goat which would jump on the back of a donkey and stand there whilst one had a keep-sake photo taken, the seller of home-knit sweaters and the ice-lolly merchant; she paused for a minute at the lookout slab. From here the eye could marvel at the myriad seabirds in their unceasing display of flight: terns, black-backed monster gulls, puffins, cormorants, and every now and then a scattering when a flock of gannets with close-held wings dropped almost vertically until they entered the waters far below. Turning, Aideen leaned into the wind and started the long climb up to O'Brien's Tower. Such a panorama could never be stale. From this height, looking down onto the rising swell, the wildness of the waves became reduced so much that they were little more than stitches in an immense tapestry at the centre of which were the Aran islands; closest was Inisheer, a little farther back was Inishmaan, and then tailing away into the afternoon mist was Inishmore. For a moment the three of them gave her the impression of a small flotilla of age-old vessels steaming in line ahead into Galway Bay.

Spreading the rug against a small hillock Aideen sat down and for several minutes let Moher take over to try and sort out the traumatic events taking place in her own life.

It was now mid-August. Four months ago, she and her mother, Louise, had come back from a shopping trip to Limerick and had entered Mellick to find a long white envelope propped up against the rose-bowl on the small pie-crust table in the hall. It was addressed to both of them in her father's slightly exaggerated hand. The blunt message was clear from the first sentence: investments had gone wrong, gambles had failed, he had had to clear the joint-account for travel expenses...hoped they would forgive him...better if he was out of the way. The house and land Louise could do what she liked with. No mention made of where he was going, no hint left of an address.

In those first moments, Louise showed an unexpected strength. She walked over to the telephone and called her local Bank of Ireland manager. She fired off a few very direct questions. There was a long pause before she thanked the Manager and replaced the receiver.

'Well, darling, it's just like he says, and with a few additions. Not only is the joint account cleared; must have been quite bulky for him to carry £7,047 in notes, but he's also taken all the share certificates. We've nothing left.'

She tottered over to the couch beside the fireplace and collapsed into a series of numbing sobs followed by silent weeping. Aideen waited until the blow had lessened before she went over to sit beside her mother.

Louise wiped her eyes and took her daughter's hand:

'It's actually even a bit worse than that,' she said. 'The way George Flaherty was talking I'm afraid that Daddy has let us in for a lot more than it seems.'

Louise's grey eyes caught those of her daughter and filled up with tears again.

'How much have you got in your own account, darling?'

'About £120'. Aideen allowed herself a wry smile. She felt strangely unreal as if this was all happening to a ghost of herself.

'I expect that he's taken the other car as well.' Louise rose. 'Let's go and look.'

At the door they met Neptune Blood coming up the entrance steps. The last of what would have been called the outside staff — gone were the days of coachman and grooms, of head-gardener and under gardeners. Now they had just the one faithful who so loved the place that he managed to keep the great lawns, cultivate the flower beds and grow enough vegetables to feed them. Neptune's family had served the Uniackes of Mellick ever since the house had been built in 1763 to the design of one of Richard Castle's talented assistants. Somehow just seeing Neptune brought a soothing effect. Aideen had often thought that Neptune must have descended from one of those Irish giants whose graves are turned up now and then in the hills. He looked about six feet seven inches with the breadth of a stable door to his shoulders. He had arms that could wrestle a fly-maddened cow to stillness and his clenched fist had the force of an oaken mallet, as one or two had found out when they ended on the wrong side in an argument. His hair was the colour of rust, his eyes a clear, honest blue that at that moment spoke of something close to compassion.

'Afternoon, Ma'am' he said, and then quite simply he reached out towards them and gently took their hands.

'Forgive me saying so — but I know'. He had all the sight of things done and not spoken that is a birthright of the Irish.

'Did you see any of this?' Louise asked him.

'Yes Ma'am. I was tidying up around the summerhouse at the back of the lawn and a big grey car drove up — German I think it was, the number plate wasn't Irish. The master was in it with two other men. He got out with one of them and they went into the house and after about fifteen minutes came out again with three big suitcases which they carried round to the garage. A couple of minutes later the master and one of the men are driving out in his Bentley with the other man following.'

'Thank you, Neptune.' Louise looked back up at him from the direction of the drive where she had followed his pointing arm. 'Have you seen Mary?'

'She's gone down to her mother and is due back any minute.'

Mary Dancy, like Neptune, was a remainder — the last of the indoor staff. For several years now she had cooked, washed and cleaned for the family.

'Neptune,' Louise continued, 'we are going to have to do some sorting out and it's going to affect all four of us. Miss Aideen and I will be in the drawing-room. When Mary comes back do bring us in that fruit cake I was keeping with a pot of Bewley's Ceylon — make it really strong — and four of those big harvest cups.'

On the way to the drawing room Aideen found herself marvelling at her mother's composure. She herself felt that she was desperately trying to refocus to the image she had been a few hours before. Once in the room she raised the blind and got busy making the Pembroke table ready by the window. She had barely spread its leaves when there was a tap at the door. First came in a red-eyed Mary carrying a lace cloth which she spread on the table, then Neptune close behind carrying with all the dignity and devotion of a butler cum altar boy the best and biggest silver tray. He lowered it on to the table and then stood back a step or two. Mary went over to Louise and with a little bob of a curtsey said,

'Mr. Neptune told me Ma'am — I'm so sorry.'

'Now come on you two, this is a council of war. Sit yourselves down and let's have a good cuppa. Will you cut the cake, Neptune?'

For a few minutes there was an awkward jerky conversation; this was a strange do for the staff — tea with the family and poured out from the silver pot. They ate and drank delicately as if at some great feast. As the rich brown liquid settled the nerves, they relaxed and it all became easy. Louise took command, explaining the bare facts and what they entailed.

After giving the run-down on her husband's debts, which were being estimated in hundreds of thousands, Louise took a deep breath before pronouncing: 'We shall have to sell Mellick and most of the contents and move to the cottage.'

Aideen found herself nodding, struck by the sheer simplicity of the statement. The others thought of the cottage, Quin Cottage it was called, usually let to holiday-makers but empty at the moment. The Uniackes and they would soon become neighbours for it lay outside the demesne towards Lough Graney beyond the other two Mellick cottages in which they lived themselves, each with their mother. But Louise was continuing unabated:

'I have decided that you shall both have the freehold of your places and I shall be telling Mr. Fyrken to make out the deeds as soon as possible. I'm afraid I can't offer you much but there will be something in the way of a sum.'

Neptune broke in,

'Ma'am, what are you saying — you mean you want us to up and leave the Uniackes — no Blood is going to do that. I know that Mary thinks the same. Giving us the cottages just seals the bargain.'

'What bargain, Neptune?'

'Just this, Mrs. Uniacke and you, Miss Aideen. In a way we are part of the family — please forgive me for so speaking — but you've got a bond here that you're not going to break, Ma'am. We'll stand by you and do anything we can.'

Aideen looked across at her mother and then at Mary who was nodding tearfully and then back at Neptune whose eyes were shining and earnest. She got up and said, decisively and with a smile:

'Mary, we need four tumblers and a jug of water. Neptune, there's a bottle on the sideboard in the dining-room.' A few moments later and the four of them were standing to clink glasses and look to the future.

*   *   *   *   *   *

Louise, who never seemed to have done more than wander around dispensing light chatter and doing things of little consequence, now showed a surprising capacity for organisation. It was as though she had donned the mantle of head of the family. In the following weeks everything happened. Neptune was given the responsibility for making Quin Cottage ready for them. Aideen had been up there once and found the whole place taken over by him, his brother from Feakle, a sister and her sixteen-year-old son from Scarriff, and Katty, Neptune's mother. The lad was working on the garden, the two women were inside with scrubbing brushes while Neptune and his brother were painting the woodwork outside.

There had also been a number of visits to Myles Fyrken's office in Ennis. This gentleman, whose ways and appearance had always worried Aideen, was putting on a fine show of what he probably believed to be competent professionalism. For the sale of the contents he advised against local men, in fact he felt that it would even be better not to use a Dublin firm but to go to someone in London who would be accustomed to dealing with a quality house. 'It calls for a man of taste and knowledge', as he said. He had given this idea some considerable time and felt that he had been guided to a firm that was just right.

'Who is that?' asked Louise.

Myles went through his rather odd mannerisms before he made a reply. Rising from his chair behind the desk he stood up and clasped his hands across his chest, pursed his lips and then opened and shut them several times before making a sound. The sound when it came was not words at first but a rather high-pitched whine that lasted for all of five seconds, then the rather too mauve face cracked all over and settled into the Fyrken smile which was only used when dealing with those he felt were of lower mentality.

'Yes, my dear ladies, thanks be that I am here to give you what advice I can. Your dear husband, if I may say so, chose carefully.' The high pitched whine started again and then stopped.

'Yes, I must say that this matter has used up an inordinate amount of my time — but I always promised ...'

Louise broke in with unexpected candour, 'Yes Myles, all that is taken as read. Who please?'

Aideen watched the man from where she was sitting to one side against the window. The sharpness of her mother's query had made him drop his guard. Her eyes watched his feet, his funny, totally out of proportion little feet, about size four she thought; they were now moving through odd steps and twists. From Aideen's experience this was a sure give-away that their owner was up to no good.

'Ah!' began Myles, 'the firm I would recommend is Percival Mangon and Partners; their offices are not all that far from Lord's Cricket ground; which has proved a satisfactory choice since so many of their clients have an interest in the game, you know. I have their brochure for you.'

He handed Louise a glossy and outwardly slightly over-gilt publication.

'I have made arrangements for none less than Percival Mangon the principal to give this matter his personal attention. He will be coming over with his clerk to undertake the preparation of the catalogue in three days' time. With regard to the sale of the house, the demesne and the various buildings, I am sure someone over here will make the best bid. Your husband left me clear instructions on this. Hopefully I shall have a prospective buyer who could come over and see the place on the same day.'

When the day for the cataloguing arrived Louise seemed very despondent, her sparkle gone. Myles Fyrken had arrived at just after nine thirty with his prospective buyer whose appearance reeked of money and little else. He had the not altogether encouraging name of Peterson Hudden and Myles kept referring to him as Pet. Aideen reckoned that he must have spent hundreds on his clothes, none of which suited either each other or him. One of those shiny nylon threaded suits, a heavy dark red woollen shirt with a striped pink and navy bow tie and blue suede shoes. But it was his jewellery that said it all — three over-large rings on the left hand, a heavy would-be signet ring on the little finger of the right hand and on the forefinger of this hand a huge stone that she judged to be an amethyst, cut round and smooth and set in what looked like platinum miniature vine leaves supported by a triple gold band. Clearly Mr. Hudden was a superstitious man because all the time he was talking he kept up a constant kissing of this awful ring. Louise had opted out and had asked Aideen to handle things.

Hudden clearly approved and with little more than a glance in her direction declared that it was just what he needed. Then the two of them had walked out of the hall and down to his sleek metallic silver Rolls which was parked beside a somewhat rickety blue Cortina that was all that Myles ran to; a sly move really because it quite effectively gave the incorrect impression that Myles was a hard working man who made little in the way of profits. Through the open door Aideen clearly heard Hudden congratulating Myles and saying something about great possibilities for expansion, plenty of room for chalets, a swimming pool and games places, that the stables would convert for self catering and that the grounds in general would soon shape up the way he saw it.

Aideen winced, thinking of her beloved Mellick; a warm red brick with Portland stone dressing around the windows, a perfect scale Doric portico, low pitched slate roof with wide overhanging eaves. Each room holding something for and of herself; the warmth of the great fireplace on those long drawn-out, damp winter days; the scent of lilac and roses in their seasons combining with beeswax patina on the yew and the oak; the creaking sound when the storms from the west during the equinoxes bullied their way up from the ocean and threw themselves against the walls, every now and then forcing the close-shuttered windows to drum and quiver. Since that day of the envelope by the roses there had been no word. Father had just completely vanished — every effort at tracing him had met with failure. The only sign of his past activities had been the arrival of unpaid accounts first to Mellick and later to the bank and to Fyrken's office, and the thought of Fyrken handling all this made Aideen frown.

Half an hour after Hudden had left, a very long black Cadillac drew up and two figures emerged from behind the tinted glass side windows. Myles Fyrken positively bounced out of the hall door and down the stone steps.

'Percival, it's so good to see you again. Last time I saw you must have been the autumn fair.'

'Correct, Myles.' Turning to the clerk-type character at his side, Mangon pronounced, 'Oh Alfred, would you bring in the recorder and the other bits and pieces.'

'Come in, Percy and meet the young lady of the house.' Myles ushered Mr. Mangon into the drawing-room and introduced him to Aideen. She recalled afterwards that she had not been sure quite what she was expecting but she was certain that her imaginings in no way fitted the person whose hand she was shaking. The first impression of Percival, or Percy, Mangon was of a certain rather controlled and careful respectability. His immaculate starched wing collar was adorned with a carefully tied expensive silk cravat that carried in just the right place a large pearl pin that had the matt hue that only genuine pearls have. He aroused a sense of unease in Aideen. She thought that the pearl was akin to a sleepy opening eye that gave a promise not altogether pleasant. Saville Row could have produced no better suit nor could Jermyn Street have improved on the shoes. If only Daddy was here — these were the kind of people he could sort out. Mangon's head was almost a perfect sphere; he had hair that at first she thought was real auburn, but then it became obvious some crafty operator in a salon gave it timely retouchings. He stood a fraction under five feet nine, which comfortingly meant that he had to look up to catch her gaze. His waist was possibly corseted to keep the line of the pale lavender cavalry twill waistcoat. The hands threw her, however, she just managed to hold back a tremor. His nails were perfectly manicured, but the fingers were so short it was almost as though they had all lost their top joints; the hands themselves seemed to have an odd outward cast that left her thinking that they vaguely resembled the little front digging paws of a mole. She disengaged the clasp perhaps fractionally too quickly for good manners — she couldn't be sure whether or not he had noticed. Percy Mangon turned and introduced his clerk, 'Miss Uniacke, Mr. Brigg.'

Mr. Brigg, Mr. Alfred Brigg, was not everybody's idea of a suave auctioneer's clerk from London. He was a shade taller than his boss and at first glance could have been a slightly scaled down version of Neptune Blood, except that evidence of hard living around his eyes and an unpleasant pallor pointed to poor condition. His hair was a genuine blond, short cut and frizzled. Eyes a brown so dark that the cornea and pupil blended. An odd and unnerving combination, the pale fair hair and those brown eyes — more than this, Alfred Brigg did not seem to blink; his eyes stayed at all times wide open, not that they were necessarily staring, although Aideen found it impossible to be sure.

Alfie Brigg had been with Mr. Mangon for just over six years. His earlier career started when at the age of sixteen he acted as a model for Home Gymnastic Apparatus; this was followed with a year long stint as an assistant to a blacksmith; then for five years he sailed with a deep sea Arctic trawler acting as cook and general emergency hand and lastly for four and a half years he had been a bouncer for a Soho betting shop by day and 'moonlighting' in the same trade for the night spot where Mangon had met him. His knowledge of the secrets of fine art and antiques was purposely kept slight by his employer who had trained the bruiser to just act on his instructions and not so far to think for himself.

The previous day Louise and Aideen had been round the house labelling those pieces they would be taking with them to Quin Cottage. Aideen told Mr. Mangon this and suggested that he and Mr. Brigg should complete their tour on their own. Fyrken had left and she settled down to her embroidery frame in front of one of the long windows in the drawing-room. At one o'clock Mary Dancy brought in a tray of sandwiches and assorted drinks. At Aideen's suggestion she went and told the auctioneer and shortly afterwards he and Brigg joined her. Louise she knew had retired to the summerhouse with *The Irish Times* and *The Lady*, a thermos full of strong Bewley's coffee and a tin of their shortbread.

Although Percy and Alfred were clearly gratified, perhaps a little mystified to be offered smoked wild salmon and soda bread, an assortment of Irish cheeses and a fine bottle of Sancerre, the luncheon would not have qualified as a social success. The crumbly rough bread broke in Alfred's fingers, as did the cork of the wine when he misunderstood the operation of an elaborate mechanical cork-screw. During the snack Percy explained that they were getting through matters very well — tape-recorders saved a lot of time. He would, he mentioned, be sending a photographer to take a few shots to hype up the catalogue. 'Good enough stuff,' he exclaimed patronisingly, 'but it will probably need a few lifts here and there.' Aideen had little idea as to what he meant by this but did not feel inclined to ask.

By half past four they were finished and she thankfully saw them off.

* * * * * *

A spatter of rain, a bluster of wind and a chill of approaching autumn brought Aideen back from her reverie. She got up and gathered up the rug and walked quickly down the slope on the south side of O'Brien's Tower — pausing for just one more look at those incomparable heights which appeared darker still as the shower had soaked their faces. Many of the birds had either gone fishing farther out or settled in to nest-ledges for the night. It was already nearly seven and she had promised Louise to be back not too late. Nevertheless it took her a good hour to make Mellick by eight-thirty. There she found a peat and log fire burning in the hall, another in the dining-room and a third in the drawing-room. Louise had done her chameleon act again. She stood, rather magnificent, in her finest evening gown of malachite green velvet with her one real treasure, a superb diamond and sapphire star, pinned to her right shoulder. Beside her on the Kingwood and tulipwood stool rested a silver tray with two deep-cut Waterford goblets and an ice-bucket, the gilt head and shoulders of what must be their last bottle of Laurent Perrier just showing. She had timed it all to perfection. As Aideen walked towards her the gramophone came on with the glorious opening chords of the Toccata in D Minor by Bach. Aideen started to speak but Louise leant towards her and gently pressed a finger to her lips. Stepping back she opened the champagne and filled the two goblets.

Passing one to Aideen she held hers level with her eyes and they both drank to their private thoughts at what seemed to be the passing of Mellick.

'Mary and Neptune have been magnificent. They borrowed a van and his brother came over and helped them take out all the furniture and bits and pieces we wanted. Quin is ready for us, Aideen, carpets laid, our own clothes in the presses and ward-robes. I gather Mary has even stocked up the larder and Katty Blood has sent along one of her special cheeses,' said Louise. Neptune's mother Katty had been making her strong cheeses since Louise was a girl.

'That should discourage the evil ones,' replied Aideen, remind-ed by the cheese of the cold supper she had seen laid out in the dining-room. 'Let's go and have our final Mellick meal, Mother, we've an early start tomorrow.' They went through, bringing their goblets and the opened bottle. The rest of the champagne served as a foil to the chicken and chicory salad and Aideen blessed Mary for her thoughtfulness in leaving a crème brûlée dessert — her favourite.

By half past nine they were drifting into sleep, each of them happy in the knowledge that the other was coping well enough with the break from Mellick.

* * * * * *

Down at the 'Salmon's Leap' on the back road to Feakle, business had never been so good for Pat and Bridget Tierney. The car park was jammed with Volvo Estates, at least eight Ford Transits and a couple of other vans all sporting enormous roofracks. The conversation was a mix of Liverpudlian, Brum, Cockney and a concoction of Irish accents. In the front snug Gladys and Rutty had taken over and were holding court getting appreciative glances from the new arrivals who found Clare was new territory.

Terry Dick, who kept a stall going at practically every town in the Home Counties, broke in:

'Well, what have you got then — you've bin over 'ere four days — I bet you've cleaned out the locals?' Before either could reply there was a chuckle from Reg Dainty from Shadwell:

'I bet they've not got wot I 'ave.'

'Get out of it Reg, you was always the one to play the trumpet. Let's see then, show up wot you think you've got.'

Reg lifted an ancient Gladstone bag and partly opened one side, slipping in his hand which reappeared with a delicate silver teaspoon. Rutty took it gently and fumbled in his pocket for his loupe, found it and screwed the powerful magnifier into his right eye. For a minute or more he examined it and then gave it back to Reg.

'I apologize, old lad. That's the goods all right — about 1625 London Assay I make it. What you want for it, mate?' The rest of those present whistled and sat silent.

'Don't rush me, Rutty — there's more and you'd better take a look.' Reg then pulled out eleven more teaspoons, a lovely cream jug and a plain silver bowl. 'Mind you, they were black as pitch wiv tarnish, I couldn't be sure, Glad.'

'Where did you fall on these then?'

'Well, it was nowhere near here. It was a small village outside some place called Nenagh. I see this fine house over the road and I got one of those feelings, you know, and went over and gave the door the old tap.'

'Don't muck about, what was the place then?' said Terry Dick.

'Surprise my lads — surprise — it was a convent.'

Rutty sat up:

'A convent! Reg, you mean to say you've knocked up a convent? Are you right out of your miniature mind? Convent people and all that lot — they're everywhere over 'ere. You're goin' to give us all a bad name. Well go on, you knocked the top reverend sister over the 'ead I suppose?'

'Hold on, Rutty, I gave good money for those bits. I asked the nice little young nun, novice I suppose she was, if they had any old metal scraps they didn't want. She said oh yes. In fact the Reverend Mother wanted a bit of extra cash for new curtains and things round the place. So she fumbles around in a cupboard and brings out these things — which mind you didn't look much — cos I've cleaned 'em up a bit since. I looks them over and says "well they're not much dear are they?" She says no but any little bit will help. So right out I says as it's a nice day, how about twenty quid for the lot. The girl said, "Oh my", as much as to say Oh I don't think I should. I says, "now, go on," hands her four fivers, and she puts the loot in a supermarket carrier, and I'm off down the road to here.'

'Do you know what that little lot is worth, Reg?' said Gladys who fancied herself as a bit of a silver pro.

'Come on Rutty, where's the roll? We'll give you four hundred right now.'

Terry pricked up his ears: 'Add a fifty.'

'No, you don't,' said Rutty, 'we spoke first. Five hundred and that's it Reg, and I'll forget where they came from, all right boy?' The deal was struck.

* * * * * *

At about six-thirty the next morning Aideen heard a gentle knock on her door. There was enough light filtering through the curtains to show up the splendid figure that entered. Louise was still in the gorgeous green velvet gown with the sapphire and diamond star, her hair now rather dishevelled.

'My dear, I can't do anything else. I forgot to keep something to wear; Mary cleared it all out. Can you give my hair a bit of a straightening? I don't think I'll wait for the sale. I 've arranged with Neptune to drive me over to Quin just after eight. I'll go and get us a bite from the kitchen.'

As they drank a rather weak cup of coffee and ate some slightly stale bread, all kinds of noises could be heard from the hall and garden. Going over to the window Aideen could see that a gang of men were erecting a large marquee and a smaller tent on the lawn across from the shingled turn around for the

drive. Heavy mallets drove huge wooden pegs into the fine turf.
Then a van from a caterer in Ennis drove up and trestle tables
and chairs were carried into the smaller tent followed by cases
and cases of liquid and hampers of food. Another van brought
more trestles for the marquee and the rostrum for the auctioneer
and a great many folding chairs. Louise took one look, kissed
Aideen and said,

'I'll be off now — you'll be well able to handle everything I'm
sure.'

She opened the door which led out on to the landing and the
main stairs. Within twenty seconds a silence fell. Nobody moved.
Rough lads they might be, but they'd never seen anything quite
like this. Louise came down the broad staircase with her shoulders squared, one hand gently guiding her gown over the steps,
giving every now and then a slight turn of the head to left and
right. Her eyes were levelled over the heads of her audience.
Queen Maeve could not have made her exit more effectively. At
that moment the television engineer switched on the huge t.v.
lights. The effect was stunning. The jewelled star flashed, the
folds of velvet gleamed. But Louise did not falter in her progress
towards the front door. When she was about five paces from it,
one man came to and leapt to open it. Louise gave a tiny inclina-
tion of her head and lifted her skirt slightly to descend the steps.
Below, Neptune stood rigid awaiting the Lady of Mellick.

* * * * * *

By nine o'clock the carousel was well and truly moving. Aideen
had given rushed interviews for television and radio. Unavoidably
the disappearance of her father cropped up and she tried to divert
the prying questions of the interviewers by using something
suitably vague.

One presenter unintentionally helped her by saying:

'Obviously it must be a matter of some undercover business?'

Aideen adopted this line for the rest of the day.

The sale was due to start at 1100 hours. At ten o'clock Percival
Mangon and Alfie Brigg arrived with a girl of around thirty who
looked like she had stepped off the pages of Vogue: cropped salon
blond hair, fiercely made-up eyes and oversize dark rimmed
glasses. Her jump-suit however wore a slightly crumpled appearance. She had clearly picked it as being the right thing for the

wilds of Clare. Rachel Hollow was her name and she gave a handshake to Aideen that felt like a touch from a Dover Sole.

'Rachel will give me a hand with the ceramics, which are very much her field, and she'll also tail off with the odds and ends at the close,' said Mangon. 'Now, can we have a few minutes somewhere quiet, Miss Uniacke?'

Such was the bustle in the house that they settled for the back seat of the Cadillac. Mangon wasted no time and took everything at a gallop:

'First, a couple of catalogues for you — needn't bother to go through them right now. One or two points though, you'll see I've indicated the reserves. Tricky business that, we have to leave plenty of leeway for the auctioneer.' Aideen looked at one or two items; a Georgian Irish Giltwood mirror surmounted by a lambrequin frieze had a reserve of £350; a Regency pollard oak Drum table, £120; a pair of ormolu and Sèvres candelabra with lightly draped *putti* and flowering branches, £300.

'Mr. Mangon,' Aideen tried to keep her voice strong and level, 'these are nowhere near the figures we discussed with Mr. Fyrken at the original meeting, and there are quite a number of items here which have no connection whatsoever with Mellick. They are not in the house at all.' Aideen stopped as she knew her voice was betraying her shock and puzzlement.

'Miss Uniacke', Mangon began, 'I don't know what you know about the international auction scene but it's a highly organized and complex matter. First of all, one thing is vital — trust and faith between all parties concerned must be maintained. Trust is the way to success — a success that I am sure will be seen here today. Unless the auctioneer has the leeway I mentioned, well, I'd rather call the whole thing off. In which case, you, as you've seen by the list of conditions, will be responsible for the considerable expenses so far incurred. I don't in any way want to push matters, but you and I must be clear about my rôle. Myles, I am sure, must have spoken to you about my personal credentials and that of my firm. I trust that I may take your goodwill in this matter for granted.'

Aideen felt stumped and the enclosed space of the car seemed to be getting smaller by the second. It was true that Myles Fyrken had made a big deal of locating the right people for the job and she herself had overheard snippets of Mangon dictating data to

Briggs about pieces that she had almost forgotten were there. He sounded knowledgeable alright. 'Yes', she said in a clipped tone, 'but what about these extra items that are not ours?'

'Those we have got together with the sole purpose of bulling certain areas of the sale along.'

'And what about some of the items I've got here on the first list? They don't seem to be in the catalogue at all.'

'Miss Uniacke, with more than five hundred lots, there would be little point in putting in objects that will only clear a pound or so.' Aideen felt quashed for her ignorance and seeing nothing to be gained by further discussion, she got out of the car leaving Mangon to glide off and supervise the final minutes before the first Lot came up. Mangon, of course, did not mention the arrangements he had made for 'buy ins' from assorted clients in London.

Mellick was transformed. The house seemed to bulge with throngs of people holding catalogues and pencils, taking a quick view. Outside, the drive was totally blocked with estate cars and mini-vans — the parking had had to overflow down the road and was now covering the meadow opposite. She could see Neptune trying to sort matters out with the help of the local Gardaí.

Aideen was almost certain that she could pick out the dealers; they had a look of confidence about them and a knowledgeable manner. The lower order of 'knockers' and 'bell-boys' were easily spotted. She registered the fact that probably all the major fine art houses had sent a representative and she felt a wave of regret that many of the pieces would most likely be leaving Ireland. As she walked through the crowd towards the marquee stray snatches caught her ear: 'watch out that you've got it right with Percy that he puts you down for the trade figure'...'I've got Rachel bidding for that one'...'keep an eye on old Mangon that he doesn't catch you with "puffing"...'he's a good boy, he'll look after the dealers.'

At eleven o'clock exactly, Alfie Brigg called for order by ringing a large handbell. Percival Mangon made some rather daft opening remarks about County Clare and then as though he was conducting a Bingo session called: 'Right then, eyes down for Lot 1.' Then there was no stopping as he and Rachel, who took over while Mangon stepped down for a drink, rattled through at a rate just short of three lots a minute. Aideen, for a time, stood slightly to one side and tried to take the measure of just what was happening. There was little doubt Percival Mangon was certainly an expert at the high speed auction. She felt that he must be up to something. He was in fact. But her innocent eye could not have hoped to pin it down. No one was more expert than Percy at taking phantom bids from the top of the marquee, or at surreptitiously favouring the 'ring'. He was a master at making sure to sell low to the dealers and at passing the lesser lots at knock-down figures to the 'container' boys who would put them on route to the hotel trade, to Europe and the U.S.A. To Mangon's stated commission could be added quite a number of 'sweeteners', that only the sharpest of eyes could pick up.

After about half an hour Aideen tired of the exhibition and retired with a sandwich and a thermos to the summerhouse. At about twenty minutes past six there was a general starting of engines and slamming of doors; final good-byes were shouted and the stream of vehicles poured itself away. Hired labour brought down the tents; chairs and tables were loaded and soon they too were gone. She came out to survey the wreckage. The lawns and even flower beds had all been run through. Neptune walked towards her looking concerned:

'Come on Miss, I've got the car in the stableyard.'

Two

At two thirty the following afternoon Aideen and Louise arrived at Myles Fyrken's office in Ennis. Myles at his most unctuous rose from his seat and beckoned them to two chairs placed near a small round table, whilst he lowered himself into a third.

'Not a bad day at all, Mrs. Uniacke,' he began.

Aideen caught her mother's eye and knew that Louise was all set for a rough passage.

'Dreadful day isn't it? It's been since eight this morning. That wind is remarkably cold for this time of year.'

'Shall we hear what we came for?' retorted Louise.

This riposte was clearly not expected by the solicitor. For a moment or two his little feet scrubbed the floor. Then, the lip movements started and the high-pitched whine came, which procedure obviously helped him to begin speaking again: 'Of course, my dear ladies now, I have it all here'. He picked up a folder from the table and thumbing the papers began to read:

'I have managed to agree a figure with Mr. Hudden for the land, Mellick House and outer buildings. This figure is £180,000, which, less the normal commission and other reimbursements, fees due to this firm, telephones, postage and sundry items leaves a comfortable sum of £173,000.42.'

Louise came in with one of her most glacial looks: 'What date are you putting on this document, Myles?'

'I am not sure that I follow?'

'I mean what year; is it 1970? There are no less than six hundred and fifty seven acres at Mellick.'

'I know, Mrs. Uniacke. I had them surveyed and the result indicated that more than half is what might be called sour-land, over a hundred are under blanket bog and what arable land there is suffers from rock and stone problems.' Aideen and Louise could only answer with silence.

'If I may continue? Mr. Mangon, myself and our clerks worked late last night to have these figures for you. The grand total for all the effects from Mellick after the auctioneer's percentage and his sundry already agreed expenses have been deducted comes out as £114,000. So we have £287,000.42 to play with.'

Louise came in again: 'Your choice of metaphor hardly does you justice. What's on the other side of the balance sheet?'

'Yes, I was coming to that. Requests for payment connected with Mr. Uniacke amount to £148,005.77.' Daddy had always played it close to the chest — the union with Mummy, had been a desultory romance. Now his real deviousness was coming into light.

'Pay those forthwith please, and how much is outstanding on your own account?'

'I beg your pardon.' Fyrken stuttered as much at the coldness of Louise's look as at her words. 'I'm not sure that I understand? . . .'

'I wish to pay you right up to date, today's date; shall we say as up to ten past three which gives us four minutes to leave this office? Send that account, Fyrken, with all the relevant receipts to Quin Cottage within the week.' Louise rose.

'But there is no need for all this unpleasantness, Mrs. Uniacke.' The high-pitched whine was rising.

'I feel no unpleasantness at all. In fact, I feel deliciously free from your services. In plain language, you're fired, Fyrken.' Aideen and her mother strode out of the office looking remarkably alike. Both held their heads high but both knew that the contents sale and other transactions had been entirely fixed against them.

They each separately gathered their wits and went on to the next call at the Bank of Ireland, there to meet a very different man. George Flaherty had a genuine respect for these two and took little time to show it:

'Good afternoon Mrs. Uniacke. Miss Uniacke, I expect by now your solicitor has told you the news.'

'Thank you, George,' Louise replied; looking at a page at the back of her diary, 'we have something like £137,000 plus to bring to you. Less of course what we've had to run up recently.'

George Flaherty smiled gently, 'I'll send you a statement. I have heard of auction results and methods many times but Mellick has got to be among the worst, and clearly not conducted with the best principles.'

Aideen came in for the first time allowing her anger to come to the surface: 'Yes, George, I think in basic parlance the Uniackes have been properly screwed.'

'Oh, darling, please don't use that word,' Louise winced. 'I know we have but there must be other ways of putting it.'

* * * * * *

Gladys Pilch and Rutty Evans were spending the night in Dublin before catching the early morning boat at Dun Laoghaire for Holyhead. They had picked a hotel on Wellington Quay because it not only had a lock-up garage but also an anonymous atmosphere. Their room faced on to the quays and looked down into the grey-green waters of the Liffey. Straggling along the further side was a somewhat dejected collection of old brass shops, last-hope furniture marketeers and imaginative bric-à-brac merchants among which were interspersed pubs, boarding houses and tailors, which last could, if necessary, take a measure after breakfast and deliver by supper time. Rutty and Gladys had been pushing good sirloin steaks on their way with pints of porter, and had finished with bowls of Rutty's favourite sweet, a good rich trifle. They were now in their room going through the lists of purchases and taking another joyful look at the silver Reg had passed to them at a reasonable profit.

'I like these, Rutty,' said Gladys; "specially this little jug. Lovely decoration on it, what do they call it — Repushy, ain't it? You know, I reckon it might be by that woman, Heather something.'

'Could be, Glad, I've got a fancy for the spoons myself, they're real pretty.'

The room telephone rang. A gentleman below wanted to see two old friends, said the hall porter, and if it was all right by them he would be on his way up.

'Now, who could that be? Stuff that silver under the pillow. It might be old Sean Varney who must have heard we were here and I wouldn't mind a bet he's got somethin' useful for us.'

There was a knock at the door but it wasn't Sean Varney — it was Alfie Brigg.

'Evening, glad you're in. We're staying at the Gresham and after dinner Mr. Mangon suggested I take a walk down to the quays and call in on you.'

'Well, of course Alfie, why ever not. Can Glad go and get you something?'

'No, not necessary. I'm not staying long. Mr. Mangon said he could be interested in that silver lot what you got off Reg Dainty. I expect you know what he means.'

Every time Gladys met Alfie, she found that those unblinking dark brown eyes gave her the shivers. Rutty was trying to look innocent and puzzled. Alfie carried on:

'Look maties, that stuff is right out of your area — the boss told me to get it reasonable or ...' He reached into his pocket and pulled out an unpleasant looking knuckle-duster that he slipped on to his left hand:

'Now then, Rutty Evans, stop looking like dinner weren't so good. The boss said to be generous. If our information is correct you gave Reg five hundred, so how about a bit of a mark up for you, lad, and I hands you six hundred, hmm?'

Gladys looked first at Alfie and then to Rutty:

'Go on Rutty, give him the stuff,' she knew too many stories about Alfie and his knuckle-duster: a broken jaw or a collection of broken ribs would not be a great help in their trade.

Alfie smiled approvingly, took off his favourite weapon and pulled out an over-full wallet:

'Clever girl you've got there, Rutty, I always admire clever girls.' He counted out six hundred and then added an extra fifty pound note for Gladys to buy something she fancied. Rutty retrieved the silver from under the pillow, put the pieces back into the supermarket bag and handed them over.

'That didn't take long did it? Oh well, I 'spect we'll meet again some place. Good night to you both.' Alfie opened the door and was gone.

'I'll give 'im a right chiving one day and Mister Mangon too with all his fine airs. He's only the same as ourselves. He only got what he got cos he's not so fussy as us wot he does. I reckon old Reg must have shopped us or I suppose it could have been Terry. I tell you Glad, the profession is not what it was.'

'No Rutty, but you and I have long memories — if you get my meaning.'

*   *   *   *   *

Louise and Aideen were returning to Quin Cottage. As they turned up the cul-de-sac lane between the Neptune cottage and Mary Dancy's the successor to Mellick actually seemed to be welcoming them. After a fairly stiff climb for seventy yards, they crunched to a stop on the well-raked gravel. Louise got out and took two of the carriers from the back seat and went to the door that was opened by Mary while Aideen drove round the east corner of the cottage and into the garage.

Louise asked Mary if she would mind holding the tea until about five as they had Miss Croker coming and she might be a bit late. The drawing-room was small by Mellick standards but it had an atmosphere about it that was harmonious and seemed to breathe a kind of security, a safe place to run to — a lair for a wild thing. The Axminster from the study fitted almost to the walls and the bawneen curtains had been a happy choice. In the wide hearth a mound of turf glowed in dark orange patches and smoke drifted up the chimney leaving its homely fragrance. Whoever had built Quin had done a good job well — in truth it was more of a house than a cottage. The ceilings of the drawing-room and dining-room cleared nine feet. The drawing-room had two wide sash windows facing close to due west with just a touch of the south. This allowed for a splendid light to fall cross-ways on the end wall opposite the fireplace and so it was here that they had been able to fit in the full-length portrait that Louise had commissioned from Patrick Russell about eighteen months previously. An ardent follower and admirer of the work of Sir John Lavery, Patrick had managed to capture Aideen's fiery spirit as well as her vulnerability with powerful brush-work. Louise adored the painting; for her it brought into being all the strength of the ancient romance where she had found the name for her only child. The 3rd century legendary hero Ossian was son of Finn Mac Cumhail. Ossian's own son was the brave and gentle Oscar who married Aideen. There was a fearful battle in 283 at Cabhra when Carbery, High King of Ireland, cut down the Ossianic forces and Oscar was killed. Aideen died of grief and a cromlech in Howth Castle demesne is said to mark her grave. Looking at the portrait now lit by the late afternoon sun Louise felt that it gave out a combination of so many of the qualities that were fused in her daughter. Patrick had used a very traditional mode — Aideen held a rose in her right hand and wore a long blue-grey dress. Aideen had only been persuaded to sit by the fact that the portrait would mean so much to Louise.

The quiet moment was shattered by the staccato snarl of a powerful motor bike. Amidst a splatter of loose gravel the engine died and a figure could be seen walking towards the front porch. Aideen went out into the hall to open the door. There was her favourite relation, even if she was a distant cousin on her mother's side. The Honourable Beatrice Croker pulled off her crash-helmet and gave Aideen a warm kiss on both cheeks.

'Batsy dear, lovely to see you,' said Aideen, and helped her cousin out of a heavy leather short jacket while admiring the cavalry twill breeches and the shining calf length pigskin boots. After Batsy had surveyed her fuzzed hair in the rectangular bevelled mirror, she gave up trying to stroke it into place and they went into the drawing-room where Louise rose in greeting. Batsy had always been Batsy as long as Aideen could remember. She was a true original. She had wrecked the nerves of a series of governesses before travelling across the Irish Sea to a strait-laced ladies' college where she seriously curtailed the career prospects of at least three promising teachers. In the end the governors and headmistress pleaded with her titled parents to take her away. Following this her father had thought the best plan would be handpicked tutors. She got on with the third one of these and made her way to university level. Here she founded all kinds of liberal ideas which were well ahead of those subscribed to by the University Faculty. Under the shadow of her father's title the Honourable Beatrice Croker was awarded a degree in zoology and then she left. A fortnight later she met a delightful but insincere French horn player with a leading Dublin orchestra. Through one long warm and hazy summer an intense love affair developed between them: Batsy was truly star high with passion. Then, in November, the horn player got a job with a Mid-West Orchestra in America. Unkindly he forgot to tell Batsy and just departed westward by TWA.

Batsy's grief was savage — running between shouts of horrific revenge, pleading, unstemmed tears for hours and a silent wandering along the battlements of the family castle, every now and then pausing to lean over and stare down at the rocks seventy feet below. The family went so far as to find a kind and strong-charactered priest to come and live in to try to work out a solution. The good Reverend after three soul-searching months persuaded Batsy to go on a retreat, either in Ireland or Europe. Batsy settled for Europe.

But on the journey by ferry and rail to Calais she got the father's idea of retreat and everything else totally mixed up. The result was that when she reached Calais she found humble employment with a travelling circus.

For nearly ten years Batsy stayed and was gradually promoted from a kind of usherette to the one who held the ropes for the high trapeze artistes. For this task, she wore a costume of black fishnet stockings, a short scarlet skirt, a shower of sequins on net on top, and a plastic tiara set with diamanté. The circus people were kind to this invader of their clan. There were no troublesome amours but some good friendships. Tzagor, the Hungarian knife thrower, taught her his skilled art — in fact so well that by the time she left, he admitted that Batsy was just as accurate as he himself. The two Frenchmen who rode stripped-down motor bikes round and round a fragile cylinder thrilled her and they too passed on their skills. Living with these people from a dozen countries and travelling through the heartland of Europe, Batsy became a remarkably resourceful person although to the others back home, she was crazy. She accumulated a vast knowledge of people's ways, and of all the subtleties of human interaction, a knowledge that was to serve her well.

Eight years ago Batsy had returned home to take over the family abode of Place Castle when her parents died. Since then she had worked with energy and imagination to restore the ancient pile to an enjoyable home. She had also become a very close friend to Aideen who had learnt much from her cousin that was to stand her in good stead later.

Now Batsy settled herself in a deep cretonne-covered armchair beside the fire as Mary brought in refreshments.

After her second slice of cake and third cup of well-bodied tea Batsy suddenly jumped up:

'Oh silly me — I forgot. Something for you, Aideen.' She went out to where her motor bike was parked and pulled a package out of one of the panniers. Back in the drawing-room she dropped it into Aideen's lap,

'There you are, bless you, with Croker's love.'

Aideen undid the string and pulled away the wrapping paper to bring into view a flat leather case about twelve inches square and an inch and a half deep. The skin was of the softest calf and a deep blue with exquisite gold tooled designs that climaxed in the centre with the head of a magnificent dragon.

'Batsy — no, you mustn't give me these. Please, they're yours,' Aideen exclaimed as she recognised the beautiful case.

'Go on darling, I just don't need them anymore and I want you to have them more than anyone else,' replied Batsy.

Louise leant across and fingered the case:

'Some one tell me — these, them, what are they?'

Aideen slipped the catch and lifted the lid to disclose six bright steel knives with silver wire handles and some inlaid gold work on the blades; in the lid held by loops were six plain leather scabbards with sundry straps to secure them to the arms or calves of the owner.

'Oh Batsy, they are lovely. What are they for? Foreign ones for dessert, fruit or cheese or —'.

Batsy and Aideen smiled.

'Not quite — I've always thought of them as my guardians. Tzagor, the Hungarian with the circus, gave them to me — he was the knife thrower, ' responded Batsy.

'But what on earth does she want such things for? Batsy, you mustn't do this — Aideen, give them back.' Louise was becoming agitated.

'Louise my dear, let's go into the garden. Have you got an old board or bit of wood, Aideen?'

The three of them went outside and after some searching Mary produced an old door which was leant against a stunted oak. Batsy took out some chalk and roughly lined in a kind of human figure — not quite life-sized but a fair target from eight or ten paces. She opened the case and Aideen selected two knives and stood back the full distance. The first she let fly from her shoulder and it was followed seconds later by the other with an underhand throw. Knife one went straight to the heart of the target — knife two entered the right eye.

'Oh bravo Miss,' cried Mary, who had stayed to watch.

'Mary, that's enough. I am not sure if I like this at all,' cried Louise. Having asked Mary if she would go and clear the tea things she then turned to Batsy and went on:

'You shouldn't have done this — she'll cut herself, you know. Anyway what possible use can these horrid things be to her?'

'Nonsense,' replied Batsy. 'We've been practising for days. Aideen didn't know they would be hers but from what I've heard of a certain auctioneer's behaviour, one or two near misses might have had a dramatic effect.'

Batsy was just setting Aideen up with a pencil splitting test when a dark green Citroën Safari came up the drive. Stopping alongside them, a tall fair man got out of the old but clearly well-loved machine.

'What on earth am I interrupting?' he said after a pause and, turning to Louise, began to apologise for being late.

Amidst the welcomes and explanations Louise's voice was the strongest.

'René, thank heavens you've come, perhaps you can stop the nonsense these two are playing at.'

But René had another agenda — he wanted all four of them to go out to dinner together, his treat.

Louise sighed,

'Oh, I'm not sure René, we've had rather a couple of days of things, what with the Mellick sale and dealing with that Fyrken man.'

'How about you, Aideen?' broke in Batsy, 'could be just the thing for all of us?'

'Come on mother, it's René's treat and he'll be disappointed,' pleaded Aideen.

'What about that fun place in Dromineer?' Batsy said.

'Too far,' replied René, 'If I may choose, I think the Old Ground in Ennis. Any disagreement?' All the heads were nodding. 'May I use your phone, Louise?'

When he returned he was carrying Batsy's gear:

'This I have only heard about, not seen. Let me help you into your armour.'

Batsy once jacketed and helmeted, lowered the darkened visor and bestrode her machine.

'I'm off to dress up. Don't forget to pick me up, René.' She kicked down and with a puff of white smoke and a further scattering of the gravel was away down the lane followed by René as soon as he had turned round.

Aideen and her mother went back into the house and upstairs to change.

Louise, the incurable romantic, saw René as the knight errant she was continually seeking for Aideen. He could give her dear girl all that her own husband had failed to do. She thought to herself that he was possibly aged thirty-five, but couldn't be sure. Just the kind of looks I like, she thought, good straight-forward blue eyes, fair hair. But, of course, he is an artist; that could mean Aideen would have to work. But she should find some one soon. Then her mind wandered towards more pressing issues — oh dear, if only I knew where Uniacke had gone to. It was so silly not to trust me, and just to go off like that. Let me see, Aideen's next birthday is her . . .

The door of her bedroom opened and the subject of all this musing came in and was surprised to see her mother hadn't started to change.

'Come on mother, it is after seven now! Could you lend me your amber necklace? It will go with this blouse.' Aideen was nearly ready; a long Donegal tweed skirt and a green taffeta blouse, three-quarter sleeves and a low neckline. The amber was just right, acting as a perfect foil to her lightly tanned skin.

*   *   *   *   *

By seven-thirty that evening Percival Mangon had flown back to London and was seated at his desk in the rather splendid bachelor apartment which took up the whole of the top floor of the Edwardian house that almost caught a peep of Lords. The building was used also as office, show-room and for occasional select auctions. Mangon had tried marriage twice but each 'Lot', as he referred to them had failed to meet the reserve and the hapless brides of a few months were cast out with, as the jargon has it, NSV — no sales value.

Percy had left Alfie Brigg to bring the Cadillac back which would also be carrying the rather precious nest-egg from the unfortunate convent near Nenagh. He had the evening to himself and was hard at it with sales catalogues, his own catalogue of Mellick and a pocket calculator. Percy's sales accounts were complicated and only he could really work out the final figures. Alfie Brigg had put in some crafty bidding for him at the auction and this, added to 'knock-downs' by Percy himself to names that were only in the air, had brought some good results. Totting up he found that he and the absent friends had bought thirty-three lots for which he had most honestly paid a cheque through one of his banks, which needless to say was signed with an arranged name; the sum was £17,056. The carrier should arrive within the week. The value of the objects when passed on to carefully chosen clients or placed with one of the major auction houses should very conservatively bring in a sum of around £320,000. Even when he had passed back the five per cent on profits to Fyrken it was still good business. He disliked having to pay what he felt was an excessive commission. But about three years ago Myles Fyrken had caught him out on an attempted 'cooking' of an account of a similar kind. What followed had been impossible to prove — as to whether the sender was Fyrken or someone else. Percy preferred to operate outside the protecting arm of the law. A small packet had been delivered by the afternoon post and Percy had had a very close escape — as the paper knife slipped under the flap of the package there was a slight hiss and a puff of smoke. Percy fortunately for him had a jungle sense of reaction; he instantly dropped the packet and threw himself sideways to end up behind a settee. The incendiary device flared white-hot as the phosphorus broke through the thin wax covering — the mini-blaze lasted for about thirty seconds and then died. His treasured 1780s mahogany desk still showed the scars.

*   *   *   *   *

René Culhane in his heart lived a life of divided pleasures; he was the son of Cécile, a delightful lady from Blois who had married Kevin Culhane — himself a distant but direct relation to Lord and Lady Kilbandan, or Uncle James and Aunt Laura as René had always called them, who ran one of the country's most successful stately home businesses. Kilbandan Castle was as striking as the contents which the family had managed to keep together. It stood on an escarpment within a demesne of nearly a thousand acres — well walled and served with but a single lodge and gate. Here René always had a room. His mother and father managed a small but profitable vineyard near Saumur, where he had grown up, journeying to Paris he had studied in the studio of a pupil of Matisse. For the last five years he had, like many another, sought his way into the art world. He lived alone atop a crumbling early 19th century Mansart-roofed apart-ment building in Paris. In recent years his father and mother had been spending the majority of their time in Australia where they had formed a company which was into viniculture on a large scale.

That evening as René drove up to Kilbandan, James was just shepherding the last few visitors back to their coach. He turned and came across to the Citroën.

'Great to see you, it's been a long time.'

The two men clasped each other's hands.

'My only excuses are work and travel', smiled René.

'Never grumble when you're busy.'

René opened the back of the Citroën:

'I have a soupçon for you,' he said lugging out a carton that tinkled with promise.

The older man chuckled in delight: 'Oh well, bless you for that — we'll split one between the three of us.'

'Can't tonight, I'm afraid, I'll just be going in to see Laura and change. I have a dinner date with the Uniackes and Batsy over at the Old Ground.'

*   *   *   *   *

Within twenty minutes René had put on a dark suit in deference to what he felt might be worn by Batsy. He drove over to Place Castle and picked up a vision, quite stunning against the memory of the bike gear. She was standing by a stone seat halfway down the drive swathed in a pale lavender gossamer-light shawl which covered a long evening gown of white Belgian cambric embroidered with garlands of flowers at the neck and along the bottom. On her head was a thin band of gold that carried at the front a pale tourmaline held in place with sinuous curling forms based on the La Tène. He threw open the door and she eased herself into the comfortable leather seat.

'Forgive this little touch,' she fingered the simple tiara.

'But it is charming, Batsy,' said René.

To which she responded somewhat cryptically,

'Yes, it reminds me of what I might have been and perhaps shows others something.'

The drive into Ennis was not long and they parked the car outside the Old Ground at just after a quarter past eight.

They had a table tucked away in a corner and the whole meal was spent in light-hearted merriment — the two Uniackes leaving aside their cares to enjoy the company of their friends. Afterwards they found some seclusion in a lounge and having secured a large pot of coffee and suitable liqueurs to go with it Batsy suddenly sat upright looking fearfully serious and began:

'I've had this feeling, we four are here for a reason. I've sprung this on you because I find instant impressions can be so accurate.'

The faces of the other three reflected possible thoughts as to what could be coming from this unpredictable but lovable person.

Turning to Aideen, Batsy continued:

'That Mangon person, and there must be hundreds if not thousands just like him, needs bringing to order. What protection is there for people? One thing I learnt when I was with my friends in the circus; it's knowing what matters — knowing as much as one can about everything. You are all looking at me as though the Honourable Beatrice Croker has lost her reason. Well, Aideen, I am sure you see what I am getting at?'

'I'm not sure, Batsy,' Aideen replied, 'although it does strike a chord with something I was thinking when I woke early this morning.'

'There you are, I knew it! We Celts can see things.'

René leant over:

'Come on Batsy, what is it that you two clairvoyants have got hold of?'

Batsy turned to Aideen:

'My dear, you throw first.'

'All right then. I think that I would like to have some kind of a niche in the antiques, paintings world. Those years I had in Trinity, working in the Fine Arts Department, in retrospect I realize that they were exciting ... some of the lecturers were brilliant. And it was a foundation, a basic history of art. But where does that leave me now? Teaching? No, not for me; a gallery or museum? No; these are too static. With the bit of experience I have, I know that I learn best by travelling, meeting people, exchanging ideas. So the whole field of antiques — why not?'

'Marvellous, marvellous; no need for me to say much more. Heavens girl, you've lived all your life surrounded by the things. You do need some study, but most in the field learn as they go. Alright Louise, if I continue with this?'

Louise nodded:

'I don't suppose I could stop you, Batsy dear, but in fact I don't want to, please go on.'

Batsy leant across the table and shook Louise's hand:

'Well, I suggest a couple of months or so stay in London, Aideen, and you can rustle round the Victoria and Albert, the Wallace, and the others and visit as many of the top auctions as you can. Not only studying what they are selling but also the whole thing, the way they do it. Take a good look at the catalogues with all this stuff about studio of, follower of etc. etc., the pretty strange world of provenance and all the mystic jargon of the saleroom. Sales are the last of the great free shows that are around. Louise, I can see just what you're thinking. That length of time in London, so expensive. Not a bit of it! Claude Croker has a splendid little flat just off the King's Road — somewhere like Jubilee Place, I think. All very self-contained and workable. And you know what Claude is, he's just off on another one of his archaeological digs, around Carthage this time I believe, and he'll be away for at least four months. The good lad wouldn't want any rent, he'd be glad to have someone to keep the place aired plus the fact that I can get you some useful introductions. What about it? He goes in a week's time; shall I ring him tomorrow?'

Louise spoke first.

'Yes Batsy, I think it's a marvellous idea.'

Aideen registered Batsy's excitement and somehow felt that this was for her. She looked towards her mother. 'What about you, darling?'

'I'll be just fine, dear. I'm going to have a lovely time doing all those things I have never had time for. First, Neptune and I will be having a go at the garden at Quin. Then, you'll never guess, I'm thinking about keeping bees. Katty has a way with them, you know. Neptune tells me she can talk to them!'

'Well, Aideen?' said Batsy and they all looked towards her expectantly.

'Please ... yes, do ring him,' smiled Aideen, happy yet surprised at the suddenness of everyone's decision — including her own.

'René, I'm going to buy a little something to launch this.' Batsy continued, 'And, Aideen, if you come across the Mangons again, you can think: "If you can't beat them — you join them in their little games."'

To which René added:

'And then you beat them.'

Three

Three days after Aideen returned to Quin Cottage from her visit to London a letter arrived for her from France; it was from René. He hinted that if she could manage it, a trip to Paris fairly soon could further matters with this antique business; he was anxious to discuss an idea. Aideen was in the mood to strike without delay. She had enjoyed the sojourn in London immensely. Her own fine arts background and Batsy's introductions had made it possible to get onto the inside track of the art and antiques world in a surprisingly short space of time. Now she felt ready to test herself and her new-found confidence. That evening she rang René and arranged to be over in two days' time — she would be travelling by sea and train, being as she said a traveller who liked to absorb as much as possible when she went on a journey. René, it was arranged, would book her into the Hotel des Arbres just a street away from where he had his studio.

For convenience, she took the morning boat leaving Dun Laoghaire at 8.45 for Holyhead and matched up with a rail connection to arrive at Euston at around six. Then after a restful night at the London Tara, away the next morning from Victoria Station to Dover and then the hovercraft to Calais. From there one more train and she was stepping off at Gare du Nord. As she stood in the taxi queue she sniffed the mildly intoxicating scents of Paris — good coffee, oven-fresh bread, expensive perfumes and something akin to drains. The driver of the middle-aged Renault that drew up alongside the curb jumped out, handed her bags into the boot and they were away. Most of the important buildings she recognized and between them there were quick glimpses of the great Church of Sacré Coeur, white and impressive on its hill. Trying to pick out other landmarks she was struck again by the way modern advertising with its posters, flickering neon signs, and often garish creations can transform not the spirit of a city but certainly its visual impact.

The Hotel des Arbres must have taken its name from two sturdy plane trees which shaded the pavement in front of it. It was fine; modern with services, and with just a touch of a grander past evident in the ornate and leisurely lift and in the elaborate ceiling mouldings which had enough gold leaf left to show how they must have looked once upon a time. As soon as she was in her room she called René who apologised for not coming to meet the train because he had been stuck with a client.

At just after seven René arrived and guided her towards a small restaurant which produced a good set meal, a house carafe and coffee and which allowed them to sit and take the time necessary for Aideen to consider the outline of René's idea.

The basis of this was that she might think about joining two close friends of his, Tim and Nell Sinclair, who ran a somewhat unorthodox and in many ways quite simple business for the exchanging of fine art and antiques. It allowed for suitable com-mission money for the minimum outlay and best of all, no expen-sive show places were needed. Aideen pressed him for details.

'The best way to describe the plan, I suppose, is to use the name Tim puts to it;' said René, 'for private ears only, he calls it the "Two Book Trick".'

'That makes it sound like a conjuring business.'

'No, no, nothing like that . . . Tim and Nell have two books,' René raised his right hand: 'In the green one they have details of worthwhile objects their top-grade clients want to sell.' He lifted his left, 'in the blue one they have a comprehensive list of the rich folk that are on the lookout for the rare and beautiful. They also have a superb set of photographs of the wares on offer. The mainstream of this enterprise is run from a small, two-room office under their lovely apartment in an Empire house in St. Cloud overlooking much of Paris. That, my dear, is the bones of the matter. Depending on how energetic you are, how well you can find introductions to the folk that can still hold out in mansions and castles, in Ireland and the UK, there is good money to be made and probably a lot of fun to be had.'

'I have a feeling,' said Aideen, 'that I have been measured for a suit and...', she shrugged her shoulders, 'I like the feel of the fit. How do I contact your friends?'

'I thought you would, and funnily, so did Tim and Nell. They've asked us to lunch tomorrow at their place.'

'Marvellous — you've set the old mind spinning, René. I reckon what with The Honourable Croker and a few other pillars of the realm I should be able to rustle something up, given a little time.'

'You will, I'm sure. Oh and here's a bit of news. Did you know that that Mangon character has been operating in Paris for just over a year and is now expanding his business? He's fallen in with one of those Art Assessors from the US that are arriving in droves. They seem to have just one idea — to pick up any choice pieces overlooked by the Duveens and others operating fifty or so years ago. Once found, they are removed smartly back to the States... for the delectation of the next wave of millionaires, or I suppose it's billionaires now. Dear old Europe — this business in one form or another has been going on for at least a hundred years, you'd think there would be nothing left.'

René paused to sip his wine.

'Mangon's Art Assessor goes by the name of Warren B. Westonhofer. I met him once rather by accident at a Group show I was exhibiting with. Some twit who knew me, and possibly wanting to get rid of him, introduced us. Warren B. Westonhofer's opening gambit was not one that worked with me. He looked me up and down and then exclaimed in a pitying voice: "So you're a painter; got a crowd of them back home in Detroit, what's your line then boy... fuddyduddy still life, or can you rustle me up a couple of 'noods'?" I tried to back off but he continued: "You're not all French are you — can't fool me. Here's my card. Anytime you've surplus stuff that ain't finding a market I reckon Warren can fix you up with a client. Terms strictly cash, preferably Uncle Sam's greenbacks, and it'll be fifty per cent commission and no questions." With that he walked off carried along by the aura of his own importance and the worldwide power of his native currency.'

'Is that what it all comes down to?' Aideen shuddered. 'Just money, power and forget the quality.'

*   *   *   *   *   *

Warren B. Westonhofer had indeed gone in big with Percival
Mangon. They had met first at a sale at a small château some ten
kilometres south of Rheims. It was one of those little beauties
that can happen at intervals. Somewhere along the line the publicity people had slipped up — the result being that only a poor
crowd turned up; locals, a few minor dealers, and just nobody
from the really high ranks of the trade. But as fate would have it,
Westonhofer, Percival and Alfie Brigg were there. During the walk-
round viewing, Percy was possibly more skilled than Warren. In
the main salon standing on a table against the light of a window
was a Madonna and Child painted in egg tempera on a panel
about twenty-eight inches by eighteen. Percy hardly slackened
his pace but his eyes registered at once — the quality of the paint,
the small touches of almost impressionistic groups of angels
flying above the head of the Madonna, the amazing detail of her
hair, the delicately poised hand held protectively over the Child,
the finely rendered jewellery and brocade of her costume. It had
to be German and very close to, if not by, Grünewald.

Percy was already well past when he heard a minor explosion
of sound behind him.

'By all that's ever been — my Mama should see this. Warren B.
W., this is for you.' It was the Art Assessor practising his trade!
Percy did some high-steam thinking — trying to assess just how
much knowledge the flamboyant character had behind him. He
thought he'd try a well used ploy and one that was nearly
always successful: send in Alfie Brigg. He whispered instructions he thought best suited to this case. Alfie left him and sidled
across to the American who was standing alone in the hall trying
to look at a fireback.

Alfie started off:

'Stuffy in here, ain't it — these small time sales get me — cost
of the ferry, hotel and all and nothing here to make a profit.'

Warren straightened up:

'I don't think we've met, sir. You from London?'

'Well, you could say that — I muck around — specialize in
nothing really and always on the look-out for the bad ones; built
quite a record for myself in nailing some of the rubbish these
aristos try to fob off us honest dealers with. Tricky we may be but
believe me when they set out to put one over on you — watch it,
mate.'

Warren, self-styled art assessor, knew to a fine point exactly how far his 'qualifications' stretched. He thought that he was good on 18th and 19th century painting and other objects from this period but when matters got back into real art history he knew his groundwork was patchy indeed.

'You know, sir,' he began.

Alfie Brigg gave a little wriggle of pleasure — being called sir did things for him and also with Americans it often meant the fish was off the bottom and sliding in towards something that could be handled.

Warren continued:

'You being a European,' another plus mark made with Alfie, 'might care to give me some of your expertise.' This last word spelled trouble for Alfie as he wasn't quite sure what it meant in this case.

'That little painting of a woman and child back there in the saloon place. What do you think, what do you feel, sir?'

'You mean by the window? 'said Alfie: 'Well, it should be what my friend said, early Deutsch, but he tipped me the nod not to touch it. Reason being why? I'll tell you. Did you see the state of the panel, more worm-holes than wood, so covered in retouches that whoever painted it wouldn't know it. My friend, who is one of the leading authorities on early pictures, said to me, Mr. Brigg, two thousand five hundred francs max and that's it.'

Warren thanked Alfie with genuine warmth — apart from the fact that he needed to learn a lot more about early painting, he also needed to learn a great deal more about some of the home-bred characters in the trade over here.

So Percy Mangon was able to get the beautiful, yes, quite genuine, Matthias Grünewald 'Madonna of the Pomegranates' for eleven thousand francs and at the same time to take to his heart this gentleman from Detriot who he sensed, for all his shortcomings, could be a useful partner of sorts.

*   *   *   *   *   *

The next morning Aideen revelled in the crusty, crunchy rolls, delicious blackcurrant preserve and coffee that was so strong it had to be taken in sips. When René and she had parted the night before, he had suggested that she might like to come round to his studio before they went over to St. Cloud for the lunch date.

The house with the studio was less than a hundred yards away and after she had mollified the 'concierge' that she really was a genuine friend of Monsieur Culhane she began the climb of five storeys long which ended rather surprisingly on a red-tiled landing with a glass roof that was profuse with flowering pot-plants. The single door was ajar and she heard René call out:

'Come on in, I'm just making some coffee.'

Aideen went into a small entrance hall. On one side were doors leading to his bedroom and office, on the other side was the kitchen where René was putting the pot, jug and cups on a tray.

'Go straight ahead through the double doors,' he said. She pushed the white doors open and found the studio; large, with a lofty ceiling and well-lit with north slanting skylights and broad windows on the south side that gave a view across the rooftops of lower neighbouring buildings towards distant high spots of the city. Muslin curtains could be drawn across these windows if it was necessary to concentrate the light that came from above.

Artists' Studios held a fascination for Aideen. In this one, one of those massive easels stood to one side where it could be raised and lowered with a hand-operated crank and also tilted by spinning a large wheel underneath. The picture that was on it at the moment was at a stage of near completion. The subject showed a night scene probably somewhere on the Seine — an old low-arched bridge, a row of street lights, a stream of people and traffic. But what caught her thoughts most of all was the sense of light that René had brought into being — the haze and glare from the street and river levels was rising and blending with deep, warm, almost purple shades of early night. Beside the easel was his painting table: a glorious mélange of part-used bottles of oils, varnishes and spirits, a pile of new tubes of colours, partly used tubes, jars holding brushes of all shapes and sizes, jumbles of paint rags, painting knives, and resting across this array, the palette carrying an ordered arrangement of colours towards the edge and in the middle the swirling mixtures of the tints and tones that she could pick out on the canvas above. The walls were lined with canvases leaning face inwards, with frames, and higher up shelf after shelf of all the things a painter gathers around him and which often stay for decades undiscarded in the hope that they might one day be used.

René came in with the tray and set it down on a small table near the window where they sat down.

'Bit of a mess I'm afraid, but if I get the painting right what does it matter?'

'It's perfect, René,' said Aideen. 'Mmm ... the smell of a studio plus your coffee and plus a bit of Paris ... glorious, a great contrast to the peat smoke of Clare. How much further are you going to take that canvas?'

He turned to face the easel and half-closed his eyes.

'These last strokes are always the tricky ones, get them wrong and you can throw out the whole balance. Go on too long licking up the finish and you can kill it stone dead. I think just a few strokes for accents on some of the faces, a few more reflections in the river ... and yes, I think a little scumbling towards the right-hand side of the sky to blend matters together.'

For a few minutes they drank the creamed coffee and munched some mouth-watering little patisseries. Then Aideen voiced her thoughts:

'Could I see some of those, do you think?', pointing towards the serried ranks of canvases.

'Of course,' said René, 'although I don't have many completed works here. Most of those are either just laid in or are blank.' He rose and pulled out some canvases. A view of Mont St Michel at extreme low tide; a scene only just begun of fishing boats heading into a stormy sea; a bowl of dark red roses luminous against an almost black background and half a dozen others. Then he walked over to the easel and removed the painting he was working on. Turning to Aideen he said:

'Shut your eyes.' She did so and heard him walk across the studio and pick up something and then back to the easel and a little fumbling with the securing grip.

'All right — open now.'

She did so. In front of her on the easel was a framed canvas of Mellick. He had chosen that time of early evening when the sun before descending sends a warm gilding light across the Clare hills. This had given to the brickwork of the house a luminous quality; the sky was clear of clouds save for a handful of pink-grey shreds low down, the colour of the sky a mixture of Naples yellow with just a touch of rose madder which as the eye came up blended into a pale green and which, near the top, passed through cerulean to a darker tone of blue that presaged the approaching night. Here and there he had picked out details of the house; the stone dressings to some of the windows, the portico, and in the foreground an expanse of those once well-cared-for lawns.

'Oh René,' Aideen spoke at last, ' it's beautiful and just as it was, just as it will always be for me. Whenever did you do it?'

'Rather sneakily I am afraid; on a visit sometime ago I made some watercolour sketches and this last time I crept over the final evening before I left Kilbandon and did another and then I put them all together here. I hope you think it works.'

Aideen was about to ask him rather ingenuously what he was going to do with it but René spoke first:

'It's yours if you want it.' Aideen rose and went over to the picture and stood for a few minutes absorbing. Then she turned and went back to René and taking his face in her hands she kissed him gently on the lips.

'Thank you . . . dear René.'

After a pause he took her hand and led her to sit down:

'Come, we've some time in hand and I'd like to fill you in a little on the Sinclairs.' During the next half hour René gave her an excellent run down on Tim and Nell. They were brother and sister, Nell being the elder by three years. Both were in their fifties. Tim had had the usual standard education, prep school, Charterhouse, Cambridge. Nell, after a series of governesses, had been to a respected ladies' school and then to London University followed by a session at the Courtauld Institute. Nell and Tim were not keen on the usual sports but Nell had taken a great fancy to fencing and had become really accomplished at it. Both had from as far back as they could remember read and re-read everything they could find about fine arts, antiques, craftsmanship, materials, collectors in history and the art market from its very early days. René concluded that there could be few who could challenge the scholarship of these two or, for that matter, their knowledge of the darker side of the flourishing international market.

Tim could be the more misleading of the two; he had reduced effacement to a high art. To many he could appear a dull person, grey and with little intelligence. Nell was the opposite. To René, she had the lively eyes. He felt that they radiated such awareness that one felt she was always half a dozen paces ahead of you.

'There you are, something for you to go on. Ahhhh . . . yes, there is one other point . . . I had better own up to . . . I've been with them in this business for just over a year. It was Nell who told me to look around for one more candidate for the team . . . hence our lunch . . . Come on, we'd better go. I won't take the Safari, I'll ring down for Marie to get us a taxi.'

*   *   *   *   *   *   *

Tim and Nell Sinclair were just as René had described and within minutes of her arrival, Aideen felt a genuine warm acceptance. Their apartment had a sense of measured good taste — simple furnishings representing the best from the last three centuries. The luncheon had consisted of a great platter of cold shellfish, a bowl of crisp tossed salad and for dessert, fresh fruit and cheeses. Aideen had helped Nell clear away and now the four of them were taking advantage of a mild sun-warmed afternoon and were sitting out on the balcony.

The conversation during the meal had wandered around the world of the arts. There had been no probing questions from either Tim or Nell, or not that Aideen could pick up.

'Nell, time for cards on table?' said Tim. They communicated with each other in the staccato fashion of those who know they will be completely understood.

'I expect that René has told you the outline of our activities, Aideen? In brief, Tim and I would like it very much if you would come into our little game and be the Irish axis as it were, with some activity in the UK. What do you feel?'

'I can tell you in two words,' said Aideen. 'Yes please!'

'Delighted,' 'Thrilled,' said Tim and Nell almost in unison.

'So now there will be four of us working away at the Two Book Trick.'

Nell interrupted Tim:

'Yes, it's a very secret matter and so the nickname we have for ourselves is between ourselves. If you look at it in one way we're "knockers", but if I say it myself we are "Top Knockers", so Top Knocker Aideen, let's do some talking.'

Tim got up and moved towards the glass doors back into the drawing room;

'I'll just go and fetch our most precious books.'

Nell continued:

'The established art world exists to a large degree because of a cloak of secrecy and their often vaunted code of confidence, which in lower-deck parlance means "you scratch my back and I'll scratch yours" — I must have picked that up from a matelot somewhere. They may indeed be very secretive, but then I can assure you, Aideen, so is our little outfit, only much more so. I got great joy the other evening when I was at a Private View of some very expensive modern works at one of the Majors. I happened to be standing behind two of the directors of the said Major and heard one say to the other: "I say, whatever happened to that Canaletto belonging to Lord Grassholm? I hear he's sold it to that industrial man, the one that makes machinery for mines. What I want to know is how did the chap know Grassholm had it, how did Grassholm get in touch with him and how are we to find out how much was paid for it?"'

Nell and the others laughed at her imitation of his puzzlement. 'He then proceeded to tell the other man that his chairman was worried that some of their own people were not to be trusted.' At that point Tim returned with the two books — both bound in leather, one green and the other blue. He passed them to Aideen,

'These, my dear, are our records and greater trust I cannot give you.'

Aideen took the books and opened the green one first. From the page one onwards it was a breath-taking display of the machinations of a beautifully simple plan to implement the old order of supply and demand. No tricks, just straight-forward practice. A ten per cent one way commission, no involvement with others wanting a hand-back, no publicity to alert thieves as to what had gone where. The first hundred and twenty-four pages of the green book were already filled and entries across the pages complete — these included dates, names and addresses, objects the owners wished to dispose of and the price that was feasible to go for, the price over this which had been realised and the name of the buyer. Then there were about twelve pages which showed objects that the Top Knockers had on offer. The blue book was a complement to the green in that it had similar details but this time the names of the buyers were on the left. After the pages of the completed deals there came for Aideen some of the most fascinating details. These were the long queue of people from all over the world, from a wide variety of stations, who wanted some very extraordinary and expensive items indeed: the South African manufacturer who sought Celtic gold ornaments; the prince from the Yemen who wanted a Boucher featuring if possible the delectable Miss Murphy, one of the most seductive models ever; the Managing Director of a chain of up-market magazines in New York who was almost falling over backwards to write a cheque for top rank jewellery from European Royals. After about five minutes she put the books on the table.

'Well, my dear, any questions?' asked Nell.

'Nothing very big — it is all so beautifully simple. Security must be a bit of a headache.'

'Yes and no,' Tim replied.

'You see a number of these laddies on both sides of the matter just don't want publicity of any kind — it's not for us to ask why — it may be monetary fiddles, family squabbles. They can be a funny lot up in this bracket; some are just so greedy that if we didn't have the old ten per cent urging us on we'd jolly well drop them. Others, it can be vanity. But if you read around a bit of the history of acquiring it very soon shows up that the main incentive for many a buyer is power and a sweet satisfying feeling that he or she is the only person in the world that has a particular thing. And take it from me, Aideen, the fancy prices hyped up by the Majors may sound breath-taking but we have had a good number of exchanges which make the professional gavel bashers look as though they're used to working in the sticks.'

'Can you give me the rules?' said Aideen: 'Suppose I come across someone who has a Titian they are tired of or suppose I meet someone who is clamouring for a Louis something-or-other commode, what is my next step?'

Nell took up the running:

'You carefully put them on what I would call the long and confidential hold. You contact us. We go to the safe and go through the two books. Quite often this can solve matters. If not, we shuffle through our card index of would-be but-not-quite-sure buyers. Photographs can be exchanged or discreet visits arranged. If you need to make a special visit, please keep careful details of expenses, as these are added to the commission. Oh yes, and never get involved with more details than the above, insurance, packing, removal and suchlike are all the responsibility of the buyers or sellers. The method of payment we prefer and which is nearly always understood is that the buyer pays the vendor direct — the price plus our commission and sundry expenses — and the vendor then pays us. Pleased to say no bad debts yet.'

'What about the phone?' said Aideen, 'Bugging, tapping or whatever they call it?'

Nell carried on: 'Good point. An increasing number of our clients are already into the secret communication act and they have a scrambler and so do we. As an additional cover we normally change our numbers at least every quarter, and if the balloon goes up we change every month. We also use codes; I'll give you a copy of the code-book before you go. But then, an appreciable part of the business is done face to face. A vendor calls us and says for example he will be in Bordeaux on such and such a night and would one of us like dinner or a buyer may signal he will be changing planes at Heathrow, could we meet in the VIP lounge at an arranged time and date.'

Tim came in: 'I hope that you won't think this is an operation without risk, my dear. We have to step cautiously as we're often not quite in the position to give Interpol a ring or to summon up the heavy squad from Scotland Yard or the Deuxième Bureau. Not that our activities are outside the law in any way, but you can understand. Nell and I have had our scrapes, in fact, only about three months ago I found myself in a tangle with a gentleman from the Mediterranean who thought that he could pull a fast one and do a bit of cheating and also rough me up. Dear old Nell was there with that rather pleasant looking umbrella you might have noticed in the hallstand. The poor chap was not to know that Nell almost got herself in the Olympic Squad for fencing — the umbrella holds as pretty an epée blade as you will find outside Toledo. In no time she had run him through the right bicep and put two useful holes in his backside. He departed at high speed straight through a rather weak glass door that wasn't open and spoilt his nose into the bargain.'

René chuckled:

'You haven't seen this one in action. When I called in on the family the last time I was in Clare, there's Aideen with a fabulous cousin who has spent ten years with a European circus, hurling evil-looking knives around the place with a totally unnerving accuracy. You haven't got any on you, have you?'

'Not exactly on me, but I did slip two into my bag as Batsy, that's the cousin, mentioned all kinds of things that could call for attention when travelling alone in foreign places.'

'May I?' said Nell.

'Of course;' replied Aideen and slipping her hand into an inside pocket of her handbag she passed a slim leather sheath and its contents over.

'Look at this, Tim!' cried Nell, 'What a little beauty — look at the handle.' She cautiously felt the point and blade.

'Wow, you mean to tell me you can throw these things and hit things?'

René vouched for Aideen's accuracy,

'I saw her pin-pointing a target at about twelve yards range — no bother at all. Dear Batsy gave her a set of six of them.'

'Aren't you liable to be picked up by these X-Ray things when travelling?' asked Tim.

'Not really, you see I just don't like flying — I find boats and trains so much more fun.' Nell handed Aideen the knife:

'I believe you had trouble when you had a sale some time ago. René mentioned there had been a bit of a brush with a character called Percival Mangon?'

'Yes, although a bit of a brush rather underestimates the matter. The unpleasant character took the Uniackes for a ride by using all the tricks of his trade. I am not exactly sure how he did some of it but certainly at least thirty of the best lots were bought by him or by the squalid thug who acts as his assistant, Alfie Brigg. He'd be a nasty one up a dark alley.' Aideen shivered.

'Yes, we know Mangon too, he's been operating over here for close on twelve months. Married up in the business sense with a US Art Assessor, Warren B. Westonhofer, whom René has already run into. The Brigg character appears quite often with them.' Nell gave a wry smile. 'They have engaging ways between the three of them for making middle-of-the-road collectors part with some quite nice pieces. There have been various stories, of course. An Inspector Tim knows has ideas about protection rackets which the Westonhofer character could be a specialist in.'

'If Mangon goes on as he is, it is quite possible he will feel some pressure from the trade,' said Tim.

'Yes,' said Aideen, 'Those two together with Brigg must be a really nasty trio.'

Aideen was quiet for a moment or two, and they knew she was having a flashback to the unhappy incidents surrounding the Mellick sale. Then she gathered her thoughts again and continued, 'Mmm, there is another point. Please, some advice on fakes and reproductions and on provenance, that word provenance with all the complications of history and possible fiddling.'

Tim answered this one,

'I thought you might never mention the nightmare. How do we go on this? Well, I have friends in the laboratory at the Louvre and other places, but when one is out in the field you can't really carry all the gear for scientific examination. Nell in particular is good on this area. She has a sense, a simpatico with a genuine piece. One of the truly great collectors of Europe a number of years ago said to us once, "always look long at an art object you are dealing with — if it is good it will come more and more to life as you look — if it is bad the longer you look the more it will die in front of your eyes." Provenances are another of the danger areas, so are signatures which can float on and off pictures, as can porcelain marks. Develop this sensitivity, Aideen — I know René has it in good measure and from what he has told me about you and from what we've sensed today Aideen, I feel certain you too will have that eye.' Aideen was delighted that they thought she could be a top knocker and was about to speak her thanks when Nell broke in:

'Tim, we haven't even told the poor girl what her rewards can be. I hope that the arrangement we have with René will suit you too. That is, a straight two and a half per cent or, more simply, a quarter of the commission we get plus of course full expenses.'

'Thank you both and thank you for a lovely lunch and a very good talk.'

They all rose and she and René took their leave and descending in the lift to street level, they wandered along on the look out for a taxi.

*   *   *   *   *   *

Just before they arrived back at the studio Aideen suddenly leant forward and asked the driver to stop. She got out pulling René after her and paid.

'What goes?' asked René.

'Come back this way, I saw something in a dealer's window.'

They walked back about fifty yards and then Aideen stopped in front of a lush salon with just three pieces of porcelain in the window.

'Those came from Mellick, I'm almost sure,' Aideen said, 'but I'll know for certain when I have a look under the lip. We used to put a recognition mark on the special pieces and there were some chips on one of them.'

The objects were large polychrome beaker vases with a Wan Li six-character mark in a rectangle on the exterior of the rim, Aideen's mark should be close by.

The saleslady became fulsome in her praise of the quality and the history but she was not too happy when Aideen asked to handle the precious objects. In the end there was a compromise; they gently revolved one of the vases between their combined four hands. The Uniacke mark was not there, it must have been spotted and removed, but the two minute shell-chips were there just to the right of the Wan Li mark. They were ex-Mellick all right. Aideen enquired the price.

'Oooh Mademoiselle, the three are a quarter of a million franc!'

Aideen acted perfectly the role of someone who was in love with the beautiful vases but now knew she could never afford them. With a wry smile and a shrug they left the salon.

Thirty yards down the street she stopped and opened her bag to bring out a small notebook.

'I have some of the facts and figures of Mellick here. Those vases did come from there — they may have wiped off our mark but those small chips I would know anywhere. Look at that, René.' She pointed: 'Look at that! The bastard. He bought, I think it was Brigg bidding, for two hundred and eighty pounds. If that isn't the mark up of the year!'

'Aideen, let's walk.' René linked her arm in his. 'It's not very far back to the studio and I have a flash idea. How long can you stay over here for?'

'If I ring Louise she won't mind a few days, a week or even a bit longer.'

'Right, when we get to the studio you ring County Clare first and then I shall ring a friend of mine on the French railways.'

The climb up all the stairs helped to cool off the anger Aideen felt. A quick connection through to Quin and the voice of Louise was loud in her ears telling of the arrival of five hives of absolutely beautiful bees and how Katty had come up and talked to them so now they were all happy and well; she finished by saying that Aideen should feel free to stay as long as she liked.

René then called his railway friend and made a request, if possible, for two first class seats on the TGV from the Gare de Lyon to Marseilles for the morning. In about ten minutes the friend rang back and all was reserved. A call to the Sofitel central booking ensured two rooms for the next night and possibly for a number of days to follow.

'Why are we going to Marseilles, René?'

'Because I have had another of my insights. Now where shall we dine tonight?'

'You choose. But come on, cut the mystery.'

'No — but I promise you will not be disappointed.'

Four

The next morning René arrived with a taxi as Aideen was paying her bill at the Hotel des Arbres. They were to catch the TGV that would leave the Gare de Lyon at 10.41 and arrive at Marseilles at 15.56.

As they came on to the platform the train was gliding to a stop alongside — resplendent in a spotless livery of orange, white and a cool green-grey, a splendid aerodynamic form. To Aideen, used to more elderly transport, the interior of the first class gave her wonder. Their two seats were irresistibly comfortable: side by side, reclining, personal folding table with magazine-rack; large picture windows with adjustable curtaining, personal reading lights, and all appearing to be brand new, so clean and fresh. After she had sat down, Aideen pulled out of the magazine-rack a pamphlet which gave information about this monster:

'René, is that correct, these speeds they say here? This train can do 236 miles per hour and will maintain an average to Marseilles of about 114?'

He smiled and nodded that this was so:

'But, do not worry; I have been on them before — so smooth you will hardly notice. . . . And yes, I think you'll find it best to look at the country as we go along through the window opposite, rather than the one beside you!'

At 10.41 precisely the scene outside began to change yet there hardly seemed to be any sign of passage. The suburbs of Paris fell away as the open country enveloped them. It was a grey day with tassels of silvery mist draped on the Lombardy poplars. They began to go faster still until the long long train cut through the damp air with the sureness of a sword blade. Outside were more tall poplars with at their tops rooks' nests impaled on the spiky branches. A hill appeared with a scattering of what looked like white toy houses, and aspen, birch and alders, white turkeys, white pigs and white cattle all together in one field. The line of the rail seemed to run endlessly straight, and still even at high speed there was practically no vibration.

Aideen's reverie was broken as the stewardess brought the lunch tray, previously ordered by René — cold meats and crisp salad, Evian, coffee and a bowl of fruit. Loathe to miss any of her journey, Aideen smiled at René and turned again to the window. The train was climbing now through swirling clouds of grey fog. The ascent flattened out and a long descent began and at the same time a glorious sun broke through and the whole landscape jumped to life. They were entering the Rhone valley and running alongside the Autoroute. For a moment a tiny cameo — roaring along the road a super special sports car with driver showing its paces to a girl; then disgrace, his proud steed was passed rather quickly by a train.

The scenery of the Rhone valley was a rich thing. On the west bank atop a steep crag perched a multi-turreted castle — a hideout for a French Brunhilde. The foliage was various with tints of greens, golds, silvers. This ground emanated the atmosphere of history. Hereabouts would have been the killing ground for Celt, Roman, Hun, Vandal, Goth, Visigoth leaving behind their blood that would leaven the men and women of the future. In quick succession another castle, and another and another; who built them? The crusaders or the Templars? About here, in one frightening carnage a hundred thousand and more fell in a single battle.

The outlines of buildings became less distinct under the influence of the heat hazes that tinted the scene, as though by delicate coloured glazes put on by a painter's brush. Avignon and the wraiths of Popes. There was a feeling of entering a crucible of bygone great ones, of becoming a part of the entwining intrigues, the forces of European destiny being forged and hammered out. Down here the Rhone was as broad as the lower waters of the Rhine, but the air was balmy; then, quite suddenly, with a shock the raw beautiful cliffs of nature were exchanged for man-made cliffs of brick, stone and concrete. So gently the train came to rest — Marseilles was here and Aideen came back to today. She apologized to René and he said:

'I wouldn't have broken your dream for anything.'

Marseilles for centuries has spread out round the coast and more slowly climbed the hills to the north. Wherever one goes in this teeming city of many peoples, the eye only has to look up and there will be the looming form of the Notre-Dame-de-la-Garde. Aideen tried to analyze the scents — spices she could only guess at, animal odours from distant parts, frail sweet essences of flowers borne in by the breezes from the north, the whole unified into an exotic different thing by a dry arid smell that hung over this mixing basin for the peoples of France, the Barbary coast, Spain, Tripoli, Sicily, Venice, Greece, Turkey and more that have travelled from the East. The Phocean Greeks from Asia Minor have as good a claim as any to being the founders of the First Port of France. About 600 B.C. an expedition under the command of Protis found good anchorage here. He disembarked for talks with the chief of the local Ligurian tribe. Legend has it that he found himself the guest at a great banquet at which the Princess Gyptis was to choose her husband. Her eye settled on Protis and she brought him a dowry which included the hill which is today surmounted by the Basilica of Notre-Dame-de-la-Garde.

A dark-eyed taxi-driver took them from St Charles station at a fast clip down La Canabière Boulevard and then skirted the Vieux Port and climbed the hill to bring them to the Sofitel. Their rooms had large wide windows which took in much of the panorama of the city. It seemed to Aideen that almost every stone must conceal a fragment of history, of romance, of power and guile, of violence unguessed. A short boat passage from the mainland lies the Château d'If, with stumpy round towers and the frown of a medieval fortress; blood and suffering mark much of its early history — in the 16th and 17th century Protestants were held there before being sent to the galleys. The entrance to the Vieux Port is guarded by the twin forts of St Jean and St Nicolas; this was the original inlet into which the Phoceans had sailed; the quays and the buildings behind them are to a large degree as they were when they were constructed under the orders of Louis XII and XIII. Outside the Vieux Port are the Joliette Basins for deep sea vessels; on the landward side stands the impressive mass of the cathedral.

There was a knock at Aideen's door and René entered.

'It's quite a city — I think I see more in it each time I come back here.'

'It is so different from any other place I have been to. Look down there at the colours the men and the girls are wearing — gorgeous scarves with that deep yellow and maroon. Now René, when do I get my answer, why have we come down here? It's lovely, but such a long way.'

'Yes, I suppose I ought to tell you ... but I think what you'll see tomorrow will be the better as a surprise. ... You don't mind really, do you?'

'With so much to see, to hear, of course not. How long are we going to stay? ... I hope I will have enough clothes.'

'Well, let's think, tomorrow and possibly the next day as I really have a lot to do back in Paris. But apart from the special visit I really want you to come to the Notre-Dame-de-la-Garde and hopefully you will hear what I think is one of the most exciting organs anywhere. But now some dinner.'

'I want to sample the real Provençal *bouillabaisse* and then another dish I have read about but never tasted, that rather special Medieval fish platter, *Brandade de Morue* and to finish I will take one or two of the celebrated *caladons*, the tiny almond cakes.' said Aideen.

René smiled appreciatively,

'Let's see what the restaurant can do.'

*   *   *   *   *   *

The next morning there were whispers of an approaching visit by the Mistral — the air had a strange feel to it and the light breezes were picking up strands of mist and twirling them in and out of the towers.

René asked for a taxi, and when it came gave an address in the area of the Château Gombert some ten kilometres out of the main city and up in the hills to the north east. As the winding, climbing road left the busy commercial bustle of weekday Marseilles and found its way through the environs, the buildings changed almost imperceptibly. It seemed as though they were quietly slipping away to some secret retreat but at the same time doing it with immense dignity: the walls partly covered with flakes of whitewash, greywash and the roofs rouged with exquisite earthenware tiles.

As the taxi crossed one particularly delightful square, René said,

'That is the Château Gombert, one day I must take you there —
it is for the Art of Provence. Full of marvellous stuff, not least a
fantastic collection of Santons.'

'I've heard of those — are they tiny figures?'

'That's right — they cover I think every aspect of Provençal life
and they have a very special place with the people down here.'

The streets they were now passing through had grown quiet
and had little traffic and few pedestrians. Plane trees of considerable age were profuse, their ancient trunks flaking, the soft green
leaves making a jigsaw with sun specks across the walls and dap-
pling the surface of the road. One further right-hand turn and the
taxi entered a small square cul-de-sac. On three sides tall stone
walls rose without a window piercing them. The fourth side had a
single entrance doorway of some size with embrasures about eye-
height on each side. The door itself was massive, made from hard-
wood timbers and heavily studded. They got out of the taxi and
paid.

Aideen looked up at the rather severe façade and then turned
to René saying:

'Come on René, what is this about? What is this place, some
kind of prison?'

René laughed,

'Couldn't be farther from the truth. You have a lovely surprise
coming.'

'But there isn't even a number to the door, there is no name-
plate, there is no knocker, and I can't even see a bell.'

'Oh yes there is.'

René stepped up to the right-hand side of the doorway and
just underneath the top hinge and almost invisible was a small
brass button which he pressed.

As the notes of the bell fell silent there came a rumbling of
heavy bolts being withdrawn and a lock being turned. One half
of the door swung inwards and at the same time a truly impressive figure came through and stood on the top step of the three
that raised the entrance from the pavement. He wore the clothes
or rather the uniform of a Cossack. He must have stood six foot
six, which, with a flamboyant kind of shako, brought the entire
vision up to over seven feet. The lower half of his face and neck
was totally obscured by a dense black beard; black eyebrows
shielded his eyes but not sufficiently to hide an intimidating stare
which fortunately softened as soon as he saw René.

'Monsieur Culhane, ah welcome, it is good to see you again.' The voice was a tremendous bass to match the figure.

'Igor my friend,' said René, shaking the great hand extended towards him.

'May I introduce Mademoiselle Uniacke.' The giant Russian bowed and offered his hand.

'Igor is the one you have to get past when you come to the Ateliers. To give it the full title — Les Ateliers des Oeuvres d'Art of Madame Angélique, whom I see coming to meet us now,' continued René.

They went through the entrance and past a heavily secured gatehouse which was the hideout for Igor and his two assistants. Out of the shadows and into a pleasant courtyard and garden. Going towards Angélique, Aideen felt an unspoken approval from the mistress of this establishment. Angélique was nearly as tall as Aideen herself, a fuller figure with dark honey-blond hair, skin carrying the soft tawny tan of the Provence sun and blue eyes that shielded themselves behind the partially lowered lids which tended to give Angélique a mild appearance. Nothing could be farther from the truth, I'd wager, thought Aideen as she weighed up this attractive person in her delicate patterned silk dress which was given just a flash of rich colour from a magnificent bar brooch set with five large rubies. Angélique held on to Aideen's hand and took one step backward till they were at arm's length:

'Oh René, she is lovely. Forgive me Aideen, but to admire is a compliment, my dear. Let us go over in the shade and take coffee before I show you what I have here.'

Aideen let her gaze wander. Scattered amongst the shrubs, the flowers and trees were several statues which she judged to be either early Roman or late Greek. The buildings surrounding the garden and courtyard were three storeys with large windows in the manner of the French Empire style with wide sills supported by finely carved acanthus leaf brackets. In between the windows on the ground floor were niches about four feet high holding dark patinated bronze figures of legendary tales from the past.

Aideen was completely puzzled as to just what she was going to see. Angélique, she felt, must be one of those great but secret collectors, but what of? After the coffee, they got up and Angélique led the way through a foyer and into a Grand Salon which, she explained, was continued down through both wings around the courtyard. For an instant Aideen was held by the sheer magnificence of the quality that was all around her.

Then she turned to Angélique:

'Would I be impolite if I asked if I might wander alone? I love to meet works such as these privately at first.'

'Of course, my dear, René and I will have much to talk about; we will sit here in the foyer.'

Aideen hardly knew where to look first. On the floors were rugs so precious that she could not bear to walk on them; an exquisite Tabriz of Safavid design and towards the centre of the main room what appeared to be a Ferghan 'Zelli Sultan' rug glowing with rich bronze and crimson tints. The furniture would have sent the most opulent of collectors into spasms of desire. Her eye delighted in a Louis XV black lacquer commode with a green and dark grey mottled marble top and ormolu fittings that were rich in detail and imagination; goatsheads, sun bursts and lions' paws for feet, a piece which surely must carry the mark of the famous *ébéniste* F.-A.Mondon. In contrast was a German walnut and marquetry *bombe* commode which had the feeling of the Spindler Brothers. The finest of every period and master seemed to be gathered here. From over the Atlantic, an example of Chippendale's influence; a mahogany block-front desk or possibly dressing-table which could have come from the workshop of the Goddard-Townsend family. A George III mahogany Carlton House writing-table and another piece from the same period; a giltwood console table which just had to have come from Robert Adam and could possibly have been made by William France and John Bradburn. Another object that drew her was a *pietra dura* table top which was clearly early 17th century and probably came from the Grand Ducal workshops.

For the moment she ignored the paintings. There was so much to see. On one wall a superb Flemish *feuilles de choux* tapestry of the 16th century and facing on another wall a set of four Brussels tapestries. Standing alone a North Italian suit of half-armour sparkling with quite amazing inlay work with gold and silver wires. In a case was a Swiss wheel-lock holster pistol dating from 1640 which was likely to have come from the hand of Felix Werder of Zurich. Nearby rested an Icon of the greatest beauty; it showed the Presentation of the Virgin Mary in the Temple — a precious plaque measuring no more than twelve and a half inches by eleven, it was an enamel predominantly worked with several shades of a blue close to ultramarine and white with touches of ochre. Nearly every category of antiques seemed to be present: glass vessels and chandeliers, illuminated manuscripts, Japanese netsuke, ironwork. Everything except, it seemed, ceramics and silver objects.

Aideen now turned to the pictures. As she walked and paused a succession of masterworks held her attention. A 14th century Triptych: The Birth of Jesus, which had the feel of Pietro da Rimini. A beautiful freely brushed-in Madonna and Child with the infant Saint John the Baptist and Attendant Angels which to her gave evidence of being by Giulio Cesare Procaccini. A Village Kermesse by, she thought, the younger Peter Brueghel was hung next to what seemed to be a Willem van de Velde of Dutch Men-o'-War. Then quite harmoniously on an adjoining wall, a most nostalgic scene, she felt sure by Claude Monet, entitled Argenteuil, Fin d'Après-Midi; one of the few works which he had not signed, she thought. In the three salons there must have been some seventy first-line paintings and the value of these plus everything else must total comfortably up into the seven figures bracket if not the eight — and that was pounds sterling, not francs.

She went back to join the other two, and Angélique smiled at her:

'So Aideen, you have seen some of my treasures. What do you think?'

'What do I think! René told me I was in for a surprise but I could never have guessed anything like this.'

Angélique exchanged a look with René and then said,

'Come with me.'

She rose and walked across the main salon towards a tall door to the right-hand side. Turning the handle, she continued,

'Now what about this?'

Aideen was led through the doorway into a wide and lofty passage. Almost at once it was the smells of the place struck her. Linseed oil, varnishes, waxes, and others that she could not recognize. Then she realized that leading off the passage were numerous workshops with craftsmen of many callings — she could see half-finished pieces of furniture, tapestry looms, glass workers and down at the end she could just make out a very large studio, canvases and wooden panels in various states on easels. She knew then what the surprise was, but it was difficult to absorb.

'Angélique, am I right?' she pointed to the various workplaces and then back to the door through which they had entered.

'They are doing those?'

'Yes.'

'But why?'

'There are so many clients to satisfy — there could never be all those genuine things to find for them.'

'But surely . . .'

René came in:

'I think Aideen is troubled about the law, Angélique.'

'Quite so . . . but what does the International Law say about such things? It does not say it is illegal to make reproductions or fakes. It just says that I must not sign names and make hallmarks and then sell these things as if they were by these great masters. The dealers who buy from me know well that the objects are reproductions. If a client comes here, I do not say that a certain painting is by Boucher, or a tapestry is Gobelin. I do not have labels, as you see. No. No. I leave the vanity of the collector to do this for me. There are few people more vain in their ignorant knowledge than some of the collectors. The more money they have, the bigger the head. Tell me, Aideen or René, how many cases do you know of where a collector or a dealer admits to buying a reproduction as the real thing — or fake if you like?'

Aideen raised a point:

'What about stolen works?'

Angélique replied:

'Ah, those are outside my work. But I know plenty of people who deal with these things. Then, it is not so much a matter of vanity but of greed. When you are so rich that you cannot spend what you have, what is left but to want the things no one else has. The backwaters of the art dealing world are a long way away, I'm afraid, from the place where the artist works.'

For the next two hours Angélique led them through the workshops and studios. In the three spacious workrooms devoted to furniture it was intriguing to see at close quarters just how skilled hands go about 'creating' something that is supposed to be two hundred years or more old. Veneering now was no longer done on carcass timbers but chipboards and laminated plyboards were used. Angélique even had a large humidity chamber where pieces could be subjected to changes of temperature and humidity that would, after a couple of weeks, induce just a slight warping and thus give a more convincing look of age. The 'distressors' worked with almost a brutal disdain for the skill of their fellow craftsmen. Some of the finished pieces were subjected to bruising, scratching, abrading, staining. Nothing was left to chance: one man spent most of his time carefully making hand-made screws and working with a small anvil and hammer to produce nails of an early period. The very latest techniques with marquetry had been studied and were being so successfully applied that much time was being saved by being able to produce a perfect surface at the first application.

Angélique explained that all the craftsmen and artists she had working for her were refugees. They came from many parts of the world, often by word of mouth selection and they brought much skill and knowledge with them. The château was large enough to have made a community. They had in some cases brought their wives or husbands with them and apartments had been converted. They were paid either in kind or in money and for more than eight years now it had been a place of harmony. Doing, she said, no harm to anybody — well, perhaps lessening the weight of their wallets for the rich. The feeling that her family was happy was underlined as they went from group to group all of whom were addressed by their Christian names and who called the director of this remarkable gathering Angélique.

From furniture they went to a central workshop where the gilding experts were plying their difficult task. Giovanni, who had run some time ago from matters he did not like in Italy, explained with pride that the skill of the gilder was one of the oldest of all. It started with the Assyrians and Egyptians and then for a time much of the skill was lost sight of only to be rediscovered in its entirety by a monk in the 14th or 15th century. It all succeeds if the preliminary stages are carefully and honestly done. The building up of the gesso layers, creamy plasters of gypsum or similar substance with a weak glue which could be rabbit-skin or the curds from long-soured milk. Then the laying of a thin coat of bole, a red clay, to give richness to the frail thin gold leaves. Glair was a favourite with some for holding the gold leaf; this substance is prepared from over-beaten fresh egg-white and a little water; others preferred just plain water gilding. Last of all the quiet patience with the lifting of the leaves on a broad soft flat brush and guiding them into place — looks so easy.

Finally, the burnishing with an agate tool shaped rather like a curved dog's tooth. If the gilt panel was for use with an early painting, the artist might demand that patterns were punched into it with various shaped dies.

The tapestry looms were in the charge of a quiet little man and his sister. They had come from Belgium years ago seeking security in the factory work places of New York and had moved on to other cities as their dreams faded. Then Lise and Hans had found the trail that led them to Angélique. They were so grateful that it seemed at whatever hour she walked through the workshops, the two of them had their looms and frames clattering away. Their knowledge of the making of the various types of tapestries and rugs encompassed every angle — the picking of the right sizes of yarn, through to the whole dyeing process. She had seen a rug made by them pass without comment as the genuine thing by more than one of the top experts in this tricky field.

On through the glass manufactory where three workers from Poland were demonstrating the handling of every process the masters from the past had used. Blowing, moulding, gilding, enamelling. From one corner of this seemingly endless complex of talent a great deal of noise was coming — here two German armourers and one Austrian were at work — that day it was a suit of Nuremburg armour of the 15th century. On shelves behind them were lying in various stages of completion a fearsome array of daggers, swords, crossbows and firearms of many types and periods.

Lastly they came to the painting studio. On a large cranked easel stood a nearly finished canvas showing what would certainly be taken, when completed, as a work by John Wootton, the English 18th century animal painter. In a wooded glade stood a magnificent dark chestnut stallion — neck arched as a groom tried to restrain the spirited animal. To one side Dietrich, once of Hannover, worked on a small panel of a Madonna and Child with a circlet of angels exactly in the style of the early Flemish painter Geertgen tot St Jan.

Angélique took her leave of Dietrich and beckoned on Aideen and René, who were to join her in her private apartment for lunch.

Aideen could hardly bear to take herself away from this cave of treasures in the making. She smiled her gratitude to them all and followed the Madame who had brought into being such an incredible centre.

They went back into the foyer and up a slender staircase that brought them to a wide landing which gave straight on to an elegant drawing-room through two wide flat arches. There a further surprise awaited Aideen as Nell and Tim Sinclair rose to greet them.

'How was the flight?' asked Angélique, embracing Nell.

'I think it's possibly quite a bit slower, by the time one gets out to one airport and back in from another, than the way our friends came down,' replied Nell.

'You are surprised to see us, Aideen — but like René we wanted this fabulous place to be a surprise for you. Tim and I have been friends with Angélique for many years.'

'Let us go into lunch now and then we can have a longer talk over coffee,' suggested Angélique.

The dining-room was long and graceful with three windows, the walls a pale cool yellow, the ceiling slightly coved and decorated with low relief flower and leaf forms. In the centre was a splendid dark mahogany Chippendale table with a set of chairs from the same workshop; though whether it was all from the real Mr. Chippendale's workshop or the one downstairs Aideen didn't even venture to guess.

The meal began with a chilled soup of cucumber with tiny medallions of lamb's liver gently flavoured with garlic. This was followed by small sea bass grilled whole on a bed of fennel stalks accompanied by a salad of endive, finely sliced purple cabbage, slivers of young carrots and skinned grapefruit segments. Next came platters of fresh fruits and a board with some of the cheeses from the district including the local goat's cheese which had a soft crumbly texture and a sharp taste to the palette. After this they rose and returned to the drawing-room where the coffee tray awaited them.

'I must congratulate you, Tim and Nell, on your new recruit,' said Angélique. 'She will soon fit in. I feel we shall all have some — how you say — fun working together.'

'René found Aideen for us,' said Nell. 'But how is the business for you down here?'

'I should say pretty good,' began Angélique, 'in the last month I have taken on two good men for furniture; they came to me via that man you gave a good name for, the one in Stuttgart. Also a splendid talented girl arrived from Istanbul; she enamels with a skill I have not found before, both with *cloisonné* and the *champ-levé*. But do tell me, how is the centre of things in Paris?'

'At the moment a fury of rumours,' said Nell. 'Just after you two left yesterday morning the bell to the apartment rang and it was a very excited young lady, Cécile, who is one of our secretaries and absolutely reliable. She was bursting with news. That Percival Mangon character is really starting to stir things. Last week apparently he had a row with that Art Assessor partner of his, Westonhofer. What it was about one can only guess but the American was on a Pan Am by lunchtime. Mangon seems into something pretty deep and we heard last night that only about three hours after the Westonhofer left, someone else who could make big trouble turned up at Mangon's place. You may know her, Angélique, she is from Austria, from Vienna . . .'

'Oh no! Not Herta Poll!' Angélique broke in.

'You've got it,' said Tim.

'Yes, the greatest double-agent in the antique trade,' went on Nell. 'How she will make out with Mangon I can't imagine but they spell big trouble. They were closeted together for more than three hours. From the first reports of the playback what they have in mind could possibly throw wide open the whole world trade in antiques.'

Angélique broke in: 'What is this about playback?'

'Oh, I may not have told you, but that quiet peaceful looking character Tim at one time was in intelligence and surveillance was one of his specialities. We have one or two places fitted with bugs of the very latest sensitivity and Mangon's is one of them.'

'You English with your expressionless good looks — when it comes to the craftiness we are outside in the passage,' cried Angélique. 'So what is the heart of what they are up to?'

'We've known for some time that Herta had hatched some extraordinary scheme for marketing antiques. But what it lacked was a partner as crooked as herself. Mangon nearly convinced even us with the sales spiel he gave her. Fräulein Poll is no easy knockover but by the sound of her voice she was feeding on every word Percy could dream up — how he had this huge list of rich clients, businesses about to expand not only in London and Paris but also on the east and west coasts of the United States and in a host of other places. It sounded as though he was reading from the end pages of a catalogue from one of the Majors. Who, by the way, are just going to love this, if these characters get going. It could mash up the market — certainly from the medium range items downward which are after all the cake and jam for the Majors and the Minors everywhere.'

René came in:

'Surely they can tie him down in some way or other. What about finance?'

'I am not at all sure,' said Tim.

'After your sale in Ireland, Aideen, the man had the devil's luck. He fell in with a consortium of international moneybags — the kind of people who have arrived at a position where they can't even hope to spend what they've got. We are trying to track them down but they keep themselves very private, a fact of life I would think if they want to go on surviving. We do know three, a Korean, a Malayan and a Taiwanese. The scheme for this mad marketing seems to be related to the hypermarket plan linked with all the gimickery of special offers, give-aways, mass media publicity, sponsoring by related commercial interests etc. Those two characters could be really cooking something up. And there was another interesting pointer towards the end of the tape. Herta was burbling something about all those art thefts and the low rate of recovery by the police. She talked about where the eighty per cent of unrecovered stuff was going to and how she could perhaps track down some of this lot with the help of her pawn-broking cousin in Regensburg. Apparently he has told her of an extremely profitable side-line he's developing as a fence for these antiques. She mentioned juggernaut loads of them going round looking for buyers.'

'One thing is quite clear, the Mangon-Poll partnership must be broken up,' said Angélique. 'They cannot operate outside the rest of us! But how best to do it?'

'Can we get at him through his backers?' queried Aideen

'Possibly, but it is going to take some thinking through,' said Nell. 'I've seen these fast ones before — they break the confidence of our clients.

'Here are we trying to stabilize things — trying to bring some sense to a market that is already bursting itself. £24 million for a bunch of fading sunflowers, it isn't as if it was the only painting of sunflowers he did. That is turning money into non-money. The prices are creeping so high that proportion is lost sight of. Bank notes become just symbols; I don't know whether money is taking the place of art or art is taking the place of money, but I think it has got to be the latter. With the share prices blipping across television screens the vast majority of people are losing sight of what money is. Start one side of the globe with a full wallet and go through several bad exchange rates and that's it. Fine art and antiques with a carefully controlled pricing and value can really be the only stable security for the future.'

The others nodded in agreement. Nell was reiterating something that they all felt.

'The trouble with types like Mangon,'said Tim, 'is that there is no way they can be reasoned with. Even if they appeared to be going along with you they have the infernal cunning of a hyena and you'd be shopped at the first chance they got. No, we've got to find a way, and there must be one, to pull him down and the Herta woman with him. Now, I don't want to break this up, Angélique, but . . . ' Tim explained that Nell and he had an appointment with a woman who might have something of interest before they caught the evening plane back to Paris. The other three saw the Sinclairs to the courtyard and made their farewells.

Once Tim and Nell had been let out by Igor, the remaining three settled down in comfortable basket chairs on the shady side of the garden.

About three o'clock there was a gentle interruption to their reverie from Igor, who told Angélique that there was a man to see her, an American. His name was Hiram K. Frack and he said he had an introduction from the director of one of the big New York museums, said he'd come specially all the way from Frankfurt while he was on vacation in West Germany.

'Thank you, Igor,' said Angélique: 'I will see him here in the garden. I know what museum it probably was. He may be genuine, he may not be. Don't go far away, Igor.'

The Russian went back to the entrance and then reappeared leading Hiram K. Frack to where Angélique was standing a few yards away from Aideen and René.

The approaching figure was impressive in all the wrong ways. The dress or costume was over-loud, the Stetson was too big, the over-decorated calf-length boots didn't help. He stretched out a hand with spatulate fingers and a set of terribly broken nails.

'Hi, Maaam! The name is Hiram, the state is Arizona, the country is the good old U S of A. My, you gotten a pretty garden here.'

The opening sally had to a degree thrown the urbanity of Angélique but she came back quickly.

'It suits me, Monsieur Frack.'

'Oh come on now . . . what's all this Monsew stuff. Folks back home wud laugh me outa town.'

'You have come a long way — what can I do for you?' said Angélique.

'Well now ma'am, I'm one of those collectors that go fur things other folk don't have.'

'Are you sure you have come to the right place?'

'Sure am. I've a little commission to give you. I was told you sure have some bright fellas here. Now what I want is this — and I'm sure we're not goin' to fall out over price. You get your top man to make me the best tootin' copy of a certain girl and we're in business. The real one is not far from here. What I'm gettin' to is I jest want me a copy or reproduction or whatever you folk call the thing — of that Black Virgin they've got stashed away down here. Now, what do you say — how much and I'll add ten per cent if he's quick at the job.'

'My answer, Monsieur Frack, is no. We do not do things like that here in my ateliers.'

'Do I hear you turnin' me down, ma'am? That's not the way we do things back where I come from. My money's good; and it is, if I may say so, the man who calls the throw.'

'I'm sure it is. But the answer is no. This is my establishment and I wish you to leave.'

'You tryin' to cheat me outa something I'm tryin' to buy on the level?'

'I am most certainly not. Now, as our talk is over, you must excuse me, I have other clients to see.'

'Just a minute, ma'am. Back in my place I could show you silver idols and figures that are worth a lot more than your little old black statue. You know how I got them? Hiram's got friends around and knows some smart fellas willin' to earn a handful of green and no questions asked — there are not many places left that can't be broken into if you use professionals. Don't worry your little wavy head — I don't need your help. No ma'am, Angélique or whatever you call yourself.'

'Monsieur Frack, a last word of advice. You would be very ill-advised to try anything like that here. This is not some temple in the wilds — this is Marseilles.'

'I don't take no advice from wimmen. And you'd better keep your mouth shut about this.'

Angélique drew herself up very straight,

'I order you from my château. Get out!'

This last remark stung Hiram and he leant forward and quite brutally lashed out at Angélique. She was quick to side-step but the blow still landed heavily on her shoulder. Almost simultaneously with the blow René stood up but before he could move there was a flash of something bright and a thunk as one of Aideen's knives hissed through the air, missing Hiram's left ear by a hairsbreadth and then burying itself in a palm tree just beside him.

For a moment he appeared too shocked to move.

'Damn you, who threw that?' His eyes went past Angélique to where Aideen stood.

'You, was it? We'll see who can play funny games.' He started to reach towards the handle of the knife stuck in the palm when an ice-cold voice called out,

'I wouldn't if I were you. The next one will come much closer.'

The man from Arizona turned his head and looked towards Aideen. She was standing with her right arm raised and the hand holding a second knife. Hiram had been in some rough-houses and a base instinct always told him when he was on the losing side. As his gaze met the soul-shivering stare from those green eyes, he felt a tell-tale trickle of chilled perspiration run down his chest. Quite suddenly Hiram K. Frack cracked, crumpled as a triple pricked balloon. His lips trembled as though to say something, then rather unexpectedly he let out a sob of utter frustration.

'Igor, would you please show him out.'

When the Cossack returned from despatching the unwanted visitor he went over to the palm tree and carefully pulled out the knife. This he then wiped on a large green bandana; inspected the workmanship of the handle, tried the blade with his thumb and then returned it to Aideen:

'It is good. And Mademoiselle, whoever taught you, taught you well. Your speed and eye few could equal.' The eyes of the big man were full of admiration.

Angélique went over to Aideen and gave her a hug of gratitude.

'My dear, I could employ you full time. That's one visitor that won't return. I noticed Igor whispering something to him as he was pushed out through the door into the street. What was it, Igor?'

'I don't think he understood what I said but he knew what I meant.'

Angélique smiled and continued to Aideen,

'Now my dear, have you seen enough of what I have here?'

'I could spend days in those workshops but René has told me he has another treat in store, a visit to the Basilica of Notre-Dame-de-la-Garde, hopefully to hear the sound of the organ there,' said Aideen.

'Ah, magnificent. Now always remember, if you come to Marseilles Angélique would love to see you.' For a moment they embraced again and kissed on both cheeks.

'Thank you again. Igor will call you a taxi. René, when do you plan to return to Paris?'

'The plan is to visit some more of the special places of Marseilles tomorrow, like the Château Gombert, the Beaux Arts and the Grobet-Labadié. Then back to Paris the following day.'

'Do not be too optimistic — unless I am not feeling things quite right, the Mistral is not many hours away. Don't be unwise and venture too far.'

Igor was opening the main door as a taxi drew up outside.

'Ah, there you go.' Angélique was embracing René, 'au revoir, my friends.'

The driver must have been newly qualified because he lost his way, and they ended up in the centre of Marseilles alongside the Vieux Port and thus had to ascend the central hill again. The narrow streets climbed a gradient that must have been close to one in three and there was a succession of the tightest hairpin bends imaginable; the progress went on until it seemed they would truly end up in the sky, and then the taxi deposited them onto a tiny parking space in front of the Notre-Dame. The driver said he could do with a rest — they should not hurry — he would be right here for them.

From this altitude when looking down on the city it was as though the whole scale had changed. Fifteen storey buildings hundreds of feet high had shrunk to things made with children's building blocks. The yachts in the Vieux Port appeared to have pin-sized masts. The Grand Joliette Basins with ocean-going liners and giant tankers gave the impression that they were baths full of clockwork models. The Cathedral, which was the largest church built during the 19th century in France, had become a matchbox model of tiny domes and spires. Out to sea the Chateau d'If looked about as formidable as a toy fort.

Turning from the view, Aideen saw that the climb was not over yet — one hundred and sixty worn rock steps stretched upward. At the top a novelty, for the entrance to the church was over a drawbridge. The total height of the Notre-Dame-de-la-Garde is some one hundred and fifty feet above the summit of the hill; the belfry being topped by a thirty foot gilded statue of the Virgin Mary. Over the drawbridge and inside at last, a low arched roof, silence and an atmosphere of its own; more flights of steps and then out into the body of the church. A priest standing on a tall pulpit-like platform in the centre was just concluding a service. The congregation could probably be only found in Marseilles. There seemed to be representatives of all the races that had for centuries made Marseilles a unique city. René and Aideen chose to seat themselves towards the rear where they judged the sound would be at its best. They waited.

At last an earth-trembling chord of a bass so deep that it shook the air heralded an explosion of celestial music. Within the notes and phrases seemed to be contained passions and echoes from the whole history of church music overlaid by that indefinable touch of the great city below, which for two millenia had received the wanderers, the conquerors, the holy ones, the infidels and now a sublimation of their voices was being poured forth from this great organ. The player, Robert Martin, was improvising on a Te Deum, which was followed by Adeste Fideles, Salve Regina and at last a spirit-lifting Dies Irae. In the silence that had now returned they sat, hand-in-hand and quite still.

Without speaking they rose and walked slowly across to the steps that led to the door that gave access to the drawbridge. When they reached the top of the long flight of steps down to where they could see their taxi waiting patiently, Aideen touched René's arm.

'Thank you, René dear, that was a sublime moment. This morning with Angélique was tremendous but that almost incredible sound is right up there on its own.' They began the long descent and near the bottom they came upon a little shop where two Franciscan nuns were selling religious items, postcards and tapes of the singing and music of the great basilica. While Aideen bought some of the cards and colour transparencies René was thumbing through the tapes; he pulled out one and exclaimed:

'Here, you can take a memory back to Clare. It is the music we have just heard and it is played by Robert Martin.' He paid the smiling sister and gave it to Aideen.

'Wonderful,' she said, 'it will be lovely to have it to listen to and interesting to hear it against the atmosphere of Ireland.'

Outside once more, they walked the last paces to the taxi. Looking at the panoramic view again it seemed that the light had grown stronger. Lifting their gaze to the sky it could be seen in the last hour what clouds there had been had completely cleared away — just a vast expanse of the clearest blue, the sun a white hot fearsome ball, although there was an intensifying chill to the air — unconsciously they reacted with a shudder.

'Ah, ah, she is coming,' the driver said. 'Even now she is leaving Valence to grow rude and strong pressed between the great cliffs of the Rhone valley. Quick, into the car and I will get you back to your hotel before the Mistral gets here.' Aideen had heard of this wind which can blow roughly one day out of two, mostly in the winter; the record for Marseilles stands at one hundred and seventy-five days in one year. It can occur along the coast from the mouth of the Ebro to the Gulf of Genoa but it is in Provence and Languedoc that it is most frequent and achieves the greatest strength. The beautiful sky that was still overhead fools no one who lives there.

Even in the fifteen minutes it took the taxi to take them to the Sofitel the temperature had fallen still further; when they got out another strange phenomena was a distinct fall in the humidity, the skin of their hands felt papery with dryness.

Back inside the cosseted comfort they settled down in a lounge that had large windows viewing the Vieux Port and towards the entrance of the harbour and across to the Grand Joliette Basins. Over two long glasses of Citron Pressé they could watch, but at that moment not hear, the coming of the unwanted visitor. The surface of the sheltered water of the Vieux Port took on a strange texture that altered its appearance constantly as the wind attacked down first one street and then another. The water danced as though being sucked from above, then fell to form into the look of a coarsely raked field. Flags and pennants strained at mastheads and halliards bellied and thrummed to the force of the embryo storm. The streets that they could see were emptying fast.

Some brave souls were making last minute attempts to secure the smaller yachts and skiffs — extra lines were being secured fore and aft to the larger boats. Anything that was loose was being pushed below decks or into sheds along the quays. The Hall Porter came over to them.

'Good evening, Mademoiselle and Monsieur, you are not going out tonight I hope. This Mistral will be a bad one. Already there are reports from along the nearby coasts of great damage building up. The seas are coming inland and chimneys and roofs are flying — some have already gone.'

René replied:

'No, we are certainly not going out, I think that a good dinner here is in order.' He looked at Aideen and received her vigorous nod of approval.

Now they could hear the angry voice of the storm even through the heavy glazing of the windows. There was a distinct mumbling roar that seemed to be coming from all directions at once, and was slowly rising in pitch. The early Mistral had deceived the automatic central heating of the hotel and the room became chilled. They decided to take an early dinner and after this they watched the television which was screening the first reports of the damage. It was indeed serious and one of the worst for many years. Countless small craft were swept out to sea or battered to wood-pulp where they were; parts of break-waters and sea walls torn to pieces by the combined force of the wind and monstrous waves. The forecast optimistically claimed that the Mistral would wear itself out by the next morning.

But during the night it certainly did not sound as though the storm would end. The bass howling rose to a baritone and then a tenor before bursting into high soprano screeches and screams. Even the hotel was giving a tremble now and then as some fist of the gale battered up against the walls. It was difficult to tell who tired first, the guests in their rooms or the titanic force outside. Aideen thought afterwards that she had through sheer weariness fallen asleep about three-thirty. The next thing she knew was that room service had brought her *petit déjeuner* and when the maid drew the curtains, lo and behold the storm had gone. Pleasant white wraiths of clouds were drifting casually across the sky — the Mistral had disappeared like some evil genie back into some great dark cavern way up to the north in the Massif Central.

For the people of Marseilles it was a sad night but one which by now they accepted phlegmatically as part of what was demanded from them as payment for living in the special place that is Provence.

For the day Aideen and René became carefree tourists and wandered from gallery to museum, from churches to monuments assisted by another patient taxi driver. They went on the advice of their friend to a small boutique in a narrow street off the Vieux Port. Here René found a silk scarf with striking combination of deep crimson and yellow ochre for Aideen who herself bought for Louise an embroidered handkerchief case and for Batsy a flamboyant shawl with soft grey and green tones as a background to large, deep yellow roses.

*   *   *   *   *   *

At the Mangon premises in Paris on the second floor where Percival had made himself a comfortable apartment, the coming genius of the art sales world, as he saw himself, was indulging in a favourite pursuit; going through sales records and finding out how things balanced. Since the nice little kick-off with the Mellick sale he hadn't looked back. Two weeks after that one, a large rambling nearly stately home in Yorkshire had quite literally fallen into his lap; the intended auctioneer had for no explained reason stepped down. The building itself was no great shakes but it went at a reasonable figure for some trust for adventure pursuits or the like. But the contents had turned out to be quite spectacular. Plenty of the right stuff, oak dressers, chests, gate-legged tables, magnificent Lowestoft dinner services, about two dozen assorted Meissen birds and animals of the right period, four excellent horse pieces by Ben Marshall, a Stubbs of a forest lion, an impressive array of English silver and sundries that brought the total just into seven figures. Brigg had been at his best during the bidding, so that the plus for Percy ended up just short of one hundred and sixty thousand. Only last week he had started into the house and contents sales field in France with an early 18th-century château. This was for the whole estate, not like the time when he had won the Grünewald at the place near Rheims. The contents did not appear to be much at first, mostly ceramics which Percy tended to look down on as a main provider; but during the four hours of the sale he learnt a lot about the values possible for Sèvres, Dresden, Famille Rose, Kakiemon and other manufacturers — the end result was another six figure lift to his blooming prospects.

And now out of the blue had come an approach from this mysterious woman, Herta Poll from Vienna. In fact it was she whom he was at that moment awaiting.

At precisely fifteen minutes past eight the intercom buzzer on his desk sounded. He pressed the switch to acknowledge and the voice of Alfie Brigg at its most respectable came through:

'Excuse me sir, the lady you were expecting has arrived.'

'Thank you. Please show her to the lift.' He rose and went out to the landing opposite to the lift door. The hum of the motor stopped and with a metallic sigh the door slid open and Fräulein Poll stepped out.

'Ah, Herr Mangon. I am pleased we meet at last.'

Whatever Percival had in mind as an image for Herta Poll it was nowhere near the figure that now firmly shook his hand. To start with, Herta had a thing about how she dressed; it had always to be in black, from the beret she wore very much to one side, to the coat, the blouse, the skirt, the stockings, shoes and the black leather gloves. She liked it that way. In some odd manner she felt secure all in black. Herta was fairly tall, about five feet eight, with dark red hair and then, which was slightly unnerving for a first time meeting, she had wall-eyes. The left one was a washed out pale blue, the right a dark autumnal brown. Her face had the high cheek bones that could owe their origin to far-away places to the east, while the mouth was so thin-lipped that it was hardly there at all until she spoke. When she did speak the lips drew back to display a perfectly matched array of glistening white teeth.

Mangon was pretty quick on his feet when meeting people but it did take a few seconds before his wits returned and he led his guest into the study. When he offered her a drink it was politely refused:

'Later I will have some fruit juice or a mineral water.'

After they were seated Percy continued to expand on his remarkable successes which he had already indicated to Herta over the phone. She listened with engrossed attention, and then suddenly she picked up the bulging black leather brief case with brass locks that she had placed beside her chair and deposited it on to his desk:

'I have the papers which will explain my plans and show all details with regard to publicity, commissions, catalogues and how with our joined experience we shall make for big business. I will leave this with you tonight so then tomorrow we can make a start. You tell me on the telephone that you have hopes for the sponsors. Have you news?'

'Indeed I have and it's good. After my last meeting in London, I had an introduction to a client who had bought some silver at one of the sales I had last year. He asked me to dinner as he wished to talk of ideas. What has come out of this is very good. There are three extremely rich gentlemen who are looking for investment possibilities in Europe. This client told me how they had studied the map of the Far East and saw the trade centre as Singapore. From there routes go to Seoul, Tokyo, Peking, Hong-kong, Taiwan, Thailand, India, Sri Lanka, the East Indies, all with good markets opening up for antiques and fine art, and there is also the back-door to Australia and New Zealand. I have had several long telephone calls with these men. They are very keen on your ideas. We shall have the finance we need, I'm sure. I have told them about you and I've set up this meeting tomorrow at their hotel here in Paris.'

Mangon's great plan was for a mobile fine arts showroom. Huge juggernaut lorries converted so that together they would make a display area and a workable auction room. Something for the moment to be kept secret lest others jump on the band-waggon.

'Have you any idea how much they can place with us and how they would wish to operate?'

'Their spokesman said figures would be discussed tomorrow. They would expect us to manage everything and of course there would be understood percentages for them.'

'Do you realise, Mr. Mangon — or may I make it Percival — how big this could go?'

'Please do, Herta. I am taking with me tomorrow the facts and figures of the last two years. These present a convincing graph of growth achieved.'

'Above all, Percival, secrecy must be complete. The one who strikes first with these plans will be the one who will rule the entire international art market till the year two thousand and beyond. The Majors have had too long at the top!'

'How right you are. And Herta, you know what the key of our success is going to be?'

'Ja, Ja, the commission rate.'

Percy and Herta smiled, both sure that they understood each other perfectly.

* * * * * *

By seven o'clock the following morning the memories of the Mistral had faded. The weather had relented, the skies looked kind and for a moment an odd pinky-mauve tint wrapped the still drowsy city with a gentle touch of romance and mystery. Aideen and René reached St. Charles station well ahead of the time for the early morning TGV to Paris. A petite stewardess showed them to their seats and at six minutes past eight they were on their way. The train gathered speed with all the delicacy of a cat and was almost as silent. The somewhat dismal buildings that lined the track were blurred by the speed of passage — a long very dark tunnel and then out into the blessed light that gives a unique life to the landscape of Provence. Monet, Van Gogh and how many others have found a special inspiration here.

The morning had an unreal quality, it was bright without the harsh glare of a full sun — the buildings, the trees, the cattle, the early workers in the fields were powdered with a pale warm, in places almost golden, mist. There were no hard lines, it was all a matter of forms that had a substance that defied the eye to analyse. In a short time the broad waters of the Rhone were alongside the windows, moving so smoothly that the surface could be a polished sheet of pale bronze.

The trolley had been along dispensing fruit juice, coffee and rolls. But today Aideen was not captured by the view; once breakfast arrived, they settled down to talking about plans.

Aideen remembered her painting of Mellick.

'Don't worry. I shall be over in about a month — I will bring it with me,' said René. Aideen asked if he would like to stay at Quin Cottage, 'It is not so grand as your Kilbandon Castle, but we have work to do to get this "Two Book Trick" going. I shall need to ask for your help. Come to think of it, why don't you stay over Christmas?'

René smiled, 'I would like that very much. Marvellous idea, are you sure that will be convenient to Louise as well?' Aideen was nodding. 'OK then, I'll ring you when I have my dates sorted out. I would love to take you sketching in Clare if we get a warm fine day.'

With Christmas planned, they settled down for the rest of the journey to talk through every detail of Tim and Nell's business and also of the ateliers of Angélique. In notebooks they wrote down all the possible connections that they could think of between them. It was an impressive list that included some quite unexpected addresses not only in Ireland but also England, Scotland, Wales, France and other continental countries.

Just as they were drawing into Gare de Lyon, Aideen put down her pen and looked at René:

'You know, it has only just dawned on me, the sheer simple beauty of the scheme that Tim and Nell have worked out. I know quite a few people who have fine things to sell, not necessarily because they need money, but perhaps they feel they no longer want them, or wish to change things around. A surprising number of them are shy and reticent — they would shun conventional sales; perhaps it's the walls of secrecy that surround them or perhaps all the hype, the jargon, puts them off. But along come the Top Knockers and it can all be done, very discreetly, very politely. Do you know, René, it is brilliant of those two to have worked all this out?'

On arrival they had to rush across to the Gare du Nord for Aideen to catch the hovercraft train. Between them they spotted the funny Chinese red hats of the British Hovercraft ladies who would guide them to the right platform. After a momentary kiss they waved farewell.

As the train for Boulogne roared through Etaples a cheerful chef de Train informed the passengers that the sea in Le Manche was too bump-bump-bump for the Hoverboat. So when Boulogne was reached it meant that Aideen had to face a boisterous and showery walk along the quay to a Sealink ferry that was already brimming with day-trip shoppers returning from the French Hypermarkets. A seat or part of a seat was found and after a somewhat robust crossing a landfall was made, a train found for Victoria and a comfortable bed at the Tara before ten. The next day a train, a boat and another train took Aideen to Limerick where she found Neptune, done up in his best jacket complete with tie, waiting to meet her with her Peugeot.

Five

When she awoke the next morning Aideen got up and pulled back the curtains. The Clare countryside after Paris and Marseilles was for the moment unreal. The grey barren forms of the Burren seemed as some created scene from the imagination of an early German painter who used tortured landscapes as backgrounds for often cruel and macabre representations of brutal martyrdoms. But no! This was indeed Clare; the other must be the dream. Her thought was stimulated as it had never been. Thrust in a matter of weeks into the heart of the cloistered world of the possession and disposal art market, she had been asked to be a part of it by acting in some, to her, tenuous way, just effecting introductions.

At breakfast Louise was brimming with news of the bees — Katty Blood was fantastic with them, they settled on her hands and arms but never seemed to sting. She would sit beside the hives crooning away to them; telling them to bring good honey next summer. Louise at last exhausted the subject and frowning slightly said:

'Aideen darling, I noticed that there were two of those knives missing from the case. Surely you didn't take Batsy's advice seriously and take them with you?'

'I did.' Aideen smiled at her mother's earnest face.

'I sincerely hope you didn't use them, darling.'

'Only once, dear, just one throw to frighten off a man who was being rather trying. Batsy had the right idea when she gave them to me.'

'What do you mean?' asked Louise.

'He was being unpleasant to a friend and I had to scare him a little.'

'Did you scare him?' Louise's eyes opened wide.

'Yes — in fact I think very much. He left shortly afterwards.' Aideen laughed but her mother was still serious.

'Well, you will put them away now, won't you?'

'Don't worry, mother. I'm just going to ring Batsy. Will it be all right if I ask her over for lunch?' Aideen rose, 'Oh yes, I nearly forgot, René is coming over in about a month and I have asked him to stay here at Quin over Christmas. Is that alright with you?

'Of course it will be, Aideen,' Her mother relaxed again. 'I love the idea.'

After the phone call during which an excited Batsy, who said she was longing for news, promised to be over by shortly after twelve, Aideen went into the kitchen to greet Mary Dancy and find out what could be rustled up for lunch. There was about half a honey-baked ham, enough ingredients for a mixed salad, and a deep apple and clove pie, to the pastry of which Mary was just putting the finishing touches; and she would have it all ready for lunch at one, she said.

Outside Aideen found Neptune Blood working away on a large rockery on the West side of the cottage. He must have shifted tons of earth and rocks to create what was a quite perfect setting for the small plants that would flourish in such a habitat. It was amazing how he and Louise had improved the garden since they had first arrived from Mellick. The lawn had become respectable turf, the shrubs were obviously rooting down and the whole effect was very pleasing.

'How are you, Neptune?' she asked.

'Ah, I feel great this morning, Miss Aideen. Have you been hearing about the bees?' 'Yes, indeed. Your mother has some talents. I never knew before that she was a bee lady.'

'Ah, Katty has a way with most things when she sets her mind to them. She's a wonder to me what she can get up to.' Neptune shook his great head.

After a look at the hives, Aideen returned indoors and spent the next two hours sorting out papers, looking through telephone directories, address books, and the piles of country and social magazines she had been stacking up for some time. She covered many pages from a large pad of paper with notes and details to go through with Batsy, whom she hoped was going to act as a fairy godmother with all this — as it had after all been her idea.

It was nearly half twelve when a loud snorting noise outside announced the arrival of Batsy. Aideen opened the front door and helped her cousin discard the protective clothing she wore when burning up the roads of Clare.

'I hope you have lots of good news for me, darling,' Batsy said, planting a kiss on Aideen's right ear. 'How's Louise?'

'Fine, ' replied Aideen, 'she and Katty have got a thing going with that metropolis of bees down in the little paddock — she'll be laying up a store of beeswax candles next for power-cuts.'

After lunch, Louise excused herself as she wanted to go into Ennis to the library and was then going on to have tea with a friend out at Lahinch.

'Now, my dear, start at the beginning,' said Batsy. Aideen did as she was asked and covered everything that had happened: the meeting with the Sinclairs and her enrolment with them as a Top Knocker. Reference was made to Mangon and his activities in France; here Batsy came in and mentioned that she herself had seen some references to Mangon Enterprises. Then Aideen came to the Ateliers Angélique which really titillated her cousin. There was a shriek of great delight with the description of what happened to Hiram K. Frack,

'Oh, my dear, I would have been tempted!'

Aideen went on,

'I must be truthful, I was quite shaken with the effect on him. I feel I have made two rather special friends now down in Marseilles. Angélique and yourself would get on, and Igor's eyes looked at me with what I think was real admiration — a knife-throwing female was something new in his experience.'

They settled down then to some planning. Batsy had brought over her address book. 'I never realized that I knew so many people holed up in mansions and great castles. My dear, it's funny how things pay off — you can never tell. When Mother was bringing me out with all those balls, theatre parties, and risqué moments in punts on rivers, well, I ended up with a whole host of people whom I know on Christian name terms. I suppose one tends to become a member of an establishment. From odd talks I've had around the place I think I could find a nice little handful who could use this, what do the Sinclairs call it, the "Two Book Trick". We'll have you well blooded by the time René arrives. There's one place in Westmeath, you know it, Carrig House; two

dears have it, the Findalls. Then there is dear old Charlie Drax at
Conniff Castle in Co Louth. I thought that you might do those
two and then nip over on the Holyhead boat and tackle three in
the north of England. The Nicholls at Water-meet House in
Northumberland and close by there is the most delightful house,
Fern Hill, with a true eccentric, Miss Ormiston. Be careful of her
though, she is very bright indeed. The other one is north Yorkshire, Grey Castle they call it, set on a real pinnacle with a drive
that goes up nearly vertical; most people are terrified of the
place. Owned and run in some considerable splendour by two
brothers, the Warrens. Well, there you are, all the names, the
addresses and telephone numbers. Over to you.'

Aideen was beaming.

'Batsy, you are marvellous.' She kissed her cousin. 'Can't I put
you on a commission or something?'

'Don't be so silly, dear, your cousin has quite enough for any
luxuries which she still feels she may want to enjoy. No, it will
give me the greatest pleasure to see you make a go of this.
Naughty thought — it would be fun to get that horrible couple
Mangon and Fyrken within knife range, wouldn't it? I can just
see that little creep Fyrken slithering along the floor and begging
for mercy!'

Aideen thanked Batsy again and then produced the little
package she had bought in Marseilles.

'There, a very tiny token of great gratitude,' she said.

Batsy took the packet and opened it carefully, finally drawing
out the shawl and holding it up.

'Oh it's absolutely lovely, you have excellent taste, you are
good, thank you Aideen.' They embraced warmly again and then
Aideen got busy.

'I'll book the boat from Dun Laoghaire right away and then
fix up times and dates.'

'Don't be surprised, my dear, if, once you get this moving you
find yourself being passed around the circuit. Should "A" trust
you and tell "B", odds on so will "B" do the same and so on.'

They talked for a while and then Batsy readied herself to
leave. 'I must be off, I promised Seán, the one Louise calls my
butler, not the other Seán that does the garden — very confusing
having two of them with the same name — that he could borrow
the motorbike. His old banger has broken down again and he

has to go over and see his sister in Killaloe. See you again when you get back and do let me know when René is expected.'

Batsy disappeared with the usual noise and Aideen returned inside to begin thinking about what best to pack.

* * * * * *

It had been a marvellous eleven days. And throughout it, Aideen found that her visit to Angelique's was proving to be a great help. Her eye was beginning to pick out the vital differences between an original , a copy and a fake. She found that the two latter did indeed die before her eyes on close scrutiny.

Indeed, she had drawn only one blank. The people at Fern Hill had some interesting things but felt at the moment that they would rather put matters on hold. Carrig House produced a really fine early dresser, a landscape with a view of Delft by Ruisdael, a fantasy scene showing the marriage of two allegorical figures with the whole surrounded with a lovely garland of flowers by Jan Brueghel the Second, and one of those luscious harem scenes by John Frederick Lewis. Charlie Drax at Conniff Castle said it might be rather a goose-chase as he didn't think he had anything suitable. There was though a rather awful wood panel up in the pink bedroom. When Aideen gently blew the dust from it, lo and behold, there was an exceptional Lucas Cranach the Elder with an elaborate version of his Money Changers.

Treasure again at Watermeet House in Northumberland. A great uncle had collected lithographs by Edvard Munch, also his woodcuts. A thin leather bound folio contained thirty-five fine prints in all. The Nicholls rather diffidently told her they had never really been fond of them and thought they hadn't even been worth trying to sell. When Aideen mentioned that they could be worth upwards of £10,000 each the family just about collapsed. Miss Ormiston with a Pacific Island wooden female figure just over twenty inches high and a Ying Ching wine ewer and cover, Yuan Dynasty, first quarter of the 14th century.

The last on the list, Grey Castle, which by its siting gave a distinct impression of having been built by the designer of Neuschwanstein in Bavaria, brought further surprises. She was welcomed in great style by the brothers and fed a superb luncheon over which they explained that Batsy had got it wrong.

They really didn't want to sell anything — rather they were very much in the market for certain things. In her notebook Aideen jotted down the shopping list they were after. A Turner water colour on the large size, drawings by Rembrandt, Watteau, and Cortona, a Fantin Latour, a landscape by Corinth and a Harlequin group modelled by J.J. Kandler, also if she could find it, a Deruta blue and gold lustre charger, early 16th century. Perhaps, they concluded, she would like to work away on that little lot and then they could move on from there.

When she stopped for the night on the way back to Holyhead to catch the return boat Aideen sat down in her room and totted up a rough guess at the score. She added the figures up three times — and the total was the same — wanting to sell, close on £1,000,000, wanting to buy about £900,000. The next move was to take out the little notebook which Nell had given her and which had a simple but highly secure coding for reporting back from the field to St Cloud. With a slightly trembling finger she dialled, and in less than half a minute was through and telling Nell the details. There was a pause whilst Nell decoded and then came warm words of congratulations.

'Marvellous, Aideen. We'll take over from here.'

And so back along the A5 over the Britannia Bridge, across Anglesey, on to the ferry and back to Clare. The morning following her return she was over to see Batsy and report.

After hearing the details, Batsy responded.

'You know, Aideen, somehow I felt that this business would go like this. In a way, the Mangons that are around are actually helping matters. When you went to France I nipped over to the UK and up to London — I had some business bits and pieces to look after — and I ran into a dear friend. He has really done very well and is now towards the top with one of the Majors. He took me to lunch and during the meal, funnily enough, Percival Mangon cropped up. I mentioned in passing about the trickery with the Mellick sale. He told me that Mangon and the likes of him have been playing high, wide and handsome up and down the country — and not only were they starting to upset the art market but more important was the fact that they were giving the likes of the Majors and others an increasingly bad name with regular and possible future clients.'

'I picked up much the same feeling when I was on this trip,' replied Aideen.

Batsy continued,

'Next week the Majors are having a get together, a kind of seminar or whatever they call it to air some views about presenting the market to the public. They may not say it openly but he assured me that number one in importance is just how they can put a stop to the Mangon brigade. Percival, in particular, seems to have hooked his fingers into some pretty substantial finance. So far the spies have totally failed to find where this kind of money is coming from. They've drawn a blank with all the usual sources.'

'There may be some more news from Tim and Nell and René soon,' said Aideen.'When I was over, they did mention the possibility for some oriental backing for Mangon.'

'Oh did they?' said Batsy. 'That's what my friend thought too. When did you say that dear boy is coming over again?'

'I had a card this morning.' smiled Aideen. 'All being well, he should be here on the sixteenth of December and will definitely be staying over Christmas.'

'That's good' replied Batsy. 'I met Laura the other day and she said that they are thinking of having a good old-fashioned bash — up at the castle. James has got this great idea of really putting Kilbandan in the news. Dammit, he only got just over six thousand visitors last year — won't even pay for the extra expenses of running an open house for all and sundry.'

'Any thoughts on what the big idea is?' asked Aideen.

'Oh, Laura mumbled away about something to do with silver or something.'

'I believe they've got a pretty fine collection there already. Well, if the Kilbandans are going to have a party, so are the Uniackes — may have to be on a smaller scale than before, but we can make up for that in other ways. Make a note in your diary, any idea when James and Laura are having theirs?' asked Aideen.

'Actually she did tell me. Yes, here it is, Boxing Day of all nights.'

'That's fine, the Uniackes will be at home to a select gathering on Christmas Eve.'

* * * * * *

December the 15th and 16th were foul weather-wise. René had a wet and pitching crossing over the channel, continuous rain on the drive to Holyhead, and then the Irish Sea put on a five star performance; a Force nine gusting ten thumped and bumped the high-sided ferry as she tackled the angry grey-green seas and at last, courtesy of good seamanship, sidled her way into Dun Laoghaire harbour. After a night at the Royal Marine Hotel, René set off to the west. By early afternoon some benign spirit had pulled away the rain-burdened clouds and called off the storm-winds and by the time he was crossing the Shannon at Killaloe there was scarcely breath to move the tall reeds beside the waters.

As the long bonnet of the Safari came up the lane to Quin Cottage, Mary Dancy, clearly working on intuition, had the kettle boiling and the pot on the hob. As Aideen and Louise came out to greet René, he was already out of the car and unloading the back. Besides cartons, cases and parcels of assorted sizes there was a sketching easel, canvases, water-colour paper blocks and canvas bags from which protruded brushes, palettes, rags and what a painter would call sundries. He stooped to lift up a flat package carefully protected by several thicknesses of corrugated paper and held it out to Aideen who exclaimed:

'Oh marvellous! Can I go and unpack it now — I have a special place to hang it.' Going inside she called to Louise to follow her into the dining-room. There on the end wall was a blank space with a soft cross light from a window. The wrappings came off and she leant the painting of Mellick against the wall behind the sideboard, so that it could be seen to good effect. Louise, taken unawares, gave a little cry and a couple of tears welled in her eyes. When René came in she caught his hand and then threw her arms round his neck and kissed his cheeks:

'You are a dear boy.' Her voice broke. She turned again to the picture and murmured quietly,

'Mellick, dear Mellick as you were and as you will always be to us. Do you know René, those construction developers have smothered the place in chalets, buffets, games places ... thank goodness we're at least this far away from them.'

Neptune had come in and given a hand with the luggage and parcels up to the spare-room and then asked René if he would like him to wash the car as it was smothered in muck from the flooded roads. The offer was gratefully accepted.

After tea Louise went into the kitchen to oversee Mary some-what belatedly making the Christmas puddings and fruit cake.

'Thank you again for the painting, René.' 'You saw the effect it had on Louise and I feel very much the same. It will be a constant treasure for the Uniackes. Now, what news from the Sinclairs?'

'Lots', began René. 'First of all, you exceeded their hopes on that first trip and they have already concluded three of the deals. Tim told me to tell you that a cheque is on the way to the account in Geneva he has opened in your name.' He pulled out his wallet.

'Here's the sealed envelope for you which contains the magic number of the account. Guard it well, Tim said.'

René went on. 'I had a couple of good encounters myself just over a week ago. I went down to see my mother and father who were back from Australia for a few days and they passed me right into the hands of the owner of an outstanding Zurbaran of one of the Saints, which he wished to part with, worth all of £400,000. The other was the daughter of a client whose portrait I had painted several years ago. An uncle had left her an absolutely magnificent Claude Lorraine, which meant nothing to her; a scene of woodlands in the foreground, then a wide river and a tall castle, the whole canvas absolutely drenched in that wonderful golden light which Lorraine could get — heaven knows how he did it. I've tried hard enough but can't even approach that ethereal softness. He must have done it with repeated very thin glazes using perhaps walnut oil, I just don't know. When I told Tim and Nell they went up about six feet in the air! Made me repeat it and then I produced some not very good polaroids — but they were enough. You could see the figures spinning round in their eyes. Finally, when they came down to earth I whispered how much then? They said they couldn't be sure as no Lorraine had been on the market for ages. Eventually Nell, trying to be casual, said something around five million and what was more she knew a client who would be sitting up and begging for it. So, Miss Uniacke, we will have a fine old-fashioned Christmas!'

'That's marvellous. You've beaten me hollow.'

Aideen was stunned by René's find.

'Don't worry, this game is like fishing. You never know just how big the fish are until you have them in the net.'

'And anything fresh on the Mangon-Poll axis?' enquired Aideen.

'Oh yes. The two of them are really hatching out something. The Sinclair bugs in the Mangon establishment have been working overtime and so have the typists transcribing everything. The big thing is that they are going to launch hopefully in the late spring next year something which will be called —' here René adopted a booming voice, 'TRANS EUROPEAN INTERNATIONAL FINE ART AND ANTIQUES SALES.'

'They must have really sold these orientals something. Believe it or not, they have been advanced four million to get things going — publicity, posting shots, and then a large item which isn't quite clear from the tapes. Something about mobile sale-rooms. They are leaving the Paris branch in charge of Alfie Brigg over Christmas and the New Year. The Poll one is going to Regensberg, won't be back in Paris until January 4th, and Mangon is going to be away until the 23rd.'

'Good,' replied Aideen. 'Then we can have a couple of weeks of fun-time. First sign of a fine day and you are going to take out an amateur with brushes and paints. Then I want to take you exploring, show you one or two places you may not have seen yet. Oh yes! And someone around here must have picked up something about knocking — Mary Dancy has two cousins, the Feegan sisters in Kilfenora, who rather mysteriously have some bits and pieces — their words not mine — that they think I might help with .'

René nodded. 'Could be anything, I suppose, from a real treasure to a bit of beloved junk.'

'And we must keep track of our dates, René. There's one more I've just remembered. Katty Blood, that's Neptune's mother, always holds a solstice party on the 22nd; she's asked us all round there at six. I've been to these celebrations before and I think you'll find it interesting.'

*   *   *   *   *   *

Two days later a swirl of mildness from the Gulf Stream must have lapped along the coast. At breakfast time the overnight shower clouds were clearing and there was not a blush of pink to the sky that might have been a warning sign. Aideen and René decided to take the day as it came; Mary put together some sandwiches and Louise made a flask of coffee. Water bottles were filled and all the tackle was loaded up. It was going to be a soft gentle December day so that too many coats wouldn't be necessary as one crouched over the easel.

They headed off in the direction of Corrofin and then took the road to Kilfenora turning to the right by Leamaneh Castle. As they passed, Aideen spoke.

'Always gives me a bit of a shudder. There's a bitter atmosphere that hangs around the place. I always try to guess from which of the top windows it was that Máire Rua MacMahon pushed her second husband through to his death. He was John Cooper, a cornet of horse with Cromwell's army. It may be all myth and romance of course, but when you look at that ruin — it just could be true.'

René agreed and then asked where he was being taken to.

'Forgive me, I feel a bit dramatic today,' began Aideen. 'I think it's the changing face of Clare. Change and contrast is just so stimulating. Not long ago, it was Paris and the elegance of that place of Angélique's and now out here.' She waved to the panorama. 'We're going to one of my favourites — the wonderful dolmen of Poulnabrone.' Pretty soon they had arrived and found a place to park.

Loading up with the gear, they climbed over the loose stone wall and began the approach towards the ancient tomb. Out on the Burren proper, walking requires skill. The cracked slabs of rock are often set at awkward angles and some can wobble as the foot comes down. They both recalled the magic of the place in spring and early summer. The winds of hundreds of years have slowly gathered soil into the crevices and in these unlikely grounds have grown a horticulturalist's wonder. Rare miniature blooms including the dark red Helleborine, the spring Gentian, the Pyramidal Orchid and the Bloody Cranesbill. In late May parts of the Burren can give the appearance of an enormous reversed mosaic — the colour being concentrated in the interstices while the grey slabs act as the tesserae.

Close to, Poulnabrone took over from its surrounds. Its dynamic force came from the strength of the portal slabs, Aideen thought, and the rakish angle of the capstone added to the picture. 'It measures twelve feet by seven,' she told René who was looking up, shielding his eyes from the sun. For a time they walked around the subject deciding just which would be the better view. Finally, choosing a spot that made the most of the light, they settled to work. Aideen's experience of sketching in the open had been limited and she had to overcome a slight attack of nerves, feeling René's professionalism beside her. He allowed her the minimum pencil work before going in with the brush. Very soon his skill with water colour and the gentle way with which he pointed out ways and means put her at ease. With his eye instructing hers and his experience leading her hand she became lost in the simple pure joy of seeing something happen on the paper.

Suddenly he told her to stop.

'You've done well, now is the time to study what you have done. Perhaps a few strokes of emphasis here and there — then do no more or you may kill the life you've caught. Knowing the moment to stop is the hardest lesson for any artist.' He stood back from her, 'Not bad at all. We must try and come out again.'

Aideen smiled and then shivered.

'Look at the time. We've been at it for more than two and a half hours! Brrrr, can you feel the place now? Touch the bare rock and it has the sense of the primordial. I have been out here alone sometimes and after a while something seems to happen. You know what I mean, goose-pimples and a feeling of hair raising at the back of your neck.' Aideen laughed. 'Legends do tell just how over there in that hollow, there was a really terrible massacre of hundreds if not thousands. Once when I was here in the late afternoon, there was a fiery red sunset just after a heavy shower had cleared and everything was soaked. My imagination went wild and I thought I saw pools of fresh blood all over the place. Do you know what I did? I didn't care who was looking, I just scrambled, ran, jumped my way back to the car and drove off like mad!'

René looked around the desolate scene.

'You don't even need all that imagination. I can feel your meaning. Come on, let's go back to the car and have lunch or else it will be teatime.'

'It's three now,' said Aideen, packing up. 'After a crust we'll go back by Kilfenora and there should be still light enough to take a look at the Cathedral and the Doorty Cross.'

When they got to Kilfenora they climbed over a wall and walked towards Doorty. Aideen felt that the old cross must be one of the most interesting in the country. It dates from the twelfth century. The carvings include Christ, the abbot of the world, directing his church leaders to destroy the devil, which is itself represented by a savage bird, seen violently attacking and devouring another figure.

After they had looked their fill, they decided to try and find the Feegan sisters. Following a couple of enquiries they were directed to one of the larger houses in the village. After a tug at the bell-pull the door opened just a crack, a small thin nose appeared and a pair of shining dark eyes looked out. A sharp little voice enquired as to who they might be. When Aideen explained that Mary Dancy from over Feakle way had sent them the door was opened wide and a second figure appeared behind the first. The Feegan sisters were delighted to see them; Mary had said something about the Miss Uniacke and her friend who knew all about 'teeks'.

They were ushered into what was obviously the best parlour and while the elder Feegan sat them down and began to explain matters, the younger Feegan went off to carry out the required ritual for visitors. The tea must be wetted and the cake brought out along with the best china.

The sisters told how for the last forty years they had been collecting. They had good ears and if they heard any word of things around they'd hurry off and a gentle knock on the doors nearly always brought good results. No, their line was not those old paintings or bits of silver, and furniture was too heavy for the likes of two small ladies like themselves. Their choice had been lace, embroidery, patchwork, costumes, gowns, fans, hats, handbags and shoes. In fact everything that a lady would wear on top or as they modestly put it, just underneath. As they were both spinsters and intended to stay that way, neither of them felt it would have been delicate to go around gathering men's things.

After the tea and cake Aideen and René were taken on a grand tour of the sixteen rooms in the house. As the light failed, hissing oil pressure lamps were produced. There was untold wealth here for any textile collector. Every room except their bedroom, the kitchen and the best parlour was packed from floor to ceiling with cardboard boxes and leather suitcases and in the largest bedroom on the first floor three vast wardrobe trunks that dated back into the 19th century. These were in amazingly good condition, the drawers still gliding in and out on narrow rails. There were some supreme examples of Irish lace that was scarcely made at all anymore: point lace produced under the guidance of the Poor Clares at Kenmare, Co Kerry; Carrick-macross appliqué dating from about 1825; beautiful pieces of the Limerick tambour lace and the delicate needle lace from Youghal. Various embroideries abounded. There must have been literally hundreds and hundreds of dresses, skirts, blouses, jackets and coats, as well as nightdresses and every conceivable kind of under-wear worn by ladies during the last couple of hundred years.

After the tour was over the guests were again taken back to the best parlour and when they were seated the elder Feegan selected a key on her Châtelaine and going over to a corner near the larger of the two windows, unlocked a small cupboard and produced four glasses and a dark green bottle. Since there was going to be a chill in the air for their drive back, she would like them to have a drop of the 'creature' spirit inside them, she said. She poured out four tots of a clear liquid that had just a bit of a tan to it. Glasses were raised and the fire of 'poteen' put paid to any chance of Aideen or René feeling a chill.

'Now,' said the elder Feegan, 'what's it all worth? Will there be enough for a bungalow? You see this great barn of a place is not ours, it belongs to a younger brother and he wants it back to set up home.'

'You certainly have some value here but it would take a specialist to go through it carefully,' Aideen explained.

'Could you two not do it then? We would be pleased to pay you,' the younger Miss Feegan assured them.

'No,' Aideen replied, 'this is not really our field. You have such lovely things, it must be done properly. May I suggest that you write to one of the major houses who have experts in all the fields. They will give you good advice and you will not be under obligation to sell through them, though with much of what you have here, the London International saleroom is where you would get the best results. I'll write down the address for you.' She took a sheet from her notebook and gave the address of one of the Majors and the telephone number.

'Thank you for letting us see your treasures.' The two sisters seemed well pleased with Aideen's advice and saw them off happily, standing one behind the other at the door. As they cleared Kilfenora René remarked,

'Who would have guessed those two dears could have knocked all that lot!'

Aideen agreed and they continued homeward both marvelling of the power of the 'knocker'.

The Christmas round seemed to sweep up on them. Louise for a time was withdrawn and sad. This was the first Christmas that she had been without Uniacke since they were married. As off-hand as he had been, she missed the wretched man. Over a glass one night she reached out and took Aideen's and René's hands:

'Oh my dears, thank you for being with me, I can't help just wondering where he can be, if he is all right. He was so silly about looking after himself. Perhaps the New Year will bring something.'

Katty had put on a good spread for her little party, which consisted of the three of them from Quin, Neptune of course and Mary and her mother. The mantelpiece was decorated with evergreen and bright red ribbons and underneath the everlasting turf fire was reinforced with logs. As the daylight faded a number of thick white Christmas candles were lit. When she had the mind on her Katty was quite a cook. The main piece of furniture in the kitchen-cum-living room was an old scarred oak table. Pride of place in the centre was a Katty Blood special, a large 'currany'; well-stocked with raisins, currants and sultanas, sprouting pieces of chopped peel, and well-seasoned with good whiskey. Beside this was a large platter of slices of soda bread just out of the oven spread thick with butter and sporting large dollops of sour apples, with honey and ground cloves. Smaller dishes carried cummin bread and caraway rolls. Spitting away in the iron frying-pan was a clutch of real thick pork sausages made specially for her by a local man. Finally a bog cheese that had been well flavoured with wild garlic and salt and buried for several months. Katty had for many years followed the habits of her ancestors to produce this delicacy. For the weaker hearted she also produced a bog butter. The little party set to in earnest and bravely tackled everything; René having at least three goes at the bog cheese much to the delight of Katty.

The meal over and done, the hostess cleared the dishes with some help from Aideen and René. Then she addressed Neptune:

'Come on son, what's holding you. Fetch your Granda's fiddle and give us a tune for the season.' Neptune went over to a cupboard and opening the door pulled out the fiddle that had gladdened the hearts of at least three generations of Bloods.

He stood up with his shock of hair nearly touching the ceiling, gave the beloved old instrument a bit of tuning and then raised it to his chin and laid the bow across the strings. During the next ten minutes the party sat still. René found it hard to believe what he was hearing. This great man with hands like shovels but with fingers as sensitive as a young girl's caress brought a music into the room which ran from soft poetry of sound through chords that spoke of the ancients, phrases in praise of Christmas, and finished at first with a wild ecstatic dance and then died away into a sad but loving lament. Neptune lowered his bow. It was then the time for goodnights and warm hugs before they left to walk home through the darkness which was lit with just a tint from a low moon.

Christmas Eve morning started off with a long phone call from the Warrens of Grey Castle who had been delighted with such quick service. Tim and Nell had apparently already supplied their order and they wanted two further items: a Nolde seascape and one of his flower studies, if possible with some great red poppies. Then Aideen was given instructions to contact Lady Diana Foxford at Taw Lodge near Chagford in Devon.

This contact proved to be a good one all done from the comfort of the drawing-room at Quin. Aideen could tell that Lady Foxford was clearly an action person. Freddie Warren had been on to her and she had some bits to sell and then there were some things that she would really love to have. On the sale side were four paintings: a full length portrait of the Earl of Southcastle by Van Dyck; a pair of scenes by Jean Honoré Fragonard, The Dairymaid and The Apple Gatherer; the fourth was a panoramic view across the Elbe with shipping and castles by Bernardo Bellotto. Her ladyship then blithely said that she would need something to fill up the spaces, with no more seriousness than if she had been ordering some plants for the herbaceous border. Aideen tried to match her light-heartedness as she wrote down the desired works: a wooded scene or open landscape by Hobbema, a sea and mountain scene by Ferdinand Hodler, a flower piece by Odilon Redon, and one of those studies Claude Monet did in his garden; she finished with an invitation to drop in, always a bed, if Aideen was ever her way.

With that incentive, matters proceeded smoothly and joyfully through the festive days. The Uniackes' 'at home' was very pleasant — long-standing good friends, quiet talk, an admirable buffet prepared by Mary, the last guests leaving at a respectable time past midnight. Christmas breakfast with the family was present-giving time.

René had brought perfumes, silks, gorgeous crystallized fruits and Belgian chocolates; and especially for Aideen, some difficult-to-come-by reference books on every aspect of her trade. Aideen's gift to her mother was a surprise — the keys to a little car which they had hidden behind the garage. Aideen felt that Louise would enjoy being independent and not having to ask for the Peugeot. In return, Louise had been down to the Avoca weavers when last in Dublin and had brought back cardigans, scarves and gloves for both Aideen and René.

Boxing Day began disappointingly with heavy clouds of wet clinging mist drifting around until four o'clock. It had cleared, however, in time for the drive over to Kilbandan Castle. As usual, James and Laura had asked practically everyone for miles around. The party from Quin Cottage managed to corner their host for a few minutes. He ribbed René for deserting them and then was full of his big plan:

'I think Laura may have mentioned what we are going to be up to this summer. All these places have to do something. I've been working things out with some of these historical chaps and the National Museum. They all agree that silver is the thing. After all, the Kilbandan collection by itself is one of the finest certainly in Ireland, if not the UK. Add to this the pieces that the relations have taken over the Irish Sea. Most of which, my solicitor fellow has pointed out, is really only on loan. With that back, we shall be onto a winner! I've already arranged for one of those armoured security people to go around picking up the stuff in January. Expensive glossy catalogue by an expert, postcards, slides; might even have some reproductions done in electrum. I'm delighted that you could all come — hope you have a ball, I'll catch up with you later.' With this he was whisked away by other arrivals.

It was another late night, and the sun was well up next morning when the persistent warbling of the telephone at last got through to Aideen. It was Nell. She was full of apologies but matters were hotting up and could they both come over as soon as possible after the New Year.

Six

After fond farewells to Louise they set off at ten o'clock on January the 2nd, Aideen in her Peugeot and René with his Safari. Aideen was going to need her own car on her return from Paris. The 'Two Book Trick' was flourishing for her as previous contacts would pass her on to others, trusting both her and her judgment, which pleased her greatly.

René and Aideen were spending the night at the Royal Marine in Dun Laoghaire, which made it more convenient for the morning boat to Holyhead. They were then staying the next night at the London Tara where Aideen had arranged to leave her car whilst she was in France.

After dinner on the 3rd, they switched on the news and became engrossed in an item about developments in the antique trade. The presenter announced a new coup in the salesroom world: 'Lost Rembrandt self-portrait found in stable loose-box. Inspected many times by leading experts and dismissed as student's copy.' Then the camera cut away to Percival Mangon standing beside an easel on which was displayed the Rembrandt — now somewhat cleaned up. Mangon showed beside it an enlarged photograph of how it had looked when he found it. Apparently, he had been called in to give advice on a house clearance sale up in Scotland near Perth.

'I am one of those incurable optimists,' he told the interviewer, 'who never give up, who go through every heap of rubbish.' He smirked smugly.

'It can pay off in the end. The owner told me that it had actually been in a London sale but there had been no takers. I checked back on the records in the various institutions here and in Holland, becoming more and more convinced. A full laboratory examination was given and then all the details fell into place; someone at the Hague dug up some old papers on Rembrandt which clearly pointed to the fact that experts for many years had been expecting a "lost" self-portrait to turn up.'

'And what was the next step?' asked the presenter.

'The picture has already found a new owner — my company had a client and the sale was concluded this morning.'

'Is it allowed to ask the price?'

'It is a private sale and I would be breaking confidence if I told you.'

The presenter tried a last time:

'Would I be right to guess at a seven figure sum, Mr. Mangon?'

Percival smiled: 'I suppose you could say that.' The image on the screen cut to the next item.

'How did that ignorant so-and-so pull that one?' said René, 'I'll just nip down to the shop and get the evening paper.'

On his return he handed the paper to Aideen and there on the front page was a photograph of Percy positively purring with pride and holding the Rembrandt. The accompanying headline was 'LONE EXPERT BEATS THE REST WITH FIND OF THE CENTURY'. This seemed to be slightly overdoing matters but there was no question about the fact that Percy had secured himself a place amongst the stars in the fine art world.

After an early breakfast the next morning they bought copies of all the dailies and then were away in the Citroën to be in good time to catch a mid-morning ferry for Calais. By supper time, René had left Aideen at the Hotel des Arbres to where he returned in under half an hour after dropping off his luggage and parking the car. A simple dinner at the nearby restaurant was enlivened as they worked through the papers. The pieces ranged from quotes by Mangon puffing his ego up further, to serious in-depth articles by some art critics. One went so far as to say what a benefit people such as Percival Mangon could be for protecting the art treasures of the country with their expertise. A knowledge based not only on years of study but also combined with that perceptive eye granted to only a few that worked not from signatures, provenances and suchlike but could discern the truth from the painting itself.' René went to the phone booth and rang Tim and Nell. Needless to say, they had seen the news too and were full of it. An appointment was made to meet at ten thirty the next morning.

*   *   *   *   *   *

At about the same time as Aideen and René were having their meal, Herta Poll had arrived back at the Mangon Paris establishment to relieve an impatient Alfie Brigg, who was then free to catch a plane to Heathrow. He was looking forward to catching up with his idea of seasonal celebrations, which meant a few lost days with the boys down the Elephant and Castle way.

Whilst she had been to see her cousin in Regensberg, Herta had had little time for Christmas fun. She had been absorbed in working out plans for the double-crossing intrigue that she loved. In her world of circuitous dealing and easy consciences they were all on the jungle floor. The operators might wear coronets or flat caps, but when it came to crossing the palm, few if any felt shame if they conducted piracy against other members of the secret-bound society of art dealing. Herta's time over the holiday period had been highlighted by several long trans-Atlantic calls, and a few carefully chosen dinners for two.

She tidied up Mangon's apartment and removed all traces of Brigg's enforced stay. The time was a minute or two before eight when the intercom bell from the entrance sounded. She pressed the release and waited. The lift door slid open and Warren B. Westonhofer walked across the landing and into the study.

'Gee, it is great to see you, Herta. How many years has it been?' he said.

'You should know,' she replied rather tartly. 'It was just before you were sent down by that judge in the States for three years for thinking you could sign your name spelled Gainsborough on a drawing and at the same time play funny games with provenances.'

'Oh, come now that's water under the culvert as we say back home. I reckon the best thing for you and I is if we just forget our past.'

'Ja! Ja! that is good.' Herta's smile lifted one side of her mouth.

'I saw the early news. Where's Percy right now?'

'When I last spoke to him he was still in London, but he will be coming back earlier than he thought.'

'What I reckon you and I must work out, Herta, is a play-safe situation — if you get my meaning.' Herta nodded and he continued. 'We can pick up good business on Percy's publicity. By the way, do you want to know why I pulled out on him back a while?'

'Not particularly, I am not even going to bother to guess. I would just say whatever it was, don't try doing it to me.'

'You've got me wrong — we're in the same shack on this one. Well, I guess I must be on the move. Here's the address and 'phone. For the moment I'm playing this one from the wings.' Warren gave her a white card and walked towards the lift.

* * * * * *

For the first hour at the Sinclair apartment Aideen and René listened to extracts from tapes recorded from the bug in the Mangon establishment. Some of it they had read from transcripts. But it all sounded much more real as the various voices floated out of the speaker. Towards the end of the recital Tim leant across to them,

'Here comes the crunch point.' Mangon was speaking:

'I tell you Herta, we are going to have the field to ourselves with the kind of backing the men in Singapore are talking about.'

Herta's voice came on:

'Ja. Then we bring in a seven per cent commission just for the seller and nothing for the buyer. This is going to be selling in the super-hypermarket way. Volume sales. But we will not mention too much of this in the early publicity — just suggest . . .'

Nell switched off the tape-recorder.

'When that idea breaks it is going to rock everything. The bad news for the Majors and the rest is that it could just succeed. Trans European International Fine Art and Antique Sales could roll over the opposition.'

'Surely not,' said René, 'What about the immense cost of premises, salesrooms? Mangon will never be able to maintain all that on seven per cent.'

Tim responded:

'Don't be too sure. There's a lot more on the tapes — much of it, repetitive details. But they have, or rather Herta Poll has, worked out a way that the great showrooms, the gilded salesrooms method can be got around. When we heard it the first time it sounded a bit on the lunatic fringe. In short, her idea is to have an outfit that travels round the big centres and operates from sites rented cheaply a little way out in the country rather like the really big circuses used to. The basis will be up to ten of the largest juggernaut lorries. These will be armour-protected like the security company vehicles. Some will carry the stock to be sold: one will be a mobile office with radio communications; others could be showrooms while chairs and benches will be carried in an additional one, the auctioneer's rostrum and etceteras in another, and at least two will be fitted up as living quarters for the crew needed. The idea is that those juggernauts will be laagered and then between them and over the centre a large marquee will be rigged on possibly four poles.'

'Mr Mangon is taking off, isn't he?' said Aideen. 'Is all this just words and paper or have they got further with it?'

'Considerably further, I'm afraid. Herta Poll we know has been visiting a firm suited to this kind of work, orders have been placed with Volvo and delivery dates are sometime in April. What's more, lavish brochures are already in hand with the printers. I suspect Mangon is now desperately trying to get alterations made with these to include the bonanza publicity the press and television have given him. The initial mail shot is due for mid-February and is being sent to about eight hundred thousand people across Europe with another hundred thousand going to the United States and Canada and a hundred thousand more for the Far East, Australia and New Zealand.'

Tim went on:

'That's a cool million — a small fortune in postage, not to mention buying the address lists.'

Nell came in again:

'The main point is — how can Mangon and Poll be stopped? And at the same time we'll have to keep an eye on the Weston-hofer character as well. Any bright ideas will be welcomed. I needn't tell you both that we are now not alone in this. The Majors are pulling out every stop. Trouble is, from the legal angle there doesn't seem much that can be done. We may think that some of the European financiers play things pretty close to their chests but I can tell you that they have absolutely nothing on this Singapore Syndicate. They are taking a pretty stiff gamble but they seem quite determined and Mangon and Poll are operating with a seemingly bottomless budget. The City chaps in London, who are pretty smart by any standard, have been right through it all as far as we can understand and they seem to have adopted a rather healthy respect for these operators.'

'So halting them from the financial angle is out,' surmised René. 'How about a joint publicity crack?'

'No, René,' said Tim, 'It wouldn't work. The striking point is the commission rate they are going to use. London at the moment is ten per cent each way, seller and buyer; many European sales-rooms charge more. A reduction to seven per cent straight for the seller would slash the known market to ribbons. As Herta Poll said on the tape, this is a straightforward hypermarket situation.'

For several minutes Aideen had been sitting silently staring out of a window across the neighbouring rooftops. She raised a hand:

'Can I come in?'

'Please do,' said Nell. 'We've exhausted every possibility that we can think of — that is methods that are within the law.'

'Now this may be completely dotty. But if we could find a way to puncture the Mangon image — it just might work. You know, you can almost see versions of it happening all round. The bullyboy is made to look foolish — he may punch a few heads at the time but his prestige is never quite the same again. There must be a way that we can apply this kind of basic law. Mangon is riding good and high at the moment, certainly with the Rembrandt publicity. His stock with the Singapore Syndicate will have shot up. Now, what can be the pin that bursts it all? Bear with me you professionals, I'm just the girl from Clare,' Aideen took a deep breath.

'Two ways seem open. He could be tricked into buying the wrong stuff or, perhaps more simple to operate, we all go along with his hyped-up ego and so he will be tempted to grossly over-spend and overstock. Then, and this is the part where I go out of my depth. You two would know best. Mightn't it be possible for a little fluctuation downward for the market to be arranged — quite legally of course?'

'My hat! Who's teaching whom?' exclaimed Nell. 'She could have got it! That way percentage takings for the Singapore boys would disappear and so would their interest in the Occidental antiques and fine art market. Aideen, bless you! Mr. Percival

Mangon likes house contents sales. Let's give him a contents sale he will live with forever. You've got my train haven't you,Tim?'

'You mean the Château du Bienheureux outside Clermont-Ferrand?' Tim laughed. 'Look at Aideen and René's faces — they think we've gone crazy. Stay with us for a bit, you two. Amongst our friends are some unexpected characters. I think at the moment one of them is number two in the charts, in fact. Yes, I mean Earl Silver, a most civilized young man. He turns his royalties from the sale of millions of records into places he enjoys living in. A house in California, one in the West Indies, another in the Isle of Man and a château in France. Silver bought this from another friend of ours, the Comte Michel de Pollenard. Michel is still living in one wing while he is waiting for a smaller place to be built in a corner of the estate. Bienheureux is not one of the really big ones — but it does have twenty-four bedrooms, two large drawing-rooms, a dining-hall, studies, day-rooms, a very large glass-roofed salon and other etceteras. When Silver bought the place three years ago he had to pour money into it just to keep the rain out. We helped him furnish one wing with some pretty choice pieces and some fine paintings and that's the part he lives in. Nell, you heard from Silver last, what was the news?'

'Yes he's down there at the moment doing what he calls his meditation stint. I think in the latter part of February he is off on another world tour and won't be back until July.'

Tim continued,

'He'll play along with any idea we think up and I'm sure Michel will also. I think you and I, Nell, must go down there quite soon and see both of them. The last time I was down the big salon was practically empty. Michel had some good pieces. Yes, I'll ring them this evening and fix up a visit and we can get matters moving. We can fill up the salon and other vacant space in the Comte's wing with some mouth-watering lots for Mr. Percival. There's not all that much time but we'll get the stock together.'

'Hold it a minute,' said Nell. 'How do we get this stunning news to Mangon?'

'That's all right,' continued Tim.

'Don't forget we've got it one on of the tapes that the first mail shot goes out in mid-February. I would think Michel is certain to be on the address list. Mangon will be after any good stock he can get hold of and if it is attached to a title, all the better. So our Comte Michel de Pollenard rings Mangon and says he has seen his literature and arranges for him to go down to the Château at whatever date we work out when everything will be ready. If Michel is moving into a smaller place, he is certain to have stuff he will want to sell. And Nell, when Silver was here to dinner at the end of November didn't he make noises about some items he wanted to get rid of himself? So what could be better — we move in a few loads of goodies and then interlard the whole lot together!'

All four of them laughed with delight at the ingenuity of the plan.

Nell came in,

'Oh Aideen, René, this really is a good one! The château is imposing; turrets, classic style window treatment, flight of steps bordered with elaborate stone urns leading up to magnificent panelled doors with bronze fittings. The entrance to the estate is through an embattled gatehouse and then a fairly well-kept drive swings through a plantation and the final approach is down an avenue of walnut trees; right in front there is a fountain supported by white marble figures of gods and goddesses at play. We'll ring them tonight — it's the kind of thing Silver would call "great gas".'

Tim turned to René and Aideen and said,

'The way I see it is, that this is going to be our show — we will be shouldering the organisation, and the finance side will be ours and in no way will you two be responsible. Anyhow, I think you are both getting pretty booked up. You told me, René, you have this commission for some fifty odd illustrations for a book on the German Schloss. How long is that likely to take you?'

'I haven't scheduled it completely yet,' said René, 'but I would think something like three to four months.'

Nell looked towards Aideen:

'And you mentioned there are quite a number of people waiting to see you in the UK and Ireland — certainly enough to keep you busy. But this is important — both of you do keep in touch — perhaps phone once every fortnight. We'd definitely like you around when the great sale comes up. We should all be together wherever it is.'

* * * * * *

From mid-February onward Percival Mangon's outfit was in top gear. The proprietor, whose personal esteem now reached great heights nourished by numerous television and radio interviews plus flattering comments in the papers and periodicals that mattered, was becoming 'expensive' to speak to. But he was not too elevated that he would not take a telephone call when his secretary buzzed to say that she had The Comte Michel de Pollenard on the line.

The voice that greeted Percy was one that he would have given his soul to have — very calm, quiet but with a well controlled edge of command:

'Ah, Mr. Mangon, I have your most attractive pamphlet here on my desk — I must say it is very comprehensive and straightforward. I don't know if you know Bienheureux, it's been in my family for more centuries than I can recall.'

For a moment Percy paused; he was not at all sure how he should address such a person — until quite recently his associates had been more mundane. He took a breath and plunged in,

'No, Comte Pollenard, it is one of the important places I have yet to see.'

'Ah, the Michelin map I'm sure will guide you. I'm about ten kilometres outside Clermont-Ferrand, Puy-de-Dôme — pretty well roughly due south of Paris. It will be a fairly mixed bag on offer — some interesting Italian paintings, some Spanish — a few Dutch and a lively collection of etchings and engravings — the odd tapestry, a good lot of Louis XV furniture and some quite unique German and Spanish full suits of armour plus some fine swords and daggers. Do you think you could be interested?'

'Most certainly,' a slightly flummoxed Percy exclaimed and then forgot himself by finishing with, 'Yes sir, I would.'

'Fine. How is your diary for the early part of March, say somewhere around the 5th or 6th?'

To regain his composure, Percy studied almost blank appointments pages for these dates and then felt strong enough to answer,

'How about the 5th then?'

'Excellent, the 5th it is. I will expect you about two-thirty after luncheon.' The telephone clicked as the Comte hung up.

* * * * * *

The visit to Bienheureux for Percival was a breathtaking success. First of all he was greatly impressed by the estate, the gatehouse and then the great château itself. But then the door was opened by an extremely dignified butler, whom Percy almost took to be the Comte. Fortunately, the man greeted him with

'Good afternoon, sir, my master is expecting you,' which saved him from a serious gaffe. The entrance hall thrilled him — armour, swords, banners, classic statues and rare rugs carelessly strewn around. Then he was ushered into the presence of the Comte. A slim striking figure, ramrod straight, with an immaculately trimmed moustache and silver grey hair, eyes aloof, he greeted Percival:

'Charming of you to have come all this way. Now, there is quite a bit to see. Shall we begin? We are not concerned with the east wing as that has the private apartments of Mr. Earl Silver. I've made a rough list with the bare details of what's available — things that I really do wish to shift and there are some things also included that Mr. Earl Silver wants to dispense with.'

It was five thirty before the tour was completed. Percy was bowled over. The Comte assured him that he would rather trust the whole arrangement to just one firm. Treasure after treasure had gone before his eyes. Several times the Comte had said or gently indicated that he thought possibly some of the objects might really be beyond Mr. Mangon's intentions or resources. Percival hastened to reassure the Comte that such was not the case. He was frantically trying to keep a tally of possible values in his mind.

When they got back to the Comte's private study he felt rather as though he was about to make a bid for an entire museum collection of some importance.

'Well, Mr. Mangon, what do you think of what I have shown you?'

'Magnificent or . . .', catching himself quickly and not wanting to appear to be too impressed, 'Certainly mostly of quality.'

'So would you like to handle it?' The Comte asked.

'Most certainly.'

'Then we better talk some figures, I suppose. What kind of an offer would you care to make?'

'Might I just have a moment?' said Percy who felt he was in danger of being out-classed.

'Please do, by all means.'

For a rather hectic few minutes Percy struggled with a pocket calculator feeding in his hurried estimates from the walkabout. He tried hard not to blanch when he pressed the total button and the small electronic figures flashed up. The sum was up in eight figures.

Trying to be nonchalant he said:

'Mmm — I've got to take into consideration possible market movements as you can imagine. I propose £16 million.'

'Ah, not quite there I am afraid.' The Comte shook his head. 'I am looking for more as I've some important projects in mind. You're saying £16 million, I will say £26 million. Perhaps we can work towards each other?'

After a pretty tricky three minutes the two opponents had worked toward each other. Unfortunately for Percy he was up against a seasoned player and he had to go to £22 million.

After they had shaken hands, he explained that to completely consummate matters he would like to bring one of the principal backers of the firm down for just a short visit. Assured that this would be fine, he decided that it could be arranged in about six days' time, but he would ring the Comte as soon as it was fixed.

When Mangon got back to Paris he put through a call to Singapore and explained how things stood, quoting from the catalogue listing, and then paused when the crunch point was reached. The senior member of the Singapore Syndicate calmly asked the total. His voice betrayed nothing of what he thought. A few seconds later he just said:

'All right, Mr. Mangon, I will be with you in Paris the day after tomorrow and I will then see the château. It sounds to me as though you really have done rather well.'

Everything went without a hitch. The leader of the Syndicate was impressed and after they had been through all the individual figures and he had approved them, he said that the payment would be made at once after he had contacted the other partners in the Syndicate. The Comte agreed to this arrangement, but stressed that the objects could not of course be released until the payment had been received and everything satisfactorily cleared. The gentleman from Singapore signified his understanding and agreement. And that was it. The Comte courteously rang for the butler who brought in a decanter of fine old Armagnac and three glasses. The gentleman from Singapore excused himself on religious grounds and Percy put it down in one swallow rather to the disgust of the butler. Shortly afterwards they departed for Paris. The next day the syndicate leader left for Singapore with just one comment:

'You have done well, Mr. Mangon, and now you will have plenty to do. The Syndicate will of course be relying on your judgment.'

* * * * * *

When Herta Poll returned from the juggernaut people, Percy could not resist making her guess at the size of his triumph. When it did come out, Herta asked,

'Percival, are you talking in French Francs?'

'No, Sterling.'

'You have gone too high.' moaned Herta

'No I'm sure of it. If we cannot double this figure, I'll be amazed.'

* * * * * *

From that moment until the sale, the Mangon outfit was in overdrive. Much of the detailed planning he left in the capable hands of Herta and she worked at it with inspired energy. A top rank photographer was sent down to Bienheureux to take shots for the catalogue illustrations. Percy could only trust himself to write and produce the catalogue. It was to be an expensive item, possibly retailing at £15 or more. For a full week Percy laboured on the text. He used all the imagination he could muster. Wading through reference books and catalogues of his competitors in the international art scene he was able to contrive a credible introduction followed by descriptions and provenances for the list of lots that totalled, in the end, four hundred and eighty-two. Strangely, it was discovered later that Percy had overlooked one vital point.

Seven

The first of June was fine to warm giving a promise of good weather for the launching of TRANS-EUROPEAN INTERNATIONAL FINE ART AND ANTIQUES SALES which was to be the next day. Percival and Herta had spent some considerable time choosing the ideal place. They had both felt that atmosphere was essential; somewhere that spoke of past greatness, culture, romance, the great ones of history. Where better than beside the Loire — the land to the north and the south bearing a succession of great châteaux of which the names recalled memories of not only France itself but also many of the leading families of Europe. Buildings such as Cheverny, Chenonceaux, Chambord, Ussé all had attractions to serve as backcloths for this enterprise, but much had had to be considered: accessibility by road, the availability of suitable land that could be rented — and then lengthy consultations with local authorities. At last a site had been found that was everything that Percy had envisaged. It was on the south side of the Loire about seven kilometres from Amboise and three kilometres to the north of the small town of Bléré. Off the D31 there was a well metalled side-road which ended by a good sound, level, field. To the north could be seen the delicate rearing grace of the multi-storeyed Chanteloup Pagoda; an expensive architectural fantasy, one hundred and twenty-five feet high, reminiscent of the Orient, but surely the only pagoda with wrought iron balconies, Louis XVI decoration and classical colonnade. Behind this in the mid-distance was the shape of the Château of Amboise half-hidden by the rich foliage of the trees along the banks of the river.

At the moment the site presented a scene of some chaos. Just after breakfast the imposing convoy of the ten Volvo juggernauts had arrived under the command of Alfie Brigg. He had been up the previous day with a party of truck drivers to the agents in Paris to collect the imposing looking vehicles, their bodywork a dark blue with a single gold stripe two inches wide down each side and the words 'Trans European International Fine Art and Antiques Sales' in gold Roman lettering. Alfie was busily engaged in manoeuvring the huge vehicles into a 'U' plan. At the bottom of the 'U' had to be the one which carried the rostrum, while the two on each side of it had been specially constructed so that their sides could be lowered and then supported on legs to form display areas. Next, on one side, came the two accommodation vehicles and on the opposite side two further trucks that served as storage and packing centres. The tenth Volvo was carefully guided into position behind the rostrum truck; this one was the nerve centre with radio communication, computers, account clerks and also a room at one end to act as press office.

Alfie was as happy as he had ever been while working for Mangon. At this stage he was the bossman. He had recruited thirty extremely strong thugs from various areas of London — most were long-standing acquaintances and all, despite their own pugilistic prowess, had a complete understanding of Brigg built on their respect for his hammer-like fists and the brass 'comforter' as he called the knuckle-duster that he always carried. He had insisted that Mangon pay this crew well and in their own way they were responding. Quite a number of them were reasonably expert at rigging shows such as this, having worked with circuses and fairs. They were demonstrating their skills now. As soon as the Volvos were in position, the tall poles for the marquee were raised and secured with guys; then up went the big top, edges fastened to rings on the juggernauts and at the open end of the 'U' these were supported on smaller poles about ten feet high. Along this side, the edge of the marquee carried what could only be described as an enormous pelmet, shaped and painted to represent a long battlement. To one side stood a small booth for checking ticket-holders and for the selling of catalogues and this was in the form of a medieval gatehouse.

As soon as this part of the operation was completed, a series of security trucks began arriving and these brought the stock that was to be sold the next day. Brigg's crew turned to and carried the objects over to the juggernauts as indicated by two clerks who were checking to be sure that everything did arrive and that it was all stored so as to be ready and easily accessible for handling during the progress of the sale.

Next came the erection of a tent for refreshments which would include an expensive buffet of local delicacies; behind this, and discreetly screened, were placed a row of portable conveniences. To the right of the entrance went up a small pavilion-like tent with tables and chairs for use by the security guards and gendarmes. While some of the crew were tidying up outside the marquee, others had unloaded the large number of gilt cane-seated chairs which were being assembled in rows.

Shortly before midday, Percival Mangon and Herta Poll arrived in some splendour. Percy had discarded his black Cadillac in favour of a metallic gold Jaguar with dark blue leather upholstery and 3.6 litres of power under the bonnet. The two partners got out and walked slowly round the site.

As they came to the front Percy turned to Herta:

'I have to hand it to you, Herta. You certainly know your stuff and I would recommend you as a designer any day. I can't think of anything I could wish added that could be an improvement.'

The Austrian met his gaze,

'Thank you, Percival. It is good to be appreciated. Tomorrow you will show me what you can do with your little — what do you call it — gavel.' Herta gave herself the luxury of a full-face smile, the effect of which with her wall-eyes, broad expanse of very white teeth and the all black clothes was to nearly cause a passing waiter from the refreshment tent to trip over a rope.

One of Brigg's crew remarked, fortunately out of earshot of Herta Poll,

'Say Alfie, who's that then, somethin' out of a freak-show? Phooo, look at those choppers you could crack a steak bone wiv' em. And the eyeballs!'

Alfie replied in a half-whisper,

'Watch it, Ernie, that's the partner with Mr. Mangon. Must say, not over keen myself, but we've got to play along.'

'Howse this job goin' to go you reckon Alfie? Is there good prospects? I like this travelling around lark. You don't have to watch your P's and Q's, mate, as if you woz back home.'

'From the amount of money somebody is throwing into all this I'd say there must be something for the future. Them ten Volvos must have totted up a fair old price. I've been on some shenanigans with old Percy but never anything to approach this. Do you know, Ernie, they sent out booklets to a million people all over the world — think what the stamps alone for that lot would cost. Then there's been posters everywhere, thousands of them. Advertising spots on the telly, not only here in France but also in Germany, Switzerland, Italy and the UK too. And what do you think your lovely new uniforms for tomorrow cost, all that good cloth and gold braid — no change out of three fifty or so each. someone in the office told me that at first two million was spent and now three million will have been spent before old Percy has even sold a single ruddy lot!'

By three o'clock everything was immaculate. By arrangement with the farmer, whose land it was, a sanded pathway had been laid and raked up to the entrance and the same farmer was smiling broadly as all kinds of extras over and above the straight rent of the field were totting up. In the early evening, lighting crews and generating lorries for the television coverage arrived and erected stands and gantries for the lights and the large number of cameras that were expected not only from French television but also from Germany, Italy, the UK and 'stringers' who would be covering for the various American networks. The marquee had its own lights that were powered by a small generator in one of the Volvos, but they were not sufficient for the demands of the cameramen and producers. Percy was in the midst of matters trying to make sure that he was not going to be completely dazzled when the sale started. He was approached by someone holding a microphone who was followed by a girl clutching a clipboard, and a cameraman.

'Excuse me, Mr. Mangon, would it be possible to have a short interview for the late news tonight?'

Percy disentangled himself from coils of cables and light stands:

'Oh certainly — where do you suggest?'

'Might be quieter outside, there's still plenty of light.'

A couple of chairs were brought from the security tent and placed some thirty yards in front of the marquee and to the side. The presenter explained that the idea would be for the camera to pan across the very imposing set-up that had been erected and then to close in on them.

'On you in forty seconds,' called the girl with the clipboard.

'Can we have some quiet please?' shouted the producer and much of the chatter and clatter died away.

'Good evening,' began the presenter.

'Something very special is happening down here about seven kilometres south of Amboise tomorrow. This imposing looking marquee and accompanying collection of huge trucks is not a circus, not really an exhibition; it is a fine art saleroom. A long step from the Hotel Drouot or Bond Street or King Street, or for that matter the Dorotheum but it is, I assure you, a complete, fully equipped saleroom, even down to those gilded chairs. I have with me the man who has been mainly responsible for this incredible idea, Mr. Percival Mangon. Mr. Mangon, you are not exactly unknown to us after the wonderful piece of detective work on the Rembrandt. Could you tell me how did all this arise in a pleasant field near the Loire?'

'Good evening. Well, it's a fairly long and complicated story. I think I could explain it briefly by saying that for some time I have felt that antiques and fine art were getting away from most of us. After all, I don't see why they shouldn't be given a much wider showing. So, with my partner and good friend Fräulein Herta Poll from Vienna, we worked out the mechanics of having a very large travelling saleroom that would allow for all the amenities of a normal indoor establishment.'

'What actually is included here?'

'As you have seen, an auditorium that will seat upwards of five hundred and has standing room for many more. There is my rostrum. There is adequate display area for viewing the lots, security trucks for storage. A very up-to-date office lies behind the rostrum with the latest computers, one of which is connected to the large display panel in the auditorium and indicates the totals as they are bid in French Francs, Deutschmarks, Lira, Swiss Francs, US Dollars, Yen and Sterling. There is a short wave radio communication centre and a press office. Two of the juggernauts we have had fitted up as pretty high-class accommodation for our crew which numbers just over thirty.

'Mmm, I think that's the lot', Mangon finished with a flourish, 'it's a dream fulfilled to bring great art to everyone'.

'With your reputation as a perceptive eye in the art world and, if I may say so, being a skilled art detective, can we expect some surprises for tomorrow?'

'Ah yes, you will have seen the press release?'

'I have indeed, and one wonders where all these wonderful things keep coming from.'

'You know, if I could have an hour or two with you I could amaze you. The great houses of Europe, despite all the depredations of the likes of the Duveens and others, still hold, in many cases secretly, the most incredible treasures. Masterpieces sometimes sadly rotting away either from ignorance, or more often because of lack of funds for their restoration. A part of my idea is to give owners more confidence, a greater sense of trust. Come forward, sell one piece and the result may care for ten. I am afraid I'm rambling on — getting onto a pet subject.'

'Please,' continued the presenter, 'I'm sure most would agree with you, Mr. Mangon. One last question, if I may. I know that a great many of the art world specialists are just eaten up with curiosity as to just how you have been able to launch such a project. I have heard it said that at least three million has been spent before you have sold a single thing.'

'That's a question I'm afraid I cannot answer. I would be in breach of confidence with my backers. Forgive me.'

'I understand, Mr. Mangon. May I wish you good fortune for tomorrow with what is a very exciting and courageous happening.' He turned towards the camera, 'That was Mr. Percival Mangon, directing genius of what could well be the saleroom of the future. The eyes of the art world will be riveted on this little meadow not far from the Loire. By this time tomorrow, we shall all know the results. Will auction records be broken? It is indeed possible. In the security trucks are some outstanding works: a Tintoretto, a Velasquez, a suit of fine armour worn by the King of France at the Battle of Agincourt.... I could read out from this amazing press release for an hour. Until this time tomorrow, Au revoir!'

Later, as Percy and Herta were having dinner in their hotel in Amboise, a waiter gave him a card which he said a gentleman at the far end of the room had asked him to deliver.

The card gave the name of one of the most celebrated art critics in Europe, who not only contributed to a paper that was held in the highest regard but also regularly sent reports to a leading paper in the United States. On the back of the card it just said: 'Would it be possible to spare me a little time over a coffee perhaps?' Percy knew the writer quite well, having met him over the Rembrandt affair. He half turned in his chair and saw the man watching his reaction. Percy looked straight towards him and gave a very clear thumbs up sign with a nod of the head and a smile.

An hour later the critic and he were in adjoining chairs in a secluded corner of the upstairs lounge.

'Thank you, Mr. Mangon. I feel it is a little presumptuous butting in on you like this but I have at least two editors who are twisting my arm for news.'

'It's a pleasure to meet you again. You fire away,' replied Mangon.

'Do you mind if I use a small recorder — it saves a lot of writer's cramp?'

'Certainly not. Carry on.' Mangon was in an affable mood.

'I have your press releases and I must say right away that seldom have I seen what seems to be a collection of such outstanding rarity being gathered together in one sale. I didn't arrive down here until just before dinner and consequently I have seen none of the objects yet. A pleasure I look forward to with some interest. Now I, and I'm sure a number of colleagues in the art world are the same, am fascinated to know where you found all these treasures. To the established art circle you must probably be seen as a maverick.'

'I don't mind that name at all,' Mangon began, 'for what does it actually mean? I seem to remember having looked it up one day and the dictionary stated: "maverick — a person of independent or unorthodox views." That I think in a nutshell describes yours truly. I am not an establishment person and I think that a breeze of independence won't do any harm at all.'

'That's sound enough reasoning,' the critic acknowledged. 'You won't mind I hope if I ask you some pretty direct questions?'

Given the go-ahead by Mangon he began,

'For some time I've had a query running in my mind whenever I come across these big, big sales. Now I don't mean your mammoth affair tomorrow, but all the others as well who bring on these masterpieces. Your release states there will be four hundred and eighty two lots and nearly all of them are up in the five star class. Curiosity is a hard master for a writer, he has to satisfy it. I just wonder are some of the fabulously rich families having to sell to meet their undoubtedly vast overheads and are some of the rich institutions, who have had untold treasures left to them, in the same boat? Or perhaps is the Vatican itself raising capital in a quiet and cautious manner?'

'This is difficult for me to answer very directly,' Mangon began in a low voice. 'I freely admit to you that the objects mentioned have come to me from quite widely divergent sources. But I know you will understand that trust and the right kind of secrecy is an absolute bed rock of the trade.'

'One other thought nags me too.' The critic had expected the evasion. 'Art thefts seem to have become part of the regular fare for the readers. I don't know what the round-the-world total would add up to but it must be colossal. Recovery rate is depressingly low — possibly as much as fifteen per cent and no more. Where does this vast hoard go to? One is tempted to think that a sale such as yours tomorrow must be a target for the thieves to off-load their loot through?'

'You are striking a very sensitive nerve here,' said Mangon, 'for I think practically every auctioneer must have this fear somewhere at the back of his mind. Of course, I can only speak from personal experience. Over the years that Mangon Enterprises have operated, we have found that the thief with valuable objects will tend to avoid a large organisation like ours, and certainly a sale such as the one tomorrow, for a very simple reason. That is, there is too much publicity and too many top experts like yourself around. The last thing they want is discovery. Thus they will choose the smaller operators, third-rank dealers. Of course, that way the price dips considerably. There are so many bent men in the middle of these transactions taking big cuts that I believe the thief, at the end, often gets little more than about fifteen per cent.'

'Another rumour I've heard is that when a really big robbery is made, the paintings or whatever, may be used as collateral for a loan; the inference being that there are opulent individuals around, or even possibly private banks, who are not too choosy and will advance pretty healthy loans against what they would think are gilt-edged works of art. Obviously the interest and repayment rates would be sky-high. But, say, if one takes along something worth ten million and it means an advance of five million is forthcoming, it can be an attractive idea; more so, if the transactions are taking place in an area where they can be blurred, smudged over with some clever paperwork that will successfully bury all the details.'

Percy nodded his head.

'If you get a glimpse of the list of first-rank masterpieces that have gone missing, certainly in the last thirty years, it's scarcely believable. Although officialdom vigorously denies the concept of the commissioned theft, I don't think there would be many who would declare on oath that it just doesn't exist. Read up accounts of thefts. Time and time again the villain has obviously been selective. Every sign points to the fact that certainly some jobs are being done to order. Off the record, if you don't mind, with this bit — but I'm sure we both know that the prime encouragement for this kind of activity comes from over the Atlantic.'

'I absolutely agree,' replied the critic, stopping the tape. 'Quite blatant accounts and admissions have appeared from time to time from people very high up, presumably labouring under the illusion that vast wealth is a wall of security for any activity they may want to indulge in. You've been most co-operative, Percival, may I wish you very good luck for tomorrow.'

'Thank you. But do you think that I need it?'

The critic shrugged,

'In this game you never know. Well, I'm for the bed. Good night to you and thanks.'

* * * * * *

At seven-thirty the next morning the inter-room phone rang just as Mangon was completing a rather careful shave. Dabbing away the soap he walked across the room and lifted the receiver to hear the voice of Herta:

'Percival,' she positively purred, 'forgive me for calling so early. But I had an idea. This is our big, big day. I wondered would you like to share a private breakfast with me in my room. We need something substantial — I have ordered what I would call a full Bavarian breakfast. Quite informal please — I think dressing-gowns should be worn. May I expect you shortly?'

Percival was somewhat shaken by the request but he answered: 'I would like that, Herta. Thank you, I'll be along.'

Thank goodness, he thought, as he put the phone down that I brought my new satin dressing-gown rather than my old battered towelling wrap.

In answer to his knock, the door was opened by a Herta he hadn't realized existed before. She took his hand and gently pulled him into the room at the same time brushing his cheek with a fleeting kiss. The expensive perfume she was wearing found its mark — something stirred, an excitement that was strange, an emotion that he had almost forgotten rose within him. All he could see before him was a new Herta, not the coldly efficient and over-bearing Herta Poll. No. She stood looking into his eyes while still holding his hand. She wore a fine black silk dressing-gown embroidered with fantastic dragons in gold thread; they jumped and fought together from the bottom of the gown right up to her shoulders.

Herta turned. 'Come, they have set the breakfast for us by the window.' Percival looked at the table and the full Bavarian breakfast. Hard-boiled eggs, half a dozen varieties of sliced meats and sausages, four different cheeses, assorted rolls, jams, fruit juices and a huge pot of coffee.

As he sat down he noticed on his plate a small leather case.

'Ah . . . that is for you, Percival, as a good fortune talisman for today . . . to look after things.'

Percival lifted the case and pressed a small button on the side and the lid opened. Inside, nestling into a piece of crumpled blue velvet, was a delicately wrought tie-pin in the likeness of a small spray of edelweiss in gold with sapphires.

For a moment Percival looked at the beautiful thing and then across the table to Herta.

'This is really for me?' He felt unsure, almost nervous in the presence of this Herta who seemed to have totally transformed herself.

'Herta, my dear Herta, this is lovely, but I have nothing for you. Oh, what can I do?'

'Nothing, Percival. Nothing at all. For me it is the woman's privilege to back the man. I am a romantic historical — smile, if you like. Richard Wagner and all those great Nordic legends and knights and supermen and their ladies. The knights go into battle carrying the favours of their ladies. Forgive me, but I get carried away. I see us today, you as my . . .but no, I must stop. Anyway will you please wear my little offering today?' For a second Percy thought Herta was going to cry but she gathered herself, swallowed a mouthful of pineapple juice and attacked a plate of meats, cheeses and eggs with a thoroughly collected and competent Germanic gusto.

'Of course I will, and if I may say so, Herta . . .with pride.' At this point he took refuge behind a similar plateful to Herta's and they both munched away in silence. Between them they practically cleared the whole tray — a last cup of coffee and Herta said,

'Well, now it is just after eight and we must not be late. I will meet you in the foyer in twenty minutes.'

When the gold Jaguar arrived at the site the sun was clear through the thin woolly clouds and the Mobile Saleroom looked quite splendid. Alfie Brigg, in his new morning coat, pepper-and-salt trousers, lavender waistcoat and oyster grey cravat, fairly breathed of dignity, confidence and trustworthiness.

He came across to the car as Mangon carefully parked it alongside the medieval gatehouse where the two girls were already installed ready to check the invitation cards and ticket holders and to sell the catalogues when they arrived.

'Good morning, both,' he rather familiarly addressed Percival and Herta, 'There you are, Mr. Mangon, the final touch.' He pointed upward to where four large royal blue pennants emblazoned with golden sunbursts floated freely in the breeze. As he got out of the car, Percy stood quite still for at least a minute, his eyes wandering over the scene from the figure of Alfie and his cohorts, who were now almost unrecognisable in their uniforms, to the mock battlements above the entrance and then up to those proud pennants. Surely, later in the day they would signify, by carrying the sign of the sunburst, the Mangon integrity. They would stand in people's memories as symbols of the triumph, the arrival of Percival Mangon — prince elect of the brotherhood of greats that ruled the world of fine art and antiques.

He walked over to Alfie and shook his hand,

'Well done, well done, Alfie.' Then he put his mouth close to Alfie's right ear and whispered very quickly,

'You'll get your cut, me old friend, for this.'

'There's one slip though,' said Alfie, 'the van carrying the catalogues has broke down near Orléans.'

'How long do they reckon it will be before they can arrive?' asked Percy.

'I got a relief van organized; but it will be after eleven I reckon, Mr. Mangon,' answered Alfie.

'Better get an announcement made right away,' said Percy.

Brigg went over to the office truck and gave a clerk the message. The speakers came to life:

'Good morning, ladies and gentlemen. One announcement. The transport bringing the catalogues has broken down at Orléans. But we do have a relief on the way. It should be here shortly after eleven. For your convenience, would you please go to the booth in the medieval gatehouse and there you may purchase a docket that can be exchanged for a catalogue as soon as they arrive. Ushers will move around the seating and other areas with the catalogues which can then be exchanged for your dockets. Thank you for your patience.'

The viewing for prospective buyers and the press was just beginning and the car park was already half-full. Mangon and Poll strolled leisurely round acknowledging recognitions from those they had met before. Inside, under the lofty marquee, it was an even more impressive sight. Practically all the lots were now on display — furniture and standing objects either on the lowered sides of the Volvos or on strips of dark blue carpet on the ground. Paintings and tapestries hung from rails along the top of the juggernauts. Small items rested on tables and everywhere the uniformed staff roamed, seemingly casual but with eyes alert. Those members of the public who wished to examine objects closely were encouraged to do so, as long as they had one of the Brigg brigade alongside them.

It was hardly surprising that in all this splendour and movement Percy did not take in the rather tatty figure of a young man who had just arrived in a beaten-up old banger and was now earnestly examining several lots. Gingerly he picked up a 16th-century Spanish morion, and then with the help of an assistant an early Sienese Madonna and Child; after that an 18th-century French prie-dieu, and an icon of the Novgorod school that had perhaps escaped the destruction of Ivan the Terrible in 1570, and he took considerable interest in the dramatic landscape in front of Burgos, which Percy's press release had claimed as being by El Greco. He scribbled away in a notebook and then hurried out and drove off. If anyone had remarked on his actions, they would have assumed he was a 'runner' for some important bidder who wanted some advance information.

* * * * * *

By dinner time the previous evening, Tim and Nell, Aideen and René had arrived from Paris at a select country house hotel on the north bank of the Loire about twelve kilometres to the west of Amboise nearly opposite MontLouis-sur-Loire. They found that Angélique had arrived earlier and was waiting for them. As Mangon would be sure to recognise Aideen, it was suggested that she should stay at the hotel during the sale with Angélique who herself might be known by some of the dealers who would undoubtedly be coming from all over the country.

At ten fifteen the next morning Tim, Nell and René were on their way to the Sale.

They arrived as part of a long queue of cars that were moving towards the site. With the help of a friendly gendarme, René got almost the last parking space in the field. It was an amazing scene. Press everywhere, photographers, film cameramen, and — much in evidence — the security guards and porters in their uniforms. Tim went over to the medieval gatehouse and bought dockets for three catalogues and was given at the same time three tickets for standing space on the right-hand side of the saleroom. They were rigging extra speakers outside the marquee to allow for bids from the considerable throng that was assembling.

Tim rejoined Nell and René and handed them a docket each.

'Do you know what that character charged for these? £15 each! Come on, it's fifteen minutes past eleven. We're going to have to stand, I'm afraid.'

* * * * * *

The somewhat tatty young man in the old banger wasn't a 'runner' at all. He was a 'stringer' for a London paper that had editions coming out throughout the day. He was now at two minutes past eleven trying desperately to get a reverse charge call through to his Editor. By four minutes past he had succeeded.

'How was it?' asked the Editor.

The 'Stringer' replied, 'Just as you thought. I got a good look at the five lots you mentioned. Quite definitely they all had it!' and the phone clicked off.

*   *   *   *   *   *

Three minutes later and the London Editor was through to a close friend with a leading French newspaper group. The same message was repeated.

'Thank you, my friend,' said the correspondent in Paris.

*   *   *   *   *   *

Another two minutes passed and the correspondent in Paris had passed the same message to the Radio and Television News Room.

*   *   *   *   *   *

By eleven fifteen every gilt chair was occupied, the previously allotted standing space was all taken up and the crowd now covered an arc forty yards deep. Mangon, behind the scenes, was becoming desperate.

'How can I have a sale without the catalogues? Brigg, can't you do something? Oh, I should have looked after this myself. Why must I always do everything myself?' Herta remained outwardly calm. Another minute passed. Then a cheer from outside told of the arrival of the van. Herta turned to the office staff,

'Outside all of you, and get those catalogues distributed!'

Somehow by twenty-seven minutes past eleven the Mangon staff had passed round to docket holders just over seven hundred catalogues and had sold another twelve hundred to the crowds outside. When Alfie whispered this to the highly charged Mangon it did much to restore some of his confidence — £28,500 just for the catalogues was a very good omen.

No one in the office or amongst the staff outside had heard a certain newsflash on a local radio programme.

Nell, who had a small transistor in her shoulderbag, had heard the brief announcement or part of it. The presenter had cut off a 'pop' record in full blast . . . .

'Here is a newsflash with regard to the big sale of antiques and fine art which is just about to take place between Amboise and Bléré. Those attending should . . .' there was a burst of static cracking and after ten seconds the voice came back again:

'I'm afraid that some of you in certain areas may have had difficulty in receiving that but we had a breakdown on transmission which has now been restored. Our next offering will be the latest from the Spindleshakers.' Nell leaned towards Tim and spoke quietly close to his left ear:

'I think it has all got through.' Tim gently squeezed her arm and smiled across to René. The time of the newsflash had been eleven twenty-six.

With four minutes to go, Nell noticed small groups of people she had assumed to be dealers scattered around the concourse talking excitedly together, gesticulating with their catalogues. It seemed to be infectious — the hubbub increased.

Tim looked up at the gantry carrying the television cameras — further evidence of excitement — producers and personal assistants were harrying the cameramen seemingly to get them to film or VTR every detail.

At exactly eleven thirty the Mangon sense of showmanship reasserted itself. Suddenly the clang of a great bell came through the speakers loud and clear. Shocked by the unexpectedness, the crowd went silent. Next came a fifteen second flourish of a recorded trumpet salute and as the notes faded away dark blue velvet curtains behind the rostrum parted and Percival Mangon stepped forward and mounted the three steps to the auctioneer's desk. Tim generously admitted afterwards that one had to hand it to the fellow. He was immaculate; charcoal grey suit, dark green doeskin waistcoat, stiff wing collar and crimson cravat in the centre of which was secured the edelweiss pin that sparkled brilliantly as the full glare of the television lights came on.

Percy raised both his arms as a welcoming salute to his audience and then the great moment came.

'My friends, good morning to you all and it is wonderful that so many should have been drawn to this, the first of what undoubtedly will be many more offerings from Trans-European International Fine Art and Antiques Sales. Let me waste no more of your time.'

Turning to the group of porters beside him Percy began, 'May I have Lot Number One; a pair of Arita Vases. Now ladies and gentlemen, we're away...an opening bid of £500...behind you madam £600, £700, in the corner £800, £900, £1,000, from outside £1200, in front £1500, behind you again £2,000, £2,500, £3,000 at the side £4,000, in the centre £5,000, beside you...no...outside again £5,500...any more any more at £5,500 once, twice...sold!' From where he was he could not make out the paddle number of the final bidder and he whispered to a clerk to confirm the details. Lot Number two; An earthenware pot by Yabu Meizan. This brought in £11,000. Lot Number three; An early Safavid silver and gold inlaid brass ewer with cover brought £19,500. Lot Number four; A Nuremberg Hausamalerie vintner's goblet, painted and with some gilding by Hermann Benckert, reached a surprising £17,000. Lot Number five; a French ivory chess-set featuring Napoleon and the Austrian Emperor Francis broke a record for such an item with a final bid of £4,250. Lot Number six....But Percy never got to what it was. Approaching fast could be heard police sirens, several of them. There were shouts from outside. Sounds of vehicles screaming to a stop. Car doors slamming. Then right at the back directly opposite to the rostrum Mangon could make out a surging amongst the standing crowds. A large number of gendarmes were appearing, their distinctive caps just visible above the heads of the audience. In their midst a solitary tall figure in a grey suit was trying to make his way to the front but the audience was packed so tight he had no chance. He stopped and signalled to the inspector who turned to his men making frantic signals to them to blow their whistles. Half a dozen of them did so with considerable force. It had the effect needed. The man in the grey suit called out:

'This sale must stop at once. I have here,' and he held up a very official looking document, 'a court order for sequestration and holding until a full enquiry has been satisfied.'

Behind Mr. Mangon four plain clothes policemen appeared holding a painting, a chair, a sword and a bronze *putti*. The attack from the law was so quick, so efficient that there could be no doubting.

The man in grey called out once more, this time to the plain-clothes men,

'What are your findings?'

The senior man shouted back,

'These four lots are all described as genuine in the catalogue... yet they bear the symbol that shows that they are definitely reproductions.'

The man in grey looked straight at Percival Mangon.

'It is my duty to charge you with fraudulently selling modern reproductions whilst claiming them in your catalogue to be genuine.' The room erupted, everyone was on their feet, shouts and oaths filled the air. People milled in all directions. The gendarmes desperately forced their way through towards the rostrum. The four plain clothes men seemed to have been swept to one side by the uniformed porters and staff.

Mangon, Herta and Brigg with the cunning of jackals crouched down and with Brigg leading butted their way with desperate speed back into the office, jumped out of the back door and still crouching sprinted along behind the parked Volvos until they came to where Mangon's Jaguar was parked beside the medieval gatehouse tent. Alfie Brigg suddenly took control and ordered,

'Give me your keys, I'm driving. Get in the back Percy, and you, Miss Poll, in the front.' He then ducked into the Security tent which was empty except for one overawed clerk who was clutching the cash box which held the takings from the sales of the catalogues. This was no time for finesse. Alfie hit the poor chap hard just under the right ear and he fell forward without a sound. Grabbing the cashbox, Alfie was out and into the driving seat of the Jaguar in seconds flat. He threw the cashbox in the back, flicked the starting key and revving the powerful engine moved towards the exit road. But it was blocked solid with police cars and crowds. Alfie hadn't survived a bringing up in Shadwell and the docklands of London by being slow and indecisive. Just to the right there was a low hedge with a slight ditch and then another flat meadow. He pushed the revs up and the gold car literally jumped at the obstacle, hitting the side of a police Renault and narrowly missing two spectators. The Jaguar was through the hedge and skidding round in a wide arc as Alfie spotted a wooden gate which gave on to the road to Bléré. He hit it at about forty, fragments shot all over the place but the car kept going.

*   *   *   *   *   *

It was well past two o'clock before Tim, Nell and René returned to the hotel where they had left Aideen and Angélique. The chaos that followed the dénouement had been almost beyond description, with upwards of six thousand people, and probably at least a thousand cars all trying to absent themselves from the site as soon as possible.

René said that he had heard what must have been Mangon's Jaguar tearing its heart out. He related the rest of the story. When they had finally got outside they could see where the car must have torn through a hedge and then careered across the next field and smashed through a wooden gate. The police cars all appeared to have been thoroughly jammed in by others. They had emerged about twenty minutes after it all happened and as far as he could judge only one Police Renault had had a try at following but this had buried its nose in the ditch by the hedge which the Jaguar under full power had managed to jump.

'Did you hear the radio flash?' asked Nell, 'we got part of it but the last bit was lost by a transmission fault.'

'We did indeed', Aideen answered, 'I made a note of it.' She produced a scrap of notepaper.

'Here we are…"With regard to the big sale of antiques and fine art which is just about to take place between Amboise and Bléré, those attending should be very careful and check their intended purchases thoroughly, as it is reported from a reliable source that all may not be well with some of the lots for sale."'

Angélique was looking through one of the catalogues they had brought back. 'You can't say that Mr. Mangon is not greedy. He must also suffer from what you say…a big head. Four hundred and eighty-two lots, of which three hundred and twenty have come from my Ateliers. He, in his catalogue, has made it that every object without doubt is by well-known master or craftsman. I don't wonder that some of the dealers were getting worried when they finally got the catalogues. Tim and Nell know what has been my practice ever since we started. We make reproductions of many kinds of work, but never do we sign them or mark them as original works by great masters. In fact, from the start and for the protection of the trade, every single item that leaves my workshop has our distinctive mark indelibly placed upon it. You ask any leading dealer. They will tell you. It is very well known; the "one-eyed lion". It's no crime to make reproductions and to sell them as reproductions, even less so when they are clearly marked with such a symbol. Mr. Mangon went deeply wrong by starting to sell them with that catalogue which states clearly that they are by masters.'

Meanwhile Tim had also been examining his catalogue:

'And why on earth didn't the idiot put in the usual disclaimer section as other people do. You know, "Mangon's make every effort to ensure the accuracy of their catalogue and the descriptions of every lot. But they do not accept responsibility for the authenticity, attribution, genuineness, date, age, condition, materials, techniques etc. etc." Was it his great big head as a world expert — or some awful printer's error? After all the catalogues were late! I don't think I'd like to be in Percy's shoes. No, not with oriental backers chasing me and waving an IOU for twenty-two million pounds plus. Let's have a celebration dinner.' Tim looked around at the smiling faces.

Just at that moment the phone rang. Nell answered it and she recognized the voice at once,

'You lot have taken an age to track down. Sounds to me from the early news as if a very thorough dismantling of "our friend" Mangon has taken place. I have fixed it with the manager of your hotel that your party is to have the finest meal with all accompaniments he can produce and the bill is on us. Bye for now, Nell dear.'

'Who was that?' asked René.

'Oh someone I had lunch with not very long ago in London,' replied Nell, 'he is in a way connected with the trade.' Angélique smiled.

*   *   *   *   *   *

The gold Jaguar, thanks to the frantic confusion at the site, did in the end have a clear seventeen minute start on the police pursuit. Alfie drove in silence with a concentration that marked him down as a true expert. In those precious seventeen minutes he covered slightly over twenty-nine kilometres. Through Bléré, St. Avertin and down to Montrésor and Loches and cutting a way through little used side roads to Poitiers and then on towards La Rochelle. Somehow he felt the opposition would be looking out on the roads either to the Channel ports or a straight run down to the Spanish border.

Following the southern bank of the river Seure and now at a more leisurely pace, he kept his eye open as the river passed through a long and twisting course. Suddenly he stopped and told the other two to get out and pushed the cash box after them, and Mangon's brief case and Herta's holdall.

'What are you going to do?' asked Percy.

'Do?' said Alfie, 'get rid of this...this giveaway. Haven't you noticed there don't seem to be many golden jaguars around with dark blue upholstery?' Slowly he edged the car towards the top of the river bank until he felt the gradient. Then he put on the brake, got out, leant over and released the brake and the weight of the car caused it to dive deep into the muddy waters.

Percy shouted, 'You so-and-so, that cost me more than £28,000.'

'Shut up Percy,' said Herta.

'By your big headedness and conceit and phoney knowledge you've dropped us right into it, haven't you?' spat Alfie. 'And what about all me mates back at the site, eh?'

'Come on,' broke in Herta, 'I presume, Mr. Brigg, you have a plan for something and that is why we are on the way to La Rochelle.'

'Before we start let's see what the exchequer stands at, shall we,' said Alfie. 'There should be more than £28,000 in that box. What have you got to add, Mr. Mangon?'

'I have about £120 in my wallet and another £2,000 in the brief case.'

'And you, Miss Poll, please?'

'I have no more than £1200,' said Herta. She leant towards Mangon and grabbed at the edelweiss tie pin. 'I'll have that back, you stupid, stupid man.'

'Let's see what I have got,' said Alfie. 'Had quite a night with the local talent and some cards...yes £4,800. Now I suggest we split it up — equal shares and let's get to Rochelle. Someone I knew a few years ago was on the run in France for a bit of a mis-understanding with a jeweller's shop. He told me the fishermen or some of them down there were not too fussy about trips if it was worthwhile. The best ones to try are the deep sea boats that chase the mackerel up to the Cornish coast or over to the south-west of Ireland. So shall we be on our way? Over to you, Miss Poll, as I'm sure you have the lingo.'

It was five kilometres to La Rochelle. As they left the river bank Alfie discarded his morning coat and they began to walk. After about half a kilometre a heavily loaded farmer's truck stopped and gave them a lift all the way. The time now was coming to evening, but still there were some shops open. With the assistance of Herta the three fugitives managed to buy the bare necessities: toilet gear, a change of clothes, a navy polo sweater for Alfie. They got to the quays just as the darkness came down. Herta went about her task with skill and energy. After the fourth enquiry she came back smiling with achievement.

'I have found a boat that will take us to Ireland, to Dingle. Please, I want contributions from both of you — the cost will be £6,000.' Between them they counted out the notes by the dim light of a street lamp. She went back to the café and then returned.

'The Captain will be along in a minute. He says to go along the quay. His boat is called "La Reine d'Or".'

They found the boat, a medium deep-sea trawler, some thirty metres long and looking as though she was last cleaned shortly after the war. But she was a way out and had to be brought to shore for boarding.

The captain and his three crewmen turned out to be friendly as well they might be after the sum paid over. The trip took the best part of four days and four nights. The ancient vessel wallowed magnificently and pitched with determination. She stank of mackerel, but in the end the coughing, spluttering diesel got them to Dingle. As they sidled alongside the quay in the very early, still-dark hours of the morning, the three escapees were hidden in the rope and tackle locker. 'La Reine d'Or', registered at La Rochelle, made fast and one after the other the three slunk ashore and disappeared into the shadows.

Eight

During the voyage from France they had decided to split up, Herta would go it alone and despite what he had said to Percival Mangon, Alfie was staying with him; but by mutual assent they exchanged contact numbers. Dingle, at this early hour, slept. The heights of Brandon and the Stradbally mountains were but the vaguest of dark forms against the sky. Herta Poll had found a fish shed with an open door. Inside were a chair and table and more importantly a sink and tap. She got out her sponge-bag and scented French soap and for ten minutes revelled in her efforts to rid herself of the odour from that awful boat. The silver grey light of the false dawn penetrated enough for her to look round the shed. On a shelf was a jar of instant coffee, and a battered old tin that held some biscuits. On a table in a corner was a small electric ring. She put some water in the kettle and put it on the ring and in a few minutes she was able to make a cup of black coffee. It was not the best cup of coffee she had had, but after those four days on 'La Reine d'Or', it was sheer delight. She filled a pocket with some biscuits and went out on to the quay again.

There was no sign of Mangon and Brigg, nor for that matter anyone else. She was desperate to ring Warren B. Westonhofer but had no Irish coins to fit the call boxes; she did not feel sure enough of herself to try making a reverse charge call. So, a little braced up she decided to set out for the village of Anascaul which was signposted outside Dingle as nine miles away. The time was now five thirty. Munching biscuits and striding out towards the brightening dawn, Herta felt much better; the exercise toned up her muscles and stimulated her mind. When she arrived in Anascaul the time was approaching half past eight. The landlord of the 'South Pole' was clearing tables in front of his inn and greeted her cheerfully.

'Tis going to be a great day. Sure, you've made an early start.'

'It is a good day. Yes, I am early. I have had a good walk.'

The landlord continued, 'It's from Dingle you've come, on a holiday exploration no doubt.'

'Yes,' said Herta. 'You could say that. Is it possible I could use your telephone if you please?'

'Sure. Help yourself. In through the saloon entrance and on the right.'

The landlord went back to his clearing up.

'Oh, excuse me,' said Herta, 'I have no coins.'

'Give Marie a shout, she's in the kitchen,' said the landlord.

Marie did provide the change necessary, exchanging the sterling gladly, and in fairly quick time Herta got through to Warren. He was responsive and full of friendliness. He asked where she was and she told him. He paused for a moment and then said, 'Gee, that's not so far. I must have known where you would pitch up. I'm at one of those farmhouses that let rooms; great people and they'll have a room for you. It is near a place called Abbeyfeale — looks like about forty miles. Honey, I'll be with you in about an hour.' Herta put the phone down and as she walked towards the kitchen Marie called out, 'Would you be thinking of using a good breakfast? I could have it ready for you in about ten minutes.'

Herta smiled, 'That would be good. Please, you are kind.'

Marie may have lacked some of the finer points of cuisine but the breakfast she produced was very good. A large pot of strong tea, steps of home-made soda bread, a jar of marmalade and a large platter of rashers of bacon, slices of black and white pudding, mushrooms, tomatoes, a lamb chop and two eggs. After that lot had been washed on its way with three cups of tea Herta felt herself rebuilt, and as she sat on a seat outside waiting for Warren the world began to be a better place.

* * * * * *

Percy, along with Alfie Brigg, after they had slunk off down the quay, found a bus-shelter which was closed in on three sides. Here they compounded the misery of the sea passage by huddling in opposite corners and trying to shrug off the early morning chill.

It was not until nearly two hours later that they heard someone stirring at a cafe just close by. They walked over and were able to get hot drinks and a fry-up. Mangon found some English coins at the back of his wallet which he found fitted the telephone coinbox. Fortunately, the phone was in a front room that was empty, so when in a sleepy voice Myles Fyrken answered, Percy was able to speak fairly openly.

'Help, Percy, do you know what the time is?' said Myles, 'Oh, look man, I was late last night.'

Percy responded, 'So were we. You've no idea how I've been screwed. I was right well conned, Myles.'

'Yes,' said Myles. 'I rather gathered that from the TV and what the papers have been saying. Headlines like "Biggest Art Scandal in History". You've certainly made it!'

'Come on, Myles. I need help. Can you find us, Alfie and me, a little safe house somewhere not too far from Ennis? I have some ideas to go through with you.'

Myles came back at him,

'I'll bet you have with that IOU fluttering around! You're lucky. I've got a small cottage that will do; it's free for about four months. Down just outside Kilrush.' He gave the address and continued, 'You hire a car, and I'll leave the keys with Mrs. O'Mahony who lives three doors away from the house.'

Finally, Myles told Mangon to be in touch in a couple of days by which time he felt Percy would have calmed down.

* * * * * *

The day after the débâcle down by the Loire, Tim, Nell, Aideen and René returned to Paris, and Angélique to Marseilles. René had a couple of portrait commissions to complete and then he was coming over to Ireland to work with Aideen on the trade. After two nights in Paris, Aideen was on her way back to Clare.

Arriving at Quin Cottage she found Louise in high spirits; apparently the warm weather had encouraged the flowers that mattered for the bees and Katty was spending most evenings by the hives talking and crooning away to her friends. It took Aideen quite a time to tell the complete story of the fall of Mangon; at the end Louise said,

'I sincerely hope that that will be the last of a very unpleasant man. By the way, my dear, I heard in Ennis the other day that

that rotter Myles Fyrken has got himself in big with these development people. He's becoming very much one of the nobs.'

'I see from the card in the hall that James and Laura have got their silver display getting under way down at Kilbandan,' Aideen replied, while smiling at her mother's venom, 'the official launch day is June the 21st. Nice of them to ask us. You'll come, won't you? It's at Jury's Hotel. Tell you what, let's have a little spree — I'll stand us both a couple of nights there and a lobster supper in the Kish.'

*   *   *   *   *   *

Warren B. Westonhofer was punctual, and gratefully Herta climbed into the rented Ford Granada beside him.

'Shake my hand, Herta. You've been through it. I guess now you have a fair idea why I walked out on Mangon. You say that he and that hood Alfie were on the boat with you. Any idea where they've gone or what they are going to be doing?'

'I have the idea that Mangon will contact that solicitor Fyrken in Ennis. They will get in together. Mangon needs big money fast if he's going to stay in one piece.'

'Well now, I reckon the programme for today is this: you have got to get yourself a change of rig. What you are wearing is a trademark and you never know who'll be around. I suggest we have a day out. I'm going to head for Cork, there are some good shops down there and good eating places. You don't mind a suggestion now, do you? I think an outfit of local knitwear and tweed is what is needed.'

'Yes, it will be fun to try.' Herta showed off her white teeth.

Warren took the road to Killarney and then over the Derrynasaggart Mountains to Macroom and into Cork where they were in time to catch a quality outfitter before lunch. Warren asked Herta if she needed money but she told him that for the moment she was in funds. While he waited he strolled over to a call-box and rang the Arbutus Lodge Restaurant and managed to book a table for two. Half an hour later a transformed Herta appeared carrying several large carriers and looking very nearly like a fashion plate for Irish produce. She had chosen a high-necked knitted jumper in emerald green with a tweed skirt of a darker tone.

'You sure look swell, honey,' said Warren. This was the first time he had seen her out of black.

'Now, I've booked us a table where we'll get the best lunch in town.'

He was not over-stating. The meal was quite something. A local speciality to start with — delicately flavoured nettle soup, followed by fillets of sea bass with ginger and saffron sauce, and then new season's lamb, pink and so tender it almost dissolved in the mouth, with to finish, some superb *milles-feuilles*.

Their conversation during lunch was non-committal. It wasn't until they were back in the car and on the way to the farmhouse near Abbeyfeale that Warren suggested they stop when they came to a parking place up in the mountains where they could have a serious talk.

This turned out to be for about the first half hour a monologue by Warren. As his plan unfolded, Herta found herself admiring this bombastic character.

Since she had seen him in Paris he had been very busy indeed. It had all started when he joined up with a group of his country-men who were over in Ireland doing the 'stately home' round under the direction of an outfit that called itself 'Destiny Tours.' The group numbered twelve and they were driven around in one of those mini-coaches. Two things had cropped up. The first happened when they were going over Ballymalloon House up in Cavan. He had got talking to the owner and had let it be known that he was an Art Assessor back home in Detroit. One thing had kind of led to another. The owner asked him if he knew about some outfit in Paris that was running a very helpful business for the likes of himself who wanted to dispose of works of art with-out all the thing of going through auction rooms and dealers. Warren had kept the old chap talking and got quite a lot out of him. Not least that the operator the Paris bunch used for the UK was based somewhere in Ireland. Warren felt that Herta and himself should look into the possibility of taking some of the action; it sounded a soft touch.

The other matter, which had, as he put it, dropped right into his lap, was an exhibition of Irish silver that was being got ready at Kilbandan castle. As a favour to the tour, which would be terminating its current visit shortly, Lord Kilbandan had arranged a special opening. Warren had continued to Herta that if there was one thing that had a quick-fire sale back in the States it was honest-to-goodness Irish silver. And Lord and Lady Kilbandan certainly had a five star exhibition there, from early church-plate with chalices and thuribles to examples of practically everything the silversmiths of Dublin, Cork and Limerick had made. Mouth-watering it was: Coffee-pots, tea-pots, chocolate-pots, cream jugs, sugar bowls, tableware, cake baskets, epergnes, and a wonderful array of those Irish specialities, the dish rings — many of them showing fantastic skill with repoussé, pierced and engraved work. Gee, he had gone on, he couldn't even begin to tally up what it could be worth — but certainly in the States it would bring in four to five million dollars. Then Warren had stopped, looked hard at Herta and said.

'You know, my friend, that is just where it's going to go. And I reckon you deserve a cut.'

'You mean, Warren — you— I — we are going to take it just like that from a castle,' gasped Herta.

'Yes, you could say that,' came the reply. 'Just you wait while I tell you the rest of the idea. I've put some hard thinking into this. A few more items like this and I am going to hang up my hat on the art assessor game. What you say? Are we in this together?'

'Let me hear everything first, then I will decide,' said Herta.

Warren continued with the details for his plan. He had found Lord Kilbandan and his wife Laura quite charming, real gentle-folk. Again, as with the people at Ballymalloon, he had hung back and got them talking. And again he had used the Art Assessor title, saying that he was linked with this and that and how his real love was silver. Then Lord Kilbandan had asked him to stay on for a spot of supper and said he would drive him back after-wards to the Old Ground in Ennis, where the group was staying for the night. He then had taken Warren through the old castle from bottom to top. In the cellar area he showed the gateway to the tunnel that they used to bring in the donkey cartloads of peat for the heating. He even took him up in the old-fashioned, pull-rope balanced lift from the cellars to the first floor where the fabulous show of silver was being staged.

'What next do you think?' Warren asked Herta , 'He says he guesses I'd like a real close look at some of the pieces. He goes over to a cupboard in the corner by the lift and opened the latch. There are all the switches for the entire internal alarm system throughout the castle and for the exhibition cases. It was not too difficult to see which switches he pulled and also how the whole place could be made wide open! So that was the first most important step,' continued Warren. 'Then what next? Well, on June 21st, his Lordship tells me, there is a big official do for launching the exhibition. He and Laura are closing the castle to visitors from the 19th to the 22nd June, and taking a few pieces up for the party display. Going to be a big do: the Irish Tourist Board, Government Ministers and everybody who is anybody is going to be there at Jury's Hotel, Ballsbridge. Who's left at the castle: His Lordship's butler and his wife who is the housekeeper and their niece. No one else. The only other bod is an ancient gamekeeper at the lodge, nearly half a mile away.'

'We are going to need help on this one, Herta, and not local talent; some professionals are in order. There's an agency back in Detroit that offers a selection of services and who don't ask what's what. I have arranged for them to send four guys over on the 15th. The way out is through that tunnel which comes to the surface, believe it or not, in a lane just outside the estate wall. Now, where does one get donkeys and carts from? I happened to drop in on one of the local creamery places where some of the small farmers still use the old donkey transport. I pick a likely looking guy and tell him I'm making a film documentary on the great places of Ireland and I need a couple of donkeys and carts to show how they used these tunnels. Hundred pounds and the old chap promised to teach my chaps how to drive and handle the beasts and that was that. I calculated that four large wooden packing cases should take the whole show, so I have those being made up.' Warren was beaming at his own resourcefulness. He carried on, anticipating a question from Herta:

'How do we get the staff out of the way and open the alarm system for the entrance doors? Around four hundred yards across a park in front of the castle there is a large group of timber buildings; barns, store-sheds and things like that. When we're ready, on the day we pick, one of the Detroit experts goes over there with a can or two of gasoline and a few fire crackers — poooph, up it goes — out come the staff leaving the door open; they probably try to put the fire out by themselves first. In we go. They come back in to ring for the fire engine. Funny, the phones don't work. We grab them and lock them in a closet. Silver into cases and down the lift onto the donkey carts, off down the tunnel into a van and we are away. I'm nearly there, Herta, just bear with me a bit longer.' Herta nodded and Warren took a breath.

'Now, I've got a good friend in the cargo shipping world. He has a vessel leaving Rotterdam on a suitable date, which will be passing the Fastnet Rock at the right time. So the next move is to get the van down there to the south. I've had a guess at which roads the cops will be watching when they all wake up. So our van is going to do a roundabout trip — Tuamgraney, Mount-shannon, Portumna, Roscrea, Thurles, Cashel, Mallow, Macroom and then to a quaint little place called Goleen. If you turn left down a side road for a few hundred yards there's a place called Herons Cove. An inlet shaped like a frying pan — a narrow way in from the sea and a sheltered basin some thirty or forty yards across. At the right tide there's enough water for the boat. I said I've been busy, Herta, and it's all worked out. Tides. Moon. The arrival of the fellow from Rotterdam off the Fastnet. The wooden cases will have rope handles for easy carrying. The Detroit gang will have them on board in minutes. Yeah, I've already bought the boat — an old whaler, broad in the beam and a nice quiet little converted V8 engine. Even if it lops up a bit , she'll ride it. Out to the cargo ship which swings out a derrick and up go the cases followed by the Detroit lads; last one out of the whaler knocks out the bung and after about ten minutes down she goes. Next stop for the silver will be a private warehouse in New Orleans tagged in my name. We ditch the van and drive clear of the action in this car. Then we're going to lie low for a few weeks or so, for I have a feeling that the Mangon fella is going to surface with something that might be interesting.'

He turned to Herta,

'So what's the verdict? Are you in?'

'Ja. It is a new departure for me, but ja.'

'Come. Come. What's this about something new for you? You think I haven't got my ear to the Austrian grapevine? Let me see, what was that about the collection of gold plate from Weissberg Castle?

'Ah ah, Warren, we will work well together.'

*　*　*　*　*　*

The reception at Jury's was going splendidly. The minister concerned with the Arts had made his speech pointing to the importance of this exhibition at Kilbandan for the country, not only to attract tourists but also as a prestige cultural contribution. Lord Kilbandan and his wife were to be congratulated. The formal part of the evening was over. James and Laura were engaged in conversation with Aideen and René. James was telling of the visit of the Destiny Tours party and in particular one chap who seemed a good sort. Fact was he knew a great deal about silver, and they had asked him to stay to dinner.

'You would have got on well with him, René. He really knew the art world,' said James.

'What was his name?' asked René.

James replied. 'Let me see . . . oh yes. Warren B . . .' He was interrupted by René.

'Oh no, not Westonhofer!'

'Yes. Why, do you know the chap?'

'Enough . . . just how much did you tell him?' René's tone was urgent.

'Oh dear, has old James put his left foot in it? I took him more or less right over the castle, showed him the old turf tunnel and he just loved the ancient lift.'

'Did he handle any of the silver?' asked Aideen.

'Well yes.' James was beginning to look worried.

'Did he see where the alarm switchboard was?' René continued.

'Couldn't be sure. I suppose the chap might have looked over my shoulder.'

'Yes, he might have done just that.'

'Oh, I say, what are you getting at, old man? I tell you he was a registered member of one of the American Art Assessors Societies Incorporated . . . he told me.'

At that moment their conversation was broken into be the Hall Porter who told Lord Kilbandan he was wanted on the telephone. James pushed his way through the crowd and took the call on one of the phones on the reception desk.

'Is that you, your Lordship?'

'Yes, speaking . . . who is that? Is that Seamus?'

'Yes, your Lordship.' There was a sob. 'It's burning and it's gone.'

'What do you mean, Seamus . . . what's burning and what's gone?'

'Oh sir, come back quick. It's gone.'

'Pull yourself together, Seamus. First, what's burning?'

'The barns and places out in the park and there have been terrible things going on.'

'What's gone then?'

'Your Lordship, it's gone, all of it.'

'Dammit . . . Seamus, what has gone?'

Seamus became calmer,

'The silver, your Lordship. All of it.'

James went back to his wife and Aideen and René. His face was a tone paler than when he had left them. All he said was,

'It looks as though you could be right, René.'

*   *   *   *   *   *

The Westonhofer plan had proceeded with military efficiency and timing. The fire and general noise had drawn out the staff. When they returned they had been overpowered and locked in a large cupboard under the stairs. The two drivers of the donkey carts were similarly treated as they came into the cellar area. The two were locked away with his Lordship's best claret. Wooden cases were packed and went down in the lift and onto the carts which moved quite silently on their rubber tyres, the farmer having even bound the donkeys' hooves with sacking to enter completely into the spirit of things. Down the tunnel and the cases were into the van and driven off followed by Warren and Herta in the Granada.

It had taken Seamus nearly an hour and three-quarters to break out of the cupboard and get to a phone that was working. After ringing his master he got through to the Garda Síochána. By the time Chief Superintendent Con Murphy arrived on the scene, the van had had a start of over two hours and there were an awful lot of roads that it might be travelling on. Going round to the tunnel entrance, all Con Murphy found were two slightly puzzled looking donkeys still harnessed to their carts.

At a quarter to midnight the 'Everglades Trader' stopped engines as she drew abreast the Fastnet. There was an exchange of pin-point torch flashes and a slight bump as the whaler came alongside. A derrick and tackles were rigged and up came the cases. The four Detroit men clambered aboard, the last one opening the sea-cocks in the whaler. Within twelve minutes the ship gathered way and the abandoned whaler was already settling down into the gentle Atlantic swell.

The 'Everglades Trader', registered in Panama, was a very old lady, a survivor from the end of the war, one of the last to roll around in the vast Henry Kaiser shipyard. By any sane mariner's reasoning she should have gone to the breaker's yard twenty years ago. The rusty hull must, to a degree, have been held together by the annual coats of paint. Her engines would have been an affront to any certified engineer. She was a floating mess, but working with a scratch crew of non-union labour, men who had barely enough sea-time to qualify for a habour ferry, she made money for her owners. She was one of those pitiful hulks that tramped around the world doing the jobs her more modern sisters wouldn't do, carrying cargoes of goodness knows what without asking questions.

At half past midnight she was heading vaguely south west from Mizen Head and the Fastnet to get back on to the regular course for the Gulf of Mexico. At ten minutes past midnight the sleepy eyed quarter-master had noticed that the barometer was falling rather steeply but he hadn't told the officer on watch who was out on a wing of the bridge with a large mug of well-laced coffee. The gentle breeze they had enjoyed during the pick-up was now gusting up to Force 6. The course the 'Everglades Trader' was on went right across the 'Devil's Hole', a fearsome stretch of sea, avoided often as not by sailors. The gusts reached Force 9. One of those freak mid-summer storms had them in its grasp. The seas became enormous. Then, from out of the dark on her starboard beam came a seventh wave; it made little noise as it grew and grew until it towered way above the bridge of the lonely old ship. Then this massive mountain of thousands of tons of water collapsed with a thunderous crash over the 'Everglades Trader'. Why she did not founder no one knew. As the waters streamed off her deck the damage became apparent. All steerage gone, lifeboats crushed in their slings, number 3 hold collapsed and water pouring into the forepeak from a split in the deckhead. The captain managed to get out a May Day signal which was picked up by a coast guard and by early dawn a helicopter had found her. By then the crew had managed to repair some of the damage but there was no way that she could steam anywhere. A message came through at eight that one of the large Dutch ocean going salvage tugs was on its way from Falmouth.

The tug arrived late the following afternoon and rigged a quarter-mile line of six-inch manilla to the badly damaged vessel. The tow back to Falmouth was going to be a brute — but they made it after some seventy-two hours of skilled seamanship.

*   *   *   *   *   *

At breakfast in the farmhouse the morning after the heist Warren switched on for the radio news. Following the political round and other pieces the voice of the reader brought him upright in his chair,

'The cargo ship that got into severe difficulties very early this morning has now been identified as the "Everglades Trader" registered in Panama. She had apparently lost all steerage and must be close to foundering, although the captain and crew refused lift-offs from a helicopter. A Dutch salvage tug is on the way from Falmouth in Cornwall.'

Warren and Herta stared at each other.

'What do we do now?' ask Herta.

'We gotta sit it out and keep in touch with the news.' Only scraps came through as the tow went on. But what sealed matters was when the ship arrived at Falmouth and was secured to the trot. It was announced that Customs and Immigration people had gone aboard with police. There was some mystery as the loading manifest didn't match up with some packing cases on board, nor did the crew list have any details of four extra men on board. The cases had been opened and appeared to contain a very valuable collection of silver.

'Well, this is where you and I do a very quick flit,' said Warren.

'No,' answered Herta. 'This is where you take a flit — not for me.'

'What do you mean you little croucher, are you thinking of crossing me? Well don't!' threatened Warren.

For some minutes they argued angrily and then Warren stomped out and headed for Shannon Airport where he hoped to pick up a seat for the States. Herta arranged to hire a car in Abbeyfeale and went back to an earlier plan she had worked out.

Nine

Early in July the newspapers and the radio and television news came up with a startling announcement:

'Secret papers regarding the theft and disposal of the "Irish Crown Jewels" discovered amongst surplus musical scores in the belfry of St. Patrick's Cathedral.'

For eighty years the Jewels had defied every effort to find them. It was on July the 6th in 1907 that their loss was discovered. Since then there had been concentrated investigations, the following of theories and even the employment of a medium to hold a seance which might disclose their whereabouts.

The 'Irish Crown Jewels' included the Star and Badge of the Order of St Patrick, both set liberally with the finest Brazilian diamonds. The story of these diamonds is that they had been given to one of his mistresses by George IV. When this monarch died the lady in question chivalrously returned them to the Royal Family. It was William IV who had presented them to the Order of St Patrick in 1830. Other items were the five magnificent gold and enamelled collar badges of the Knights Companions and an assortment of smaller pieces of jewellery. An indication of the combined value in 1907 can be judged by the fact that John Lowe, Superintendent with the Dublin Metropolitan Police, offered an immediate reward of £1,000. It was Sir Arthur Vicars, KCVO, Ulster King of Arms, who was responsible for the jewels at the time of the theft.

A special strong-room had been built to hold this precious treasure in the Bedford Tower within the precincts of Dublin Castle. Something went wrong with the planning for when the strong-room was completed it was found that the door was too narrow to allow the entrance of the safe that held the Jewels. So the safe with its valuable contents was left standing in the library which was also used as a waiting room. Some strange goings on just before the theft were apparently ignored. Mrs. Farrell, the cleaning woman, said she had found the front door of the Tower unlocked; she had also seen a 'gentleman crossing the hall toward the library. She thought this was Lord Haddo, son of the Lord Lieutenant but the police got her to change this idea. In the latter part of June, Sir Arthur Vicars found the key to the Bedford Tower was missing from his ring one morning. Vicars' immediate circle included his nephew Pierce Gun Mahony, the Cork Herald; Francis Bennett-Goldney, the Athlone Pursuivant and Francis Richard Shackleton, a brother to the explorer, who was whispered to be a rogue albeit a charming one.

Inquiries in Dublin were assisted by Chief Inspector Kane who came over from Scotland Yard. He, in short order, submitted a report which named the person whom he thought was the thief. The authorities refused to believe Kane's findings and later his report vanished from police files. Vicars had been in the habit of holding late-night parties attended by all males. These were held in the Bedford Tower. Vicars had a weak head and would pass out completely after two or three drinks. It came to light that on at least one occasion when he was unconscious his keys had been taken from him. Accusations were discussed, who could it be: Shackleton or a skilled gang from London? Later a Captain Gorges who was in prison claimed he had had a part in the robbery. The case drifted along until King Edward ordered Vicars to be dismissed from his post.

So, after eighty years the hunt was on again. One of the frail stained documents recorded all the evidence above and then on its second page quoted an affidavit given by one Eilis Mehan, a sweeper of the Castle yard, that he had been given the jewels in a heavily sealed and watertight package by a masked man, who spoke with a gruff voice. His accent Mehan thought was Dublin and possibly from Terenure. Mehan was told to take the package to County Clare and he was given the address and names of two accomplices he was to meet and careful directions as to just where they were to bury the jewels on the western side of Mount Maghera. Mehan was to be paid fifteen sovereigns when the job was done. Underneath this was a small map. Photostat copies of the documents and the map were fully exposed by all the news media.

The immediate effect on certain sections of the public was to cause them to find some excuse to stop what they were doing and to grab a spade and head out to the west. The news was not lost either on Mangon or on Alfie Brigg, both of whom at the smallest mention of diamonds were brought to a state of readiness, and they agreed to go down to Clare to see just what was happening. Far away, in the boardrooms of the Majors in London, there were discussions taking place about possible involvement. After all, the 'Irish Crown Jewels' might possibly have the makings for another sale of the century, in fact be worthy successors to the publicity enjoyed by the Windsor Jewels.

* * * * * *

The inhabitants of Quin Cottage read the news with some apprehension. The site indicated on the rather rough map was a bare two miles away from them. The peat in that area that covers the sides of the mountains and high places is Blanket Bog which grows right on the mineral soil — depth can vary from a couple of feet to a formidable thickness; these facts pointed to hard work for, and possible desecration by, the multitudes coming with their spades.

Clare had produced treasure before this for those out there on the bogs; the most celebrated find being a hoard of golden objects uncovered by workmen engaged on the construction of a railway in 1854. It was close to Mooghaun in the vicinity of Dromoland Castle to the south east of Ennis. The Clare hoard, as it became known, was the largest amount of gold objects ever found together in Europe. Originally it was thought to have contained one hundred and fifty items; only twenty-six pieces have survived, the rest having been melted down. Other treasures from Clare are the Gleninsheen gold collar, two gold lock rings from Gorteenreagh and a finely wrought bronze sword recovered from the Shannon near Killaloe. The bog accepts and hides a wealth of folk objects: farm implements, fishing tackle and tools used for working with wood and metal. The authorities care for these things as they can tell much from the past, and finders are asked to report to those who can officially identify the objects.

Aideen and Louise, standing by the rockery and looking towards the valley, could make out the first arrivals. They were coming in cars and vans and even horse-drawn caravans, Neptune reported how small encampments were springing up and various factions were either joining together to make a wider search or were already quarrelling bitterly over rights of digging. Some were even trying to stake claims. A few harassed archaeologists and museum people had appeared to try and control matters, but as the volume of treasure hunters increased they had to retreat defeated.

It was rumoured that the two Majors had organised two work gangs of highly experienced turf cutters and they were setting to with a will.

René joined Aideen and Louise:

'They must be praying for this dry weather to last,' he said, 'What are the chances?'

'Katty, when I saw her last, was sure the wet was coming from the way the bees were hard at it gathering in the honey,' said Aideen.

'What a relief for James and Laura to get all that silver back. Do they know who it was that did it?' asked Louise.

'From what Chief Superintendent Con Murphy said,' began Aideen, 'it looks likely it was that Art Assessor Westonhofer René met in Paris. But he managed to slip aboard a Jumbo bound for New York before the story broke.'

'Typical,' muttered Louise.

*   *   *   *   *   *

By midday on July the 15th the dry run of summer weather stopped and the Clare skies clouded over. It was St Swithin's day and light rains began to fall.

The thought of the age-old superstition of St Swithin's day, and the possibility of forty days and nights of rain which could follow, acted as an impetus to the toiling mob to spread out over the western side of Maghera. Further excitement was aroused when a film crew from Radio Telefis Eireann arrived to make some kind of documentary about what the producer was calling 'the Irish Klondyke' — the first result of this was that the camera car got stuck in the bog and needed a tractor to pull it out, then the tractor got stuck and a call was made for some help from the diggers. Eventually, after some twenty tough men had hauled and heaved, both vehicles were rescued.

Wild cries of delight greeted any small find. At one point the Garda Síochána had to be called when a spade turned up a skeleton; but this proved to be at least two hundred years old. Then a man from a ministry appeared with warnings about disturbing ancient sites and how he couldn't condone the use of metal detectors. He might just as well have whistled at the wind. Early one morning before the light had really come, the gang of one Major accused the gang of the other Major of trespassing on their claim. There was a right set-to, especially when city-suited representatives came on the scene in an attempt to separate the factions. They only succeeded in making it worse and finished up shouting and gesticulating with tightly rolled umbrellas. One fell over backward into the mire, which didn't do much good to seven hundred pounds worth of Saville Row tailoring.

By the second week of August the curse of St Swithin showed no signs whatever of weakening. Several hundred of the hopefuls had given up and gone home but they had been replaced by other excavators, the total of which one estimate put at around twelve hundred. Reports were also coming in that thousands more were arriving on the bog areas from as far north as Lisdoonvarna and right down to Kilkee in the south of Clare. The frenzy of diamonds and gold had got hold of the people to the degree that if it was bog it could be hiding treasure.

Steadily through the third week of August the rains relentlessly increased the weight of their downpour. Camp fires were no longer a possible method for boiling a kettle; anyone who had had the foresight to bring a gas or primus heater was onto a good business — boiling water to fill a teapot was already standing at £2.00. A Hot Dog man who braved the morass was charging £1.50 each. An independent transport owner brought up his four juggernauts from Ennis to as near the scene as was safe and offered a dry night's sleep with a rough blanket and straw pillow provided for £4.00; a cup of tea and a slice of soda bread with margarine, £1.50 extra. The more wretched became the conditions, the more fighting took place. A first-aid van had arrived as had a Garda incident caravan.

*   *   *   *   *   *

The morning of August the 23rd, the final day of St. Swithin's, will always be remembered by those who saw the frightening clouds that seemed so low overhead that they were just about touching the crest of Maghera. These changed from dirty blue-grey to a strange brown colour and the winds were rising and tearing them into tattered rag-like shapes.

About ten o'clock Neptune came up to Quin Cottage and told them that he was worried that the frustrated diggers were getting nearer and nearer to the small paddocks that belonged to Quin. Aideen and René told him they would come over with him; whilst they were finding what waterproof gear they could they asked Mary to give Neptune a cup of tea. Upstairs Aideen called René into her room,

'I think things could get a bit nasty and Neptune told me last night that Mangon and Brigg had been spotted in the area. Give me a hand to strap a couple of knives to my left fore-arm.'

René demurred, 'Is that wise?'

Aideen replied; 'Don't worry . . . just the sight of them can be helpful . . . don't you remember that Hiram character in Marseilles?'

'Good point,' René agreed, 'is there anything I can have?'

'Yes, look in the umbrella stand in the hall . . . there's a whale of a heavy thorn-stick there. Help yourself.'

They called to Louise, who was in the drawing-room, and told her where they were going. Then they were joined by Neptune. The three of them went out into the downpour and buffeting winds. The rain was now coming down as though the overfull heavens were draining themselves through a thousand down-pipes. The density of the water was such that breathing was difficult and vision was blurred by the gale-driven spray. Bending forward they followed Neptune through the wicket gate that led to the paddocks and then taking what cover they could, staggered towards the wooden hay-barn that was down in the extreme corner and nearest to the action. They got down to the barn and rested in the lee of it. From here they could just make out the nearest group of diggers who, despite the frightful conditions, still drove their spades and picks into the saturated turf. Women were there as well as the men and were shouting encouragement for them to keep going. Neptune called to Aideen and René to come round to the west side of the barn where the door was. He had the key to the padlock and soon had the fastening removed and the three of them went inside and slammed the door shut on to its wooden latch. Two windows let in some light and they were able to use these to keep an eye on what was happening outside.

By midday it seemed as though the strength of the wind was still on the increase and that the rain was falling even heavier.

The skies had changed again and the clouds were very close to being a dark, almost purple grey — visibility was down to less than thirty yards. At five minutes past twelve suddenly the rains stopped and the wind fell away until a fear-laden silence gripped Maghera and those who toiled on the slopes. Then, without an overture, another elemental strength visited the area. An eye-searing flash of forked lightning hissed down from above and into the ground not fifty yards away to be followed instantly by a roar of thunder that shook the ancient timbers of the barn and brought screams of fear from the muddied ranks of the diggers. The next sound was in many ways more terrifying. It was a shriek that erupted from somewhere on the mountain behind them. Neptune froze where he was, his head tilted and eyes staring upward as though they could see through the oak planks of the barn. Again and again the shriek came, tearing forth from lungs that strained to reach up and up to notes that carried in their intensity a force that could only come from some giant goddess of a primeval tribe.

'Miss Aideen, take my hand,' whispered Neptune. As she did she felt trembling spasms raking through his body.

'Do you know who that is, Miss?'

'No . . . no I don't.'

'It's Katty . . . she's out there on her rock . . . the great rock itself. I must go to her,' gasped Neptune. He dropped Aideen's hand and went to the door, lifted the latch and followed by Aideen and René went out and round to the back of the barn. All the while the courage-curdling sounds went on — now vague words could be distinguished. Another brilliant flash flickered overhead and reflected around the mountain. In that instant a figure could be made out — it was Katty Blood, standing at the very edge of a great rock. Her long plaited hair was undone and whipped around her head by storm puffs. Her drenched clothes had wrapped themselves skin-close to her body. The next flash came seconds later and Katty had raised her arms to the heavens and still kept up her maniacal paean to prehistoric deities that she must see up there on that great rock. Katty was struggling with the forces of the storm devils that were splitting the darkened day with slashes of vivid light and numbing the senses by clap upon clap of horrific thunder.

But Neptune did not rush up the mountain to his mother — Aideen looked towards him when the next flash came and in his eyes was a look of pride for Katty — Katty up there standing against it all. She had often told him when he was a young lad about those fierce invading women warriors, the Banns; whose memorial lived on with place names such as Bantry, Bandon, Bannow and others. There was his Katty telling Clare that she was Queen of the Banns. Two more flashes came right on top of one another. Then the sounds eased and they saw Katty had turned and was stepping down from the rock.

Neptune spoke,

'She'll be all right, she'll be all right. The storm will pass. Let's be back into the barn,' The rain still fell heavy and cold, but way toward the west a frail light was coming into the sky. They went back for shelter and pushed the door shut. The light was growing in strength by the minute. The scene through the windows was one of panic. The crowds were intent on just one thing, to leave the scene, and in their haste they stumbled into bad places of the bog and went in up to their knees, their thighs and farther; screaming, beseeching for aid. Helping hands reached for theirs and pulled the mire-coated figures from the cloying suction that sought to pull them down.

Suddenly the door burst open and the mud-streaked figures of Mangon and Brigg appeared. René pulled Aideen back into the dark shadows amongst some trusses of hay. The tall figure of Neptune squared up to the invaders:

''Tis Mister Mangon isn't it, and Brigg. You're not welcome here. 'Tis private property and you are trespassing. You'd be wise to get out, the two of you.'

While Neptune was speaking Alfie Brigg had worked his way round behind the great man of Clare and was even now taking his 'comforter' from his pocket and sliding it on to his left hand, which he was now raising.

Brigg never got his fist up into a striking position; there was a slight hiss in the air as the first of Aideen's knives flashed in front of Brigg's face so close that it must have chilled those unpleasant dark brown eyes with its passage. The blade sank into the door behind Mangon.

At the same instant a cold decisive voice ripped out:

'No you don't, Brigg . . . not unless you want this one where your neck is.'

Alfie Brigg turned round and saw Aideen and René standing against the back wall of the barn, Aideen with her arm already raised and her hand grasping the second of those murderous knives.

'All right Alfie — we'll go,' Mangon broke in; the two of them reduced in an instant by the sheer menace of not just that other shimmering blade but also the look in Aideen's eyes. Brigg had seen such a look a few times and he well knew what could happen in the next few seconds if they stayed. He pushed his way past Mangon and out through the door. As Mangon was about to go, he half turned and said,

'Tell me one thing, was that old hag up there on the rock real or . . .' The next words were struck from his lips as Neptune seized him by the throat with one great hand, and put his face very close to Mangon's:

'I don't think you should have said that, Mangon . . . no you shouldn't have said that at all. That lady was my Mammy . . . my Mammy, don't you ever forget that.' Then Neptune released his grip and thrust the trembling figure of Mangon after his friend.

The full strength light for the early afternoon had returned and the view from the windows showed a spread of desolation. Here and there small groups of figures were still doggedly digging away but the crowds of the early morning had disappeared.

'We could go back to the cottage now, Miss Aideen. The rain has stopped and they'll not be giving any trouble,' said Neptune pointing out of the window. Just as the three of them were about to leave the shelter of the barn there were sounds of someone approaching. A voice, Katty's voice, could be heard calling for Neptune. He opened the door and in came a fearfully bedraggled Katty, with face drawn and eyes staring with a weird unnatural look in them.

'Oh Neptune and Miss Aideen and Mister René,' half whispered Katty; 'We must stay here. Neptune, fasten some sacks over the windows. We mustn't be seen. Shut the door . . . shut the door. They mustn't see us . . . I can hear them coming . . . Yes, they're coming, surely they will come.'

'What is it, Katty?' asked Aideen.

'Miss Aideen, I know they are coming. But if we are very quiet they won't hear us...they'll get the rest of those out there,' replied Katty.

Neptune broke in, his voice low and urgent:

'Mammy will have heard them. 'Tis the little people of the turf — she will know they are set for wickedness.'

Katty sat down on a bale of hay and again cautioned them to be silent:

'Watch for the sunlight to grow dim. The rain may be passed, but the black clouds are coming back. All of ye sit down here on the hay with me.' As she said this, the sunlight that could be seen shining through the sacks faded away and a state of twilight persisted. Katty raised a finger to her lips and strained forward listening. Like the earlier moment before the thunder and lightning a silence laden with a portent of elemental displeasure invaded the atmosphere around the little group. Even the sound of gentle breathing seemed to challenge whatever it was that was outside.

At last after about five minutes the silence was broken by a strange slithering and faint mumbling. Katty stood up holding her hands over her face and trembling from head to toe.

'They are here now ... hark ... listen.' The mumbling had increased in volume and the slithering now sounded as though masses of soaked straw and rags were being pulled over rough stones. Katty went over and pulled down the sacks from the windows.

'Look, look!' she screamed, 'Over and beyond my rock. They told me this morning they would do it. All those people digging brought the fury of the little people on them. Look.'

At first when the others looked out of the windows they did not see what she meant and then it all came into focus. Up there by her rock something was happening. The whole surface of the bog was rising and falling — a dark brown carpet being thrown about by mysterious forces from underneath.

'Aideen, look at that!' gasped René, 'it's like a lava flow.' Indeed that was what it most nearly resembled. The overriding sound now was a mighty roar. Even as they watched, a livid gash slashed across the turf up on the slope of Maghera — the gash widened to a trough, to a ditch. The bog was coming down the hill; rolling and twisting, elbowing thorn bushes, young trees and boulders out of its way or carrying them with it. The further it advanced downhill the higher grew the destructive wave of dark turf. It rolled over and reformed, jets of dark brown water spurted yards high. The spread of the menace was increasing. It came to a small peat-cutter's hut and flowed round it in an evil embrace — another surge and the hut disappeared down into the recesses of the mire.

Katty moved across to the door and forced it open. The smell of the thing came inside — it was the perfume of centuries old peat and all the things that it could have absorbed and held within itself.

'Turn away...turn away,' yelled Katty against the crescendo of noise.

'Haven't I fed you with me butter and cheese all these years. Turn away. Fairies of the turf, turn. Turn. I beseech you!'

The wave height was now eight feet or more — inexorable, unstoppable, impersonal. Yet something must have communicated. When the main force was barely thirty yards from the barn, it started to veer just a point or two to the west. The four of them crouched back into the barn where the timbers seemed strongest. Through the open door they could see the stuff was already pushing and seething past. That slight change of course was what saved them. Only a fraction of the bog attacked the barn but it was enough. They saw the planks at the side start to belly inwards — nails being torn from the supports. René pointed to the side sections as they started to totter and he rushed across to push Aideen clear. He saved her but caught his foot in an old bucket and fell to the floor to be pinned down by a mass of splintered and broken timbers. Miraculously the rest of the barn survived the onslaught and the others were untouched.

As though the incident had placated whatever force it was, the sunlight returned and the roaring died away.

Aideen crouched down beside René whose head and shoulders were visible:

'Darling...darling, we'll get you free.' She started to pluck at the debris. But René was held prisoner not just by the broken planks but by the sheer weight of an oak trunk that had been the main support for that part of the barn. She and Katty scrabbled at it, nails breaking, but there was no movement.

'Could you come away?' it was the voice of Neptune.

'Be ready to pull him clear.' The great man braced his legs across the oak, then leant forward and wrapped his arms as far round the timber as he could. For a moment he paused — testing the weight of the wood. Then with a cry he arched his back and his arms took the strain — muscles cording with the effort. Inch by inch the trunk came up. Neptune nodded his head. Then gently Aideen and Katty eased René from beneath the heap of broken planks. As his feet came clear Neptune's incredible effort broke and he and the oak trunk thumped down together.

Aideen was anxiously examining René but in some wonderful way he was not seriously injured. In fact when Neptune stood up René found that with his help he could stand on his own feet and even take a step or two.

'I think you'd be better not to walk up the hill, Mister René,' said Neptune. 'Looking at you ... you'd be no great weight. I'll have you up on my back and home in no time.'

The thickness of the mess had thinned down and it was now no more than ankle deep. The four of them slowly made their way up to Quin; Neptune bearing René with as little trouble as though he was a bag of potatoes.

Louise and Mary had the four of them into the kitchen — René being lowered into the comfortable old basket-work chair. After cups of the best tea, the nightmare began to dissolve. Looking across at the slopes of Maghera it all seemed so peaceful. The only thing wrong was that the natural colours of the turf had all gone. What remained was a great stretch of a ruddy deep brown with here and there grey rock shapes standing up — in a macabre manner the scene had the look of some gigantic flayed corpse that had strewn itself down the face of the mountain to clog the valley below. The bog in one small place in Clare on the last day of St. Swithin's had moved and left a terror behind it that would be fireside talk for years to come in the same way that the people of Mayo speak of their terror in December 1986 when one of their bogs went on the rampage and blocked a mile and a half of the road from Ballycastle to Belmullet.

Ten

At a cottage outside Kilrush the talk had gone on for the best part of two weeks, in fact ever since the bedraggled Mangon and Alfie Brigg had got back from the débâcle with the peatbog on Maghera. The house party now consisted of three, as about a week previously they had been contacted by Herta Poll, who had arrived a little chastened but still full of ideas. The main item on their agenda had remained constant; it was money — their joint holdings in cash now stood at £24,000. Comfortable for the moment, but as Mangon kept pointing out, it wasn't much in the way of funding for another operation.

The Singapore Syndicate had laid claim to all the contents of his place in Paris as well as what they hoped to rescue from the shambles of the Trans-European International Fine Art and Antiques Sales down on the Loire; the bank accounts of the firm in Paris were also included in the list of legally frozen assets; the latter hurt as the various accounts added up to at least £4,600,000. The position with his establishment in London was confused. Staff both in London and Paris were in the queue for handouts. There was a secret bright star for Percy that only he know about and that was his very private account in a Geneva bank which stood at about £700,000.

The general opinion held by the three was that they should concentrate on a single simple theft of something of high value and comparative ease of movement. This brought it down to either jewellery or a painting. After more throwing the ideas around, jewellery was tossed out, as fences always wanted something extra for handling this kind of merchandise, whereas, with a real master painting there could be more opportunities for disposal.

Banks in certain countries would accept such items as collateral for a worthwhile loan, especially where there were rather loose laws on the holding of stolen objects.

But where in Ireland was there to be found a truly great masterpiece with at least a seven figure market price? None of the three of them was exactly an expert on the contents of the great houses of the country.

Part of the answer came when Myles Fyrken arrived late one evening full of goodwill and with baskets of quality groceries and bottles to match. Perhaps he rather overdid the image of 'full of joy and beneficence' because Percy Mangon at once became suspicious.

Myles had entered the cottage using his landlord's key and surprising the trio; which was not really a wise opening gambit and might have brought him a nasty cuff to the head from Alfie who shot to his feet when he heard the front door being opened. Percy Mangon fortunately recognised the voice and told Alfie to sit down.

'Well, look what Fyrken's brought you,' Myles said.

Percy responded by first introducing Myles to Herta and then immediately saying,

'What's gone wrong then, Myles?'

Fyrken winced at the directness of the question.

'Just thought I'd drop in on you and thought you might be a bit short on rations.'

Percy told him to sit down and spill what he had on his mind.

Myles did as he was asked,

'You were always a straight-forward one, Percy. So I'll give it to you straight. Fyrken's great plans with those development boyos have come to a swift end. In fact they've taken me for a large chunk of my capital. So I thought I'd come down here and have a chat about some ideas for the future.'

Mangon broke in on him, 'How much have you got left then?'

Again Myles was more than a little put out and he glanced towards Herta and Alfie. Percy continued, 'You don't have to worry about them; we're pretty well in the same jam — we've pooled our lot, so if you think you have the ante and my partners agree, you could join our cooperative society. How much, Myles, me old son?'

'In actual notes I have a float of about £11,000 and I can get out of my various accounts another £40,000,' said Myles.

Alfie came in, 'I'd say you was elected. Anybody not agree?'

There were no objections. When Myles heard their thoughts regarding the theft of a masterpiece he was at first shaken. But after Percy had worked on him for a while he slowly became sold on the idea. In fact he saw how he could be extremely useful to the cooperative. The other three members clearly had little idea where in Ireland such a target could be found. But back in Myles Fyrken's bachelor flat was the material that could provide an answer. Since his late schooldays he had been an avid collector of periodicals associated with the fine arts; sales catalogues, yearbooks , and publications of any sort that carried information on such matters — some of his research material went back into the eighteenth century.

Percy's attitude toward Myles changed quickly,

'Myles, you really have come up with something. I suggest that Alfie stays here and that Herta and myself bring some overnight things and come back with you and we get down to some research. What do you say?'

'Sooner the better,' said Myles.

*   *   *   *   *   *

With the loving care which he received from Aideen, Louise and Mary coupled with kindly enquiries from Neptune, René recovered at speed from his experience in the barn. There had been no serious damage, just severe bruising and some strained muscles. The weather was helping and Clare seemed set to enjoy an 'Indian Summer'. Besides this, exciting prospects were coming in for both Aideen and himself concerning their business; would-be clients were making contact at a pleasing rate. But even this promise was to a degree overshadowed when one afternoon just after three Batsy arrived with an odd look in her eyes. René was sitting feet up on a settee and excused himself to Batsy who waved his words aside.

'Glad I've caught you both in,' she began, 'Need to have a word or two with you.'

Louise, sensing some business coming up which she was not a party to and which she probably wouldn't understand, begged her leave and went upstairs.

'Aideen, I'm sure you remember that painting I have in my bedroom at Place. I don't think René knows about it. Well, I have thought a great deal around the matter, and when I hear about all these robberies, I think to myself — much as I adore that picture — the time has come for it to move on. I thought the best way is for you to handle it through those dear people you have in Paris.'

'What have you been hiding away at Place?' said René. 'I seem to have seen a Fantin Latour over there and a couple of Wouvermans.'

Batsy came in again, 'Oh dear, I should have shown this to you before. It's an Albrecht Dürer.'

'Do you mean a drawing or a print?' asked René.

'No my dear, Croker means a painting,' said Batsy.

René gave a gasp. 'But there hasn't been a Dürer on the market for ages; have you any provenance on it?'

'Better provenance than most of the top pictures around the place.'

'What is the subject?'

'The "Virgin in Majesty". There is a drawing in the Kupferstichkabinett, Berlin, of the same title and it is clearly Dürer's first thoughts on the composition. There are accounts as long ago as the seventeenth century that experts were expecting a finished painting to turn up. It is on wood and measures 41 x 37 inches.' Batsy stopped and looked from one to the other to sense their reaction.

She then continued:

'Actually the most conclusive piece of evidence is that I have letters and documents that state quite clearly that the "Virgin in Majesty" by Dürer was a personal gift to Sir Alexander Croker for his services with the Austrian forces during the time of the Empress Maria Theresa. In 1758 he was made a knight of the Grand Cross Imperial Military Order, which was founded by the Empress on June 18th 1757; the Order carried with it a pension for life of 600 florins. The Empress had recalled that during an earlier meeting Alexander had particularly admired the "Virgin in Majesty" and I have at home a hand-written note by the Empress saying that she wanted him to have the picture as a sign of favour and appreciation personally from her. I also have the Order which is a splendid thing; the badge is an enamelled white cross pateé, edged with gold, enamelled with a wide fillet inscribed *Fortudini* and it is worn with a white ribbon with red borders.'

Aideen came in after this recital, 'Have you any idea what it is worth?'

'Oh, that's more your line than mine, my dear. I suppose possibly around half a million,' said Batsy.

'If you seriously do want to part with it, shall I sound out Tim and Nell in Paris?' asked Aideen.

'Please do,' answered Batsy.

Aideen went over to the telephone extension at the far end of the drawing-room and made a call to the Sinclairs. With the help of the code-book she then passed the message. This clearly caused not a little surprise in the apartment at St Cloud. She said afterwards that Nell, who had answered, asked her to repeat the coding as there seemed to be some mistake. Aideen repeated it twice and then gave a coded affirmative over provenance and other details. The upshot of all this was that Nell and Tim felt that this was so important that they would both come over. Aideen apologized that they would not have room enough at Quin but said that the Old Ground in Ennis was very good and so it was arranged that Aideen would book them in from September the 12th.

* * * * * *

The search through the archives in Myles Fyrken's flat started on the 4th September and dragged on for three very concentrated days. A number of choice surprises came to light. These included a Raphael which was not generally known to be in Ireland, also an El Greco, a Pontormo, a Botticelli, a Holbein and a Bronzino, all of them in private houses. Great pictures but ones that could be awkward to handle during a hasty removal as they were rather large. Late on the third evening Herta suddenly gave a little cry of excitement.

'Maybe I have it. Ja...Listen to this.' She read out an account of a religious painting by Dürer, the "Virgin in Majesty", being given to a Sir Alexander Croker by the Empress Maria Theresa in 1758. It went on that the picture had been hanging in the Imperial Collection since the early part of the 16th Century. Croker had been an officer with the Imperial forces and he was from Place Castle, County Clare, Ireland.

'I know that there are some good paintings still in Place Castle,' said Myles, 'But just what they are I don't know. The sole surviving member of that branch of the family is the Honourable

Beatrice Croker. She's an odd one, I can tell you. Lives all alone in that great place with a butler and his wife. I think it could be an odds on bet that the Dürer could still be there. The family has always been rich and I have never heard of any money difficulties associated with them.'

'So what is your idea for the action?' asked Herta.

Percy replied,

'I suggest Alfie and I go over there tonight and case the layout. There is a near full moon — could be just right.'

*   *   *   *   *   *

From Kilkee to Place Castle was nearly forty miles. When they came to the demesne wall they drove round it and found that there was a lane off the public road that wound among thick pines and came to a wooden bar gate and then continued seemingly towards the castle whose tower could just be made out against the clear night sky. The gate was not even locked. After parking just outside the gate they walked up the lane for about half a mile and found that it joined up with the main drive going up a slight hill toward the castle. Each side were thick plantations of conifers and some hardwoods which gave excellent cover as they moved toward the building. The moon was now so bright that details could easily be picked out. The gaunt old castle loomed up in front of them, the main block was two storeys surrounded at ground floor level by what appeared to be some kind of conservatory.

While Percy and Alfie stood back under the evergreen branches of the firs, suddenly a motor bike emerged from the back of the castle and as it roared past them they could just make out that the rider was white haired as he spurned the use of a helmet.

'Could be the butler,' whispered Percy.

Another five minutes and a small car also came round from the back and as it went past they could see two women in it.

'With any luck that could be the Croker woman and the Butler's wife,' said Alfie,

'Come on, let's go round to the back and see what's what.'

There they found a few small outbuildings and a large garage. To shield the rear entrance, two ten-foot high curtain-walls had been added and between these were a pair of stout timber gates about eight feet tall. They walked slowly round to the front and there was not a light to be seen from any of the windows.

Percy leant towards Alfie and whispered,

'Tell you what, Alfie, you go back to the plantation and keep your eyes skinned all ways. I'm going to try the front door. It can't be much of a lock, not with all that glass around. I've got the old bunch of skeleton keys with me. You remember that lot you saw advertised in that up-stage magazine — good chance to see just how good they are. Alright?'

As Alfie walked away down the grass verge of the drive, Percy crept quietly towards the front door.

There were three steps and the top one was around six feet wide. Now he was alone he began to feel just a trace uneasy. These old buildings often had an atmosphere about them. He had the feeling of being watched by many eyes — from the plantation, from the top of the tower, from the first floor windows. He rather wished he had kept Alfie with him.

Keeping his hand as steady as he could, he reached out and gripped the door handle and timidly tried the pressure. It was quite a shock when it turned easily and without the slightest noise, and it was more of a shock when the door began to open — it wasn't locked at all. This gave him courage — the thought of the great treasure that could be inside and hanging there just for the taking. He pushed the door wide open and put one foot over the threshold.

Out of the darkness seemingly from the right-hand side came a deep sepulchral voice:

'Might I have your name please?'

Percy froze and tried to penetrate the shadows — this was difficult by moonlight as the conservatory was full of large plants and creepers.

Then from the other side a high pitched soprano somewhat sharply called out;

'Yes, may we have your name?'

Then a total silence. For one minute Percy Mangon stayed as though chained to a stake not daring to move even a eyelid.

Right overhead a third voice, a high-pitched tenor yelled out:

'Yvan ... Yvan!' Almost instantly an intense white spotlight came on and illuminated the inner front door which was open. Percy heard a scrabbling sound coming across the marble tiles of the hall. It was soon explained as a large and terrifying image appeared in the doorway and stood glaring at him. What he could see of it was almost jet black with some shading of tan. Its eyes were enormous and mesmerized him. The great mouth was open with wet glistening crimson lips drawn back to expose a murderous set of huge teeth. What made it more terrifying was the fact that it was wearing protective armour; a wide collar with long spikes, chain mail for chest and shoulders and steel plates over its loins and back. The beast was starting to breathe faster and a deep and quite horrid growl issued from its throat.

At last Percy's instinct for survival broke through the hypnotic stare. He stumbled backwards, slammed the door, turned and ran towards where he hoped Alfie would be waiting for him. He found Brigg and gasped,

'Alfie boy, that place is in the hand of witches. I didn't see nobody; but there were at least three people speaking to me and . . . and that great hound. I've never seen anything like it Alfie, never.'

'You sure it weren't some kind of tape recording alarm or somethin'?' queried Alfie.

'I'm sure of one thing, Alfie. That great beast was no tape-recording', replied Percy.

'Look the light's gone out now. Come on, let's get back to the cottage.'

After their return to Herta and Myles and a steadying glass with a good feed cooked by Herta, they discussed further plans. They picked Alfie Brigg as the best one for lengthy surveillance. It was decided that he should spend some forty-eight hours tucked away in one of the plantations alongside the top of the drive; there was plenty of cover and he could get good sightings by clambering up into one of the large oak trees. Alfie wasn't very taken with the idea, but after Herta had packed him up some attractive rations and liquid refreshment, he agreed. He had bought, a few days earlier, a thick waterproofed duffel coat in Limerick, so with the deep pockets stuffed with packages and carrying a bag with a rug and ground sheet, he left with Myles who was going to run him over to Place. Arrangements were that he would be picked up at seven in the evening in two days' time.

It was generally agreed that the actual removal of the Dürer wouldn't be too difficult, but after that, what Herta termed 'diversionary tactics' would be called for. This part of the plan evolved round the idea of purchasing three not-too-elderly identical vans. These should all be of the same colour, and it should be possible to find such vehicles in the yards of second-hand dealers in Limerick. Fresh spray-painting should be avoided as it was easy to detect by look and smell. The vans would then be given some easily recognisable marks. This could be done by using self-adhesive plastic strips beloved by those who seek a sporty and distinctive look for otherwise unremarkable vehicles. Thus one van could have three yellow bands running right along each side and continuing over the doors at the back; a second could have two red, one white and two blue stripes; and the third a series of short white vertical stripes running round the top of the sides and the back. Using large self-adhesive, press-on letters name-plates could be prepared that could be fixed on the sides and back doors. These would read: 'Maloney's Garden Centre'; Delaney's Garden Mart'; and 'Magree's Garden Needs'.

Each van would carry about twelve sections of paling panels of a larger size than the Durer. The idea was that the painting would be wrapped in protective plastic-film and wadding and then concealed in the packs of the paling panels. The vans would also carry a number of plants, shrubs, bags of shredded peat, garden tools and sundries such as old empty sacks, watering-cans and overalls. The sight of these three skittering round Clare after the theft should cause some confusion as witnesses were questioned and came up with conflicting stories.

Then they started on the next part of the problem which was how to get the picture out of Ireland and over to Europe. By air was right out of the question and so, they felt, was a small fishing boat. Herta reminded Percy of her cousin's activities in Regens-berg and how for several years he had made use of the big trans-continental juggernauts. 'They have these things here, I have seen them. Many of them are on the Bavarian run with loads of meat for the American troops down there. Now such a one could be good for this. The Customs people would not be too keen on unloading tonnes of frozen meat; also not too nice for them to crawl underneath the big sides of the beef hanging inside. Such a matter should be possible to arrange.'

'You could have something there, Herta,' Percy exclaimed, 'Myles should know someone around here with a truck.'

In fact Myles did. When he got back from dropping off Alfie and was told of the idea he replied at once:

'Indeed I do know someone and he could well be just the right man. Greg Blenney and he operates from Newmarket-on-Fergus close to Shannon Airport. In fact, he owes me one as a year ago I got him cleared on a rather expensive charge of attempting to fiddle the import duties and VAT with a new truck coming in from overseas. Better still, he's a loner and an owner driver. Yes, I have a feeling Greg would be ready to play along if we offer some encouragement.'

'How much you think?' queried Herta.

'I'd make it a few thousand quid — most fellas would shut an eye for that,' replied Mangon.

Later when they had their quiet little meeting with Greg Blenney they found matters were better than they thought. His lorry was well-nigh perfect for the operation. Greg had done this kind of thing before for other 'clients' in the art world. He had constructed a well-disguised false floor right up front, close to the refrigeration unit with the only access being from the back of the truck, which meant that practically the whole of the load would have to be taken out to discover it and even then it would take a very experienced customs officer to tell the difference between the hollow sound of the real floor and the false one. More than this, the secret compartment was well insulated to protect what-ever it was hiding from damage by excessive cold. His next trip was scheduled for September 11th, which fitted in with the date they were thinking of.

Then Myles asked him how much he would want. Greg had eyed his customers. Myles, whom he knew; then there was an Englishman and some foreign female. He smelled a big job and one they were clearly quite desperate about, wanting the quickest way possible to get it over the water.

'A job like this — have to make a bit of detour to get to Regensberg. Hmm, . . . All-in, I suppose it'll have to be £25,000 and very hush-like.'

'Come on Greg,' said Myles, 'we are not running a charity . . . five.'

'Neither am I, Mr. Fyrken. We'd better forget about it then. Pity you've told me so much, ain't it,' replied Greg.

Mangon thought if only I had Alfie here he'd soon sort this clown out.

'Are you trying to tell me you could go around talking?' said Myles.

Greg Blenney didn't reply, he just shrugged his shoulders and made a quizzical face.

Herta broke in,

'All right Mr. Blenney. £10,000 when you load the painting, the rest when you deliver in good order to the address we shall give you in Regensberg. I hope for your sake that your services are as professional as your charges — you understand me, I am sure — the Bavarian mountain roads can be very difficult for such a large vehicle.'

Greg Blenney looked at this strange woman or girl or whatever she was. Then he turned away quickly — those wall-eyes struck a chill right through him. He already had qualms about the job but he could use the money. He just wished at times that he wasn't a loner.

*   *   *   *   *   *

It was the evening of September 8th and Alfie had been picked up from Place Castle and was now making his report.

'I reckon it should be a daylight do,' he said, 'Both mornings an old chap with white hair comes round from the back with that beast wot you saw, Percy. Blow me, it is big, but it's only a bloomin' dog, a Rottweiler. Mind you, he was all of a hundred yards away from me. Anyway, it and the old man goes off and both times they are away for over an hour and then comes back with the papers and a carrier bag — probably the milk and things. The first morning the boss comes an' goes off down the drive on a bloomin' motorbike, an' she's all done up with helmet and leather gear. She didn't come back until after three. Next morning she's out again and not back till one o'clock. Of the old geyser's wife I didn't see a sign. A quick tie-up job and we'll be in an' out in fifteen minutes. After that lot I could do with a good fry-up, Miss Poll.'

'Oh, could you. We have eaten and I am busy now,' said Herta. 'If you want it, you cook it, I am no servant.'

Alfie went toward the kitchen and when he was behind her back made a threatening gesture with one raised fist. Herta must have picked up the thought. She spun round and seized his lifted arm and in the next two seconds Alfie was yanked off balance and landed with a bone-shuddering crash against the door frame. She stood over him as he gasped with pain;

'I am not to be threatened. Please do not do that again. For years I am a black belt in Oriental Martial Arts. You understand.'

No one seemed quite sure just how to follow that performance. But Herta appeared unabashed,

'Now where are we? Ja. Ja...I propose we act at ten o'clock on the 10th. We must finish getting the vans ready.' The rumpled figure of Alfie lifted himself to his feet and moved towards Herta. 'That was silly of me Miss, bloomin' silly. I'm sorry...yes I'm sorry.'

For almost a full minute dark brown unblinking eyes stared into wall-eyes — the atmosphere between them ice-cold. Herta spoke first,

'Come on, Mr. Brigg. I think we both like to play rough. Now it is past. Herta will cook a good supper for you. Come. I shall be ten minutes and then we will drink to our great success. You Alfie, you Myles, you Percival and Herta, no one else just the four of us. It will be Prosit! Prosit! One thing more, how much do you think Herr Dürer's painting could be worth to the State Collections in Vienna to whom by right it could belong? How much? Well, there will be others who would be liking it. The Germanische in Nuremberg, the Alte Pinakothek in Munich, and I know at least two industrialists who would go high. We shall have a prize worth at the smallest £20 million but my thought is it will be much more than that. Now Alfie, will it be two or three eggs with your steak?'

* * * * * *

At Quin Cottage there was peace. In the small outhouse behind the garage Katty was working way on bottling the year's honey crop from her beloved bees. The wax separator hummed and rattled as the dark golden liquid filled jar after jar.

After an early breakfast on the seventh, Aideen and René had taken Louise plus ample luggage to Limerick station. She was catching a connecting train for a ferry and a train from Holyhead that would match up with other trains that would eventually get her to the New Forest. Louise had suddenly decided at tea the previous day that she would like to go and visit her two sisters who ran a pony-trekking stable close to Lyndhurst. Following the impulse she rang them and they were delighted. Neptune was dispatched to the fishmonger in Ennis for two sides of wild smoked salmon for a gift. Mary was enlisted to help with the packing and that had been that.

Later in the day, as Aideen and René sat beside the drawing-room fire, they had been for a time, silent, gazing abstractedly into the grate.

Aideen broke the moment,

'Do you feel something, René...a sense of...I'm not quite sure what? Perhaps I'm picking up Katty's thoughts. Just before lunch I went into the outhouse to see how she was getting on. She's a great worker. There are more than sixty pots of honey. But when I came in she stopped and looked right into my eyes. "Miss Aideen," she said very quietly, "we must beware. There is evil working in Clare somewhere. No, I don't mean as with the bog. I feel bad people have come to Clare. I shall stand out on my rock tonight at midnight. The little ones will come to Katty. They will know." Then, she grabbed hold of my hand and squeezed it tight and thrust her face close to mine...."Miss Aideen, be careful, very careful,"' she said.

René exclaimed, 'Old Mrs. Blood is certainly one for the fairies. But do you know I have a feeling, I don't know what it is ...all I do know is, there is a threatening sense hanging around this area. I hope dear old Batsy is all right.'

* * * * * *

Shortly after eight on the tenth, the villains from Kilrush left the cottage and walked down a lane to a cluster of sheds which served as lock-up garages for the cottage. Inside they had kept the vans which were now ready, decorated for the job ahead. Percy and Herta were travelling in one, with Alfie and Myles driving the other two. The arrangement was that they would travel at least half a mile apart and rendezvous in the side lane into the demesne of Place Castle.

The three vans made the meeting place without incident by twenty past nine. Alfie was sent along through the woods to spy out the main entrance. Forty minutes later he returned with the welcome news that the Honourable Croker had come down the drive at quarter to ten in her car and had picked up the gardener from the lodge and gone off in the direction of Ennis; a few minutes after this the butler and Rottweiler passed on their regular morning constitutional.

'Magnificent, now we are off,' said Herta. 'Come, I have the packing materials in this van. As we said last night. You stay here, Alfie, with your van. Myles, go up and put your van where this sidelane joins the main drive. Block it. Then Percival and I will do the deed. Ja. I have my chloroform and rags and cord. As they say; here we go!'

From the villains' point of view it was a triumph.

Percival and Herta drove casually up the drive and round behind the castle. The tall gates between the curtain walls were open as Sean's wife Ann was preparing to hang out her washing. It was altogether too simple. Mangon greeted the elderly lady as Herta went round behind her and roughly smothered her face with a heavily soaked rag. There had been little struggle. They gagged her, tied her arms and legs and pulled her into a wood-shed in the courtyard.

Keeping well clear of the conservatory they went swiftly through the ground floor rooms — no Dürer. Up the main stairs and into what was clearly the main bedroom still in disarray from the night. There it was, the 'Virgin in Majesty' and unques-tionably by the hand of the master — dated and with the 'AD' monogram done in the bottom left-hand corner.

For a moment Herta stood still gazing at the glorious painting with a look of total reverence. She clasped her hands under her chin and then closed her eyes.

'Come on Herta, help me with the picture,' snapped Percy. Together they wrenched the painting and heavy frame from the wall.

Herta, working with pliers and a screwdriver, took the wooden panel from the frame. Between them they carried it down the stairs and to where the van was parked just outside the rear courtyard. In ten minutes they had it swathed in a plastic protec-tive film and soft padding. It fitted perfectly in the middle of one of the paling bundles, so well in fact, that when the bundles were secured again there was no sign of anything having been added.

Percy went to the woodshed just to see if the old girl was coming to. She was, and making a great grumble about it — and if her eyes could have done anything, Percy would have been felled right where he stood.

Herta had the motor started by the time he came back and got in. Once more driving in a leisurely fashion they passed Myles with a thumbs up salute and then down the lane and the same gesture to Alfie. Again keeping well apart they drove several miles away from Place Castle before stopping in a clearing beside a minor road. The next move was for Myles to take Herta's place and join Percy in order to go over to Greg Blenney's yard and work the transfer. Meanwhile, Herta and Alfie, with the other two vans were going to circle around for several hours and return to the lock-ups at Kilrush.

It had been a great day so far but as Myles and Percy pulled into Greg's place things began to alter. Greg came out of his office and leant against the open driver's window and said,

'Things has got to be changed — the truck clutch has gone on me and the job will take three or four days — so we'd better make it the 16th for sure — I rang the ferry office and I can get a crossing then and they have onward booked me through Dover.'

'Oh boy, what do we do now?' queried Percy.

'Don't worry. Can't you lock the van up somewhere?' said Greg.

'Like nothing we can . . . the Gardaí will be round every garage in the district,' replied Myles.

'Well,' said Greg, 'you're just going to have to keep mobile, aren't you? It's only four days plus a bit.'

Myles swung the van round and headed off in Kilrush direction, wondering just how it could now work out. Percy said nothing, feeling so overwhelmed by the reversal of the situation. So nearly was the great prize within their grasp.

* * * * * *

On this morning Batsy had only been down to a nearby village to look at some flowering shrubs she had been offered by an enthusiastic amateur grower. She dropped Sean the gardener at the lodge and then drove up the drive and round to the rear of the castle. The first thing that she saw was the laundry basket on its side and washing spilt over the stone flags of the courtyard. Hurriedly braking she jumped out and then heard vague sounds of a being in discomfort coming from the woodshed. She found Ann there, in close to a serious condition. Undoing the gag from her mouth and the cords from her arms and legs she helped the poor dear to her feet and slowly walked her across to the kitchen. The kettle was singing on the iron hob and in a minute or two the old lady was supping a cup of strong brew.

When she had her voice in her once more she said,

'Oh Madam . . . I don't know who they were or what they wanted, I couldn't see from the shed. But it seemed after they had left me and gone into the house they came out with something which they took some time to wrap up before they drove away.'

Batsy cried out,

'Oh no...it mustn't be...please...please...no...no.' She ran out of the kitchen and raced up the main stairs and into her bedroom. The blank space on the wall, the empty frame across her bed told her everything.

Batsy went to one of the large windows, flung it open and screamed her sorrow out across the demesne. She found herself mouthing curses on the thieves that would keep them in Hades for an eternity. Although Batsy had already decided she would sell the painting she still loved it and was not prepared for this wanton ravaging of the masterpiece. To sell it through the good services of Aideen and the Sinclairs was one thing, to have brigands force their way into Place was quite another. She moved to a chair beside the phone on the bedside table — surely they could not have got far. According to Sean's wife, it was a bare half an hour ago.

Batsy called the Garda Síochána in Ennis and was put through to Chief Superintendent Con Murphy, a friend of some long standing. When he learnt the facts he told her to hang up and he would be out there in around forty minutes.

As she replaced the receiver there was a knock at her door, Sean the butler had returned and beside him stood Yvan. Batsy patted her knee and the huge Rottweiler trotted across and laid his head in her lap looking up into her face with soft adoring eyes.

'Well, Sean...Place Castle visited by thieves — I think it must be the first time since a branch of the O'Brien sept broke in and tried to fire the building in the sixteenth century. I am in disgrace, Sean.'

'No. No. No, madam. Mr. Murphy and his fellas will get the picture back. They will never get it out of Clare.'

'Did you see anything when you were out, anything out of the ordinary?'

'Well madam, when I was having a word with Paddy Carroll in the village, a van went through a bit on the swift side. It was some out-of-the-county gardening people, "Magree's Garden Needs" I think and then not five minutes afterwards another van, the same make, goes through only this time in the other direction and he was another garden chap "Maloney's Garden Centre" — and Paddy says to me that that's a bit on the odd side.'

'Good man Sean, make a note of the names. I have Con Murphy on the way over.'

Sean wrote the names down on an old envelope. Batsy took the crumpled paper.

'Did you see anything else?' she asked 'How many were in each of the vans?'

'Both Paddy and I saw them clear and well.' replied Sean. 'One was driven by a man and the other a woman with dark red hair. I'll tell you something else, just where the old side lane comes into the drive there are several fresh tyremarks cut into the verges.'

'Good man, Sean. You had better go and look after Ann, she's had a bad morning of it.'

'Thank you madam. Is there anything I can get you?'

'No, not just now.' Sean left Batsy and Yvan. For quite a long time she fondled the great head and stroked the beautiful satin-like coat. At last there was the sound of a car or rather two cars coming at speed up the drive. She rose, and followed by Yvan, went downstairs to greet the Chief Superintendent. She took his hand and at once felt a comfort. Con Murphy had about him a quality that spread confidence. He was another of those great men of Clare, practically out of the same mould as Neptune. When Con Murphy went after his man or woman they rarely escaped.

'This is a bad one, Miss Croker. But I have a feeling they are not going to get all that far. It was great that you could give me such early warning. As soon as I had put the phone down the order was going out for a ring of road-blocks to be thrown round Clare at once. The station contacted Limerick, Tipperary, Galway and Laois. My sergeant also got through to the Killimer Tarbert ferry people and told them not to move until the Gardaí get there. Clare, when you look at the map, is nearly three-quarters surrounded by water which makes it one of the best counties to seal off.'

Batsy gave him the information regarding the garden vans Sean had mentioned. After he had read it, Con went on,

'That could be adding up to something. A patrol car earlier made a comment about three vans passing him at intervals on the road between Labasheeda and Killadysert; he noticed how they were all gardening people and at the time he thought it a bit strange as the north bank of the Shannon just around there is not exactly a paradise for gardeners.' Con turned to the officer beside him and said,

'Get on the radio to the station and tell them to send Michael and a couple of chaps down to Greg Blenney's place at New-market-on-Fergus. I have an idea, may be nothing but it might add up. Tell them that it's a road safety check and to take their time doing it. Now, would it be all right with you, Miss Croker, if I could see where the painting was?'

'Please. Follow me. I always kept it in my bedroom.' They went from the kitchen across the hall and up the stairs. Batsy said,

'Am I allowed to ask if there could be a connection with Blenney?'

Con Murphy hesitated for a moment and then replied,

'Seeing it is you, Miss Croker, it is a possibility. Your man has not all that clean a record. Odd things like a side or two of beef which go missing between the suppliers in Clare and the people in Germany. Then there have been rumours of strange things that he might have been carrying — just rumours. So I've put him on the long finger as they say for the time being, and I can tell you there are quite a number filed away under that heading.'

When they reached Batsy's room the superintendent looked around for a bit and seemed to be drawing a blank until he walked over to the bed, went down on one knee and reached a little way underneath. With his hand wrapped in a handkerchief he picked up something and stood up again. It was a neat, well-made stainless steel folding screwdriver.

'What is that?' queried Batsy.

'It's a handy little screwdriver. Never seen one quite like it.' He held it up for closer inspection.

'That's no real wonder. It was made by a firm called Joseph Klein in Vienna.' He turned to the constable and asked for a plastic bag and then slipped the possible clue into it.

'I'll just have a word with Sean's wife if she's up to it before I go, if that is all right with you, Miss Croker.' The good lady was still in a state and not really herself. But she did remember two things; one was that the van was something to do with gardens and the other that the woman who was there had wall-eyes, one pale blue and the other a kind of warm brown.

Eleven

When the Chief Superintendent and his men had gone, Batsy ate some biscuits and cheese off the sideboard in the dining-room and then went to the cupboard under the stairs and pulled out her motor-cycling gear. Kitted up, she went into the kitchen and told Sean to see that his missus had a lie down and that she was going over to Quin Cottage and would be back before dark.

The ride through the fresh clean air was a help to her as she strove to clear her thoughts about the robbery. Was the "Virgin in Majesty" about to join the ever growing legion of the lost ones, masterpieces that had totally disappeared from collections all over Europe? It just didn't seem real to her that these things could happen. If only it had been a week later and the painting would have been safely handed over to the Sinclairs. As she came to the bottom of the narrow drive leading up to Quin Cottage, her eye caught a frantically waving figure in the garden of Neptune's cottage. It was Katty Blood. Batsy stopped and switched off the engine.

Katty came across to her,

'Are you all right, Ma'am? I saw two hooded crows pass over and headed towards Place Castle. It was just before ten this morning and they came back an hour later and one was carrying something.' She gripped Batsy's shoulder,

'Tell me, Ma'am. Something wrong has happened down at Place... there has been a bad thing done. Those birds are messengers that tell me. You have lost something. I shall go to the rock again tonight.'

Katty let go of her shoulder, came close and stared into Batsy's eyes and leant forward and kissed one of her leather gauntlets.

She then turned and ran through the wicket gate and into the cottage. After a moment Batsy re-started the engine and rode slowly up the hill toward Quin Cottage. She was glad to find both Aideen and René were in. She broke the news to them even before she had taken off her gear.

Aideen helped her take off the leather jacket and then threw her arms round her best loved cousin,

'Batsy darling, darling. How did they do it? Hmm, about ten this morning. I just wonder ... could Mangon and that Brigg have anything to do with it? Sean's wife wouldn't have known them if she had seen them, poor thing. We do know that they are in Clare, at least they were on the night of the bog-slide. Come into the drawing-room. Have you had any lunch?'

'Oh, just a crumb or two of cheese and biscuits.'

'I'll get Mary to make us some coffee and bring in cake.'

René joined in, 'This sounds a bit brash, Batsy, but I had better get on the phone to Tim and Nell as they are coming over and are due to arrive on the evening of the 12th. It would be best if they hold off for a bit.'

A call to Paris only contacted one of the secretaries at St Cloud who told René that the Sinclairs had left two days earlier and were visiting some friends in London before coming on to Clare. Unfortunately in the haste of departure, they had left no number where they could be contacted in London.

*   *   *   *   *   *

Mangon, Herta, Myles and Brigg, by the morning of the 11th, knew that their situation was grim. Rather foolhardily they had risked the night in the cottage near Kilrush but now it was time to move out. The previous evening they had worked on the three vans by torchlight in the lock-up garages. The coloured stripes had been stripped off and the nameplates removed. A second disguise had been applied. The vans now, from a casual glance, could be taken as belonging to household decorators. They all had roof-racks with ladders lashed to them. It had been left to Alfie Brigg to carry out the interior transformation. Inside the vans still carried the bundles of palings sections, one of which held the Dürer. Alfie crammed in as much as he could; papering tables, boxes of wallpapers, buckets for paste, brushes, tins of paint, tools of the trade, cans of turpentine substitute, bundles of cotton waste and rags.

Before leaving the cottage Myles made another attempt to reach Greg Blenney. After several rings Greg's voice answered,
    'Blenney's Yard.'
    'Is that you Greg?' Myles said, 'Have you any news for us?'
    'Good morning, is that Taylors factory, Portroe? If it is, it looks as though I can't manage your load until after the 27th.' The phone went dead as Greg hung up.
    'What did he say?' asked Percy, 'does the date still hold?'
    'He talked a lot of nonsense about some Taylor outfit over at Portroe,' replied Myles.
    'It could be that the Gardaí are on to him and he couldn't answer straight,' said Percy.
    'It looks like we are going to have to find another way. Let's have another look at the map of this place.' For five minutes they all stared at the possibilities for an exit from Clare. From the point of view of the land the cards were nearly all held by the Gardaí. A string of road-blocks from Ballyvaughan in the north, round by Gort, Scarriff and Killaloe and down to the Shannon at Limerick would put the net around them. Further, it was certain that they would have blocked off the Killimer Ferry.
    Myles said, 'It will be odds on that we are up against that man Con Murphy, who knows every crack in this place. I reckon what he'll be working on is to squeeze us out by tightening the blocks and the thinking will be that we'll be trying to make a dash out of here towards the east hoping that he has left a way open, which he won't have. We are not beaten yet, though. Mr. Murphy and his men have got to see a couple of the vans looking as though they are on their way to Limerick or up to the north headed for Galway. Brigg had better take one as they won't know his face, and Percy, I suppose you had better have the other. Herta will be with me and the picture. If you're stopped you should get away with it — but try to keep well back from where we think they have the blocks.'
    'What's the next bit of the plan then, Mr. Fyrken?' asked Alfie.
    'It is going to have to be the sea again. There are a few places over on the west coast where there would be a good chance of picking up a boat, Kilkee, Quilty, and Doolin. I reckon Quilty could be the best bet. A party of us had a deep-water fishing trip from there three years ago.'

*   *   *   *   *   *

At the Garda station in Ennis other eyes were scanning a map of Clare. Small flags marked the road-blocks already in position.

'I think it is a case for nice, gentle, no fuss, creep in on them,' said Con Murphy,

'Think to yourselves it'll be like pulling the string on the neck of a sponge-bag. Just in case they have ideas about taking a boat, give the fella at Quilty with that converted trawler a ring and tell him I'd like a word. There's nothing seaworthy enough at Kilkee. I wonder if they are going to try the decoy trick again.' The man in Quilty was on the line and the Chief Superintendent turned away from the map table to take the call.

'Hello, is that you, Peter . . . Con Murphy here. There may be some chancers heading down your way who would like a sea trip. No . . . no. Don't put them off. Take them on board and go to sea with them. I have already been on to the captain of a patrol vessel which is in Limerick and he'll be on his way by now down the Shannon. If it does happen he'll stand off as though bent on other business and then when he sees you clear of Mutton Island he'll come over and relieve you of your passengers . . . Have you got that, Peter? . . . Good man.'

*   *   *   *   *   *

On the evening of the 12th Aideen and René were at the Old Ground in Ennis waiting for the arrival of Tim and Nell. It was nearly seven before they saw the Sinclair's white Volvo estate drive into the park; together they went to break the news.

'Oh, so now what do we do?' cried Nell.

'Wait around for a while and give the Gardaí a chance. Clare isn't the best place to get out of if you are a fugitive,' said Aideen.

Tim exclaimed, 'After the drive from Dublin I feel like I need a good dinner. Give us a few minutes to freshen up and we will join you in the lounge.'

*   *   *   *   *   *

Brigg and Percy had spent the 11th driving round aimlessly in one direction after the other. Several times they had passed Garda patrol cars parked by the roadside, but not once had they been stopped. If they had been more observant, they would have noticed how apparently the Garda officers were doing everything they could not to notice them. As it was, they comforted themselves that the decoy trick was working well.

Meanwhile, Myles and Herta had headed towards Kilkee where on arrival they had satisfied themselves there was no boat suitable and had turned away to the north. The arrangement with the other vans was that they should come over to the west on the early evening of the12th and if they saw no sign of Herta and Myles in Kilkee they should then go up to Quilty and rendezvous in the side-turning off the quay.

Herta looked towards Myles as they munched through a couple of cheese sandwiches.

'What do you feel?' she said.

'What do you mean?' he asked.

'About us,' Herta continued, 'what else?'

Myles looked into those strange eye,

'I don't understand you. What are you trying to say?'

'Why don't we go straight on now to Quilty and get that boat, Myles?'

'Are you trying to say we go it alone?'

'Ja . . . of course . . . by ourselves there is more chance, is there not?'

'You little devil. I've known Percy Mangon for years.'

'And has he never done you a bad trick, Myles? Never?'

Myles paused for several minutes before answering,

'Not that I could really prove. But Herta, surely we could at least wait until the time we arranged?'

'I do not think so, Myles.' Her voice suddenly hardened, 'No, I think we do not wait. Either you and Herta go on or Herta will go alone.'

'Just what do you mean by that?' asked Myles.

'Only this,' replied Herta, and Myles found himself looking at the nasty end of a small Biretta automatic.

'I call it . . . how would you say . . . my last resort. It is a very small calibre but I know from experience that at such close range it is quite big enough. Now, Mr. Myles Fyrken, is it to be us or just me? And don't try any silly ideas with Herta. You saw what I did with Brigg. I have lived with much rougher company than you have, Myles.'

'What else?' said Myles resignedly, 'Shall I go on driving?'

'Of course, you amateur man.'

* * * * * *

On the morning of the 12th, Tim and Nell had found their way over to Quin Cottage and picked up Aideen and René and they were on their way to Place Castle where Batsy was waiting for them.

As they came up the drive Tim commented,

'What an extraordinary looking building with that great tower and that wide conservatory round it — it looks like some enormous umbrella upside down. Ah, this must be your Honourable Beatrice Croker. I look forward to meeting her.'

He brought the Volvo to a stop and they all got out and walked to meet Batsy who was coming round from the back of the castle. She wore her breeches and black boots with a fawn woollen blouse and cardigan.

'Forgive my working clobber,' said Batsy, 'How nice of you to come all this way. You must be Nell, lovely to meet you and of course Tim.' After the introductions were over she suggested they come round to the back to meet Sean and his wife, who had taken the brunt of the assault on Place. Tim asked several questions about the castle and its history; Batsy filling him in with facts. The first Croker had received a grant from Elizabeth the First and it was he who adapted the remains of an earlier Norman castle, giving the building the unusual hexagonal plan that it had today. Basically, the tall central tower dated from this time. The additions Batsy had made were principally the wide verandah conservatory and a heightening and embellishing of the tower. The conservatory was modelled on an idea of Sir Joseph Paxton's. She had also added the tall curtain walls at the back and had the great doors specially made.

Sean and his wife retold their versions of what had happened, and Ann described the people who had tied her up. Tim and Nell broke in almost together,

'We know who the culprits are. Certainly one of them — there cannot be two women around with dark red hair and wall-eyes, one blue and one brown!'

'Yes, Herta Poll,' said René, 'I caught a glimpse of her at the great sale fiasco.'

'Ann's description also fits Percival Mangon. Someone whom I wouldn't think is too popular in this part of Clare after his outrageous handling of Mellick,' exclaimed Nell.

Batsy led them from the kitchen across the hall and into the drawing-room. As they entered, Nell gave a little gasp of pleasure:

'Tim, look at that. I have never seen a more lovely painting of roses and it can only be by Fantin Latour. It is superb.'

The contents of the room fascinated the Sinclairs: the collection of porcelain with first-rank specimens of Sèvres, Worcester, and Nymphenburg; a small cabinet of miniatures; the fine Waterford chandelier; and numerous other notable pieces.

Tim asked Batsy about security out here in the deep country. She replied:

'I have got what I think is a unique protective system and it is one that I have only shown to a very select circle. Aideen and René have often been impressed by it but I know there seems to have been a let-down the other day. Would you like a demonstration? Perhaps, Tim, you wouldn't mind acting as the intruder? Aideen, would you be a dear and take them out through the kitchen again and wait for me by the garage.'

Five minutes later and Batsy rejoined them outside:

'Now Tim, don't worry, there is nothing that will harm you. I want you to walk casually round to the front of the castle, go up the steps and gently turn the handle of the front door into the conservatory. It is not locked and you will find that it will open easily. Then, put just one foot across the threshold and stop. Keep calm. I shall be not very far behind you.'

Tim, somewhat cautiously after these instructions, walked round to the front and mounted the three steps. He paused and looked at the door with the coat of arms and also through the glass into the conservatory. It all looked so innocent — large pots of ferns, cacti, a few orchids and thick green creepers festooning the ceiling and down the glazed walls.

Gingerly he took hold of the door handle and slowly turned it — the door swung open without a sound, and as instructed he put one foot across the threshold.

Tim, like an earlier visitor a few days ago, was not in the least prepared for what happened next.

From out of the massed foliage, seemingly to his right, a deep bass voice called out:

'Might I have your name please?'

Ten seconds afterwards a soprano voice stridently demanded:

'Yes. May we have your name?'

A further short silence and a third voice, this time a high-pitched Irish tenor, called out from apparently right over his head:

'Yvan...Yvan!' Almost at once a high-powered spotlight came on illuminating the inner front door which was open. Tim could hear a scratchy scrabbling noise from inside the hall and then the inner doorway was almost filled by a truly horrific image — some great hound, showing all its teeth, snarling and wearing what looked like medieval armour.

At this point Batsy came up behind and pushed past:

'Good boy Yvan. Good boy. It's only mother with friends. come here...there's a good Yvan. Give your paw...there, give paw.' Tim found himself shaking hands with this monster who had switched from some hell-hound to a rather lovable pet. After introductions had been made Yvan stood waiting expectantly.

'I know what Yvan wants,' said Batsy, 'Aideen, be a dear, his biscuit tin is on the sideboard in the dining-room. Could you get two of his favourite digestives. Yes Yvan — they are just coming.'

When Aideen returned, Batsy told her to give the biscuits to Tim and Nell who then somewhat timidly held them out to Yvan. The great dog approached and took them one after the other with a quite amazing display of gentleness; he then waited whilst Batsy removed his armour and the vicious looking spiked collar. When free he walked over to the corner, slumped on the floor and enjoyed the remainder of his digestive biscuits.

'Now you must meet the rest of the security force,' said Batsy. 'Can you get the stand René, it is just over there behind the fuchsias.'

René carried over the heavy metal object and set it down in front of them. It had a round base, a single upright and a cross piece about three feet long.

Batsy made sure it was standing firm, then she looked upwards and called:

'Come on my darlings . . . come down to mother. Come Clovis and Clotilde, and you Gregory. Come on, we're all friends down here...Come on my beauties.' From up in the creepers there was much bustling around, then three beautiful birds flapped down and landed on their perch. Two of them were large Hyacinth Macaws and had the most gorgeous rich blue plumage with bright yellow rings round their eyes and edges of yellow below the lower part of their savage looking beaks. Batsy had had the pair of them of a number of years and they were devoted to her. Currently such beauties are on the endangered list; only in exceptional circumstances can they be procured and their value stands at about £14,000 a pair.

Clovis and Clotilde enjoyed the whole length of the conservatory, as did the other smaller bird who suddenly felt he wasn't getting enough attention and piped up,

'I'm Gregory . . . I'm Gregory I am.' simulating a high tenor voice.

'Dear Gregory,' said Batsy, 'I think he picked up that voice when I had a young student tenor staying here during his vacation. Gregory is rather a dear and he come from Indonesia. The light effect come on, by the way, when Yvan moves towards the door and steps on a mat which has a pressure switch underneath that also switches it off after about ten minutes. Now I think we could all do with a spot of lunch. 'Fraid it's only cold.' As she led them into the hall they were followed by cries of,

'Don't forget Gregory . . . what about Gregory.'

The two Hyacinth macaws maintained a dignified silence.

Just as they were finishing their lunch a phone call came through from Con Murphy who asked if they had had any further news. Somewhat puzzled, Batsy replied that nothing else had happened if that was what he meant. But she remembered to tell him that the description Sean's wife had given of the two raiders had been enough for two friends who had just arrived from Paris to definitely identify the woman as Herta Poll and almost certainly the man as Percival Mangon.

'That's great,' exclaimed Con Murphy, 'Herta Poll is in the international wanted lists, in fact she has been there for some time. The Yard should be able to help me with something on Mangon. I think I can say that we've got them tied up somewhere in Clare. If it's a comfort to you, Miss Croker, I have eighty men and thirty-two cars working on this one.'

As the party from Quin Cottage was preparing to leave after lunch, Tim queried Batsy:

'That's certainly a fine bit of security you have for the front. But what about the rear entrance?'

Batsy appeared surprised,

'But the back quarters are in charge of Sean and his wife — they've been with me and the family for upwards of thirty-three years.' Then, with a splendid piece of logic she added,

'Tim dear, one would hardly expect callers to go round to the back door, over here it would always be the front door.' With that they said farewell for the moment and left the Croker circus in peace.

As they passed through Tulla on the way back to Quin Cottage Tim suddenly found his concentration broken by a quite extraordinary spectacle in a car-park beside a small hotel. There was a group of what appeared to be tall straw-covered objects that were highly animated. He slowed the Volvo so that they could get a good look.

'Aideen, what on earth is all that?' asked Nell.

'They're getting into a coach, what is it — a carnival?'

'No, nothing like that at all,' replied Aideen. 'It's a reminder of a real piece of old Irish folklore. They are the Clare Strawboys. It's all mixed up with beliefs and customs around marriage ceremonies. Spring and autumn are the best seasons to see them: the Easter brides, and at this time of year you have the odd goings-on in Lisdoonvarna up just to the north of Moher. Round about now the farmers have got the harvest in and the single farm lads about the middle of September make their way up to the little spa town on the look out for a bride. The festivities can go on for days and are not entirely frowned on by the church as I believe some honest wedlocks do come out of it.'

'And what are the "strawboys" then?' enquired Nell.

'The strawboys are something special, they turn up at wedding festivities and have a turn round the dance floor with the bride. The strange get up is so that they won't be recognised. What you see on their heads is a tall headgear almost like a small sheaf of straw with a couple of rough eyeholes. Straw is tied around their arms and legs; they tie a rough cape round their shoulders and chests with "sugans", which is Irish for "rope made of straw"; and finish off with more straw round their waists. They turn up in several places. Up in County Mayo, down in Clare. There are various centres that are well known for producing parties of Strawboys; over to the west there is Quilty and Milltown Malbay, up in the north there is Doolin. Our very own Neptune Blood, who you haven't met yet, was one of the greatest Strawboys in the district and he nearly always gets caught up in any sport that's going on. Lisdoovarna time really brings them out in large numbers and you could possibly have a dozen parties of twenty or more roaming around looking for a bit of excitement. There we are,' Aideen concluded, 'lecture on folklore now finished.'

* * * * * *

The hours had passed slowly and unpleasantly since Herta had drawn a gun on Myles. He had eyed her with a feeling that was only just short of terror. The Austrian vacillated from moods of silent dark threatening depression, through moments of cruel suggestion to laughter and pleasantries and sincere confidential talk. Myles was certain Herta was going, if not already gone, mad. During the early morning hours of the night he had hoped she might succumb to sleep. Whether she dozed or not he hadn't been sure but every time he stirred she shot up fully alert as some jungle predator. In the end he himself had fallen into a dreamless sleep. When he awoke it was nearly nine o'clock on the morning of the 12th. They had pulled off the road near Donegal Point the evening before. Nervously he had opened his eyes — the seat next to him was empty. Herta had gone. Shrugging himself fully awake he silently opened the door of the van and stepped out. No, Herta hadn't gone, she was some thirty yards away standing on a small hillock and looking out to sea. Quiet as Myles thought he had been, she had heard him and turned.

'Myles, come up here,' she called, 'I see something I don't like.'

Myles Fyrken walked up to where she stood.

'What is it?' he asked.

'Look there . . . do you see,' she pointed towards the south-west.

'Yes . . . what is it?' said Myles.

'I am not certain . . . if only I had some glasses . . . but I can make out that it is grey. It has some look of a small naval ship and it is going very slowly and is sailing in very close. It tells me it is trying to hide from anyone who might be on the lookout further up from here perhaps Quilty where we are going to take a boat form. You know what, Myles my friend . . . yes, my friend they are trying to trap us. That will be a patrol ship. If we sail out of Quilty and round that island, what is it, Mutton Island, they would have us . . . but they won't . . . because we shall work out other things. Ja. Ja. Now Myles, this is the time for forgetting. We shall survive and with the others too.'

Myles, quite mesmerized by this strange creature of a woman, went back to the van in her wake. They got in and slowly drove over to Quilty. Here they now waited for the arrival of Percival Mangon and Alfie Brigg. The time was drifting towards six o'clock before the other two vans arrived and stopped at one end of the quay. Myles had seen them coming and started up and slowly drove towards where they were parked. The four fugitives were beginning to look just a little shabby after the hours of driving and a night in the rough. Percy was optimistic, he had seen only three police cars and none of them had taken any notice of him; they had all been in the south-east part of the county. Alfie had actually been stopped on some trumped up excuse about checking tyres and lights. His van had been given a good looking over but the whole business had only taken ten minutes. He had seen at least nine police cars scattered about the north eastern corner of Clare. Herta reported with regard to the situation of hiring the boat in Quilty. That would be simple. What was not simple was the fact that there was a grey naval looking patrol boat skulking around on the other side of Mutton Island.

They all decided that a good hot meal would help matters and perhaps the chance of a wash and brush up. They decided to take the risk with a small establishment, the staff of which had either not read the papers or heard the news, as no special attention was paid to them. While the others were finishing, Herta went out for a breath of fresh air. She paused by the van she was travelling in and took out one of the gallon tins of turps substitute, emptied it into the gutter, and went down to a garage that was still open to have the can filled with petrol. On her way back to the van she picked up three empty milk bottles from a waste-bin. The can and bottles she put in the van she had been travelling in and went to meet the others who were returning. They were all surprised by an odd gathering that was assembling further along the quay, a group of about twenty men who were dressed up to be what looked like bundles of straw. Before they left it was decided that Mangon and Myles should switch vans and Herta would go with Percy. Their thoughts were centred on that grey boat sideling along close to the shore. A look at a map showed there was only one alternative and that was too risky; it would be to the east and then round the top end of Derg and try to make it down to Dingle.

*   *   *   *   *   *

In the control room at the county station, information was coming along quite well. Chief Superintendent Murphy had placed his pieces on the board with some considerable skill. By sightings of two of the vans with Brigg and Mangon, who had both been recognized, it was fairly clear that the villains were not going to try and make a break in the Limerick or Killaloe directions. There was another source of information and that was the grapevine of the Clare Strawboys who were very much on the move around the county as harvest home and Lisdoonvarna time came up. It could be reckoned that there might be at least a dozen groups working their way towards where the wedding parties might be. They were not really concerned with the criminal chase. Or rather they hadn't been until the morning of the 12th when a certain elder and well-loved old Strawboy called a casual meeting at Inagh. Neptune Blood was asking if the group leaders could perhaps spare a little bit of time on the way to their planned festivities in Lisdoonvarna. He said it could well be a bit of sport and would pay off some injustices done. The lads took to the idea and Neptune gave them detailed instructions with regard to timing and exactly where they should gather. He told them it would be very helpful if they could pass any bits of news back to Con Murphy whom they mostly knew pretty well. Thus an officer of the Garda station had just received a confirmation that the solicitor Fyrken, two Englishmen and an odd wall-eyed girl were in Quilty with their vans and that they had had a meal of steak, onions, fried potatoes, apple tart and custard, after which they had had a wash and brush up and had gone back to the vans. Now, Fyrken was driving one, the wall-eyed girl was in another with one English man and the other Englishman was driving the third van. The van with the girl was leading and all three of them at about two hundred yard intervals were heading up the coastal road towards Milltown Malbay.

Con Murphy was delighted by this well observed report. It meant that he could now tighten up the noose and release the officers from the east and south sides of Clare and bring them to make a concentrated wall round Liscannor Bay and South Sound areas. The villains must have spotted the patrol boat. No matter, it would be simpler to take them on land.

*   *   *   *   *   *

Later that night, Mangon and company had drawn off the N67 down a small lane that seemed only to lead to a disused quarry.

The four members of the party crammed in the back of Alfie's van and were holding an emergency meeting.

'I don't think the boat idea was all that smart, Myles,' said Percy, 'It would have been one devil of a trip from Quilty round to Dingle anyway without being chased around by some blooming patrol boat. We're now crammed over here and we seem to be running out of roads.'

'It's a right mess-up,' grunted Alfie. 'We ought to have worked things out better. With three vans we could have rammed our way through one of their blocks.'

Myles Fyrken had got the map out.

'I can see where there could be another chance. Look here, we follow the coast road through Lahinch and Liscannor. Then there are two things we can do. Doolin is a little fishing village — might be possible to get a boat there and nip across Galway Bay to Spiddal, it's not all that many miles. Or something else; if we follow the N6 and can get through to Lisdoonvarna, which will be packed solid at the moment with all this matrimonial business — you know what, it's on the cards we could get lost in the crowds. What's more there are going to be a lot of farmers' vans and lorries parked around the place. If we can find a cattle lorry, that could be fine. We fill the back with bundles of straw and tarpaulins, have Alfie up front driving and I reckon we could stand a bit of a chance.' The others nodded, tension on their faces, and then Mangon and Herta returned to their van.

'It is bad that things have come to this,' complained Herta. 'Think of the plans that we had, Percival. It could have been so good, so good.'

'We have a bare chance perhaps, I don't know,' replied Percy.

'Ah...Ah...Ah,'cried Herta, 'You call this a chance. We have millions of pounds worth of painting behind us and...I don't know. Sometimes I lose faith in Herta. She is not so clever. Percival, do you recall our breakfast together in that good hotel, the morning of what should have been our greatest day?' She paused and pulled something from her handbag.

'Please, find for me some forgivingness that I am so unkind to you.' Herta leant across and put the edelweiss pin into Percival's tie.

'Please, please, take it back.'

Percy didn't know quite what she would expect him to say. He took her hand which was unexpectedly warm and soft. Holding tightly he raised it to his lips:

'Thank you, Herta. I don't know what tomorrow will bring . . . but Herta, we must meet again. . .we could still do something big together.'

'Percival, I think I see you now as one of them. . .Sir Percival riding out in the morning to do battle. Sir Percival, be my knight.' Herta closed her eyes. 'Yes, tomorrow will be a day in which deeds will be done that will become legends. You and I, my darling, will be brave tomorrow. Promise me, Sir Percival that we shall stand together and see the others fall. My darling Percival. . .' Herta twisted herself round so that she fell sideways across Percy — her arms were round his neck and before he could resist she was kissing him with all the fire and strength that her strange soul could give. Percy was at first too terrified and then suddenly her mood got through to him and he returned in full Herta's strange force. He almost himself felt he was one of those great knights of old.

*   *   *   *   *   *

Back in Quin Cottage they were all at a meeting with Neptune Blood holding the floor. With what he had learned from the leaders of the Strawboys and odd bits of talk around the place Neptune had it all planned.

'Miss Aideen,' he began, 'I know just where we're going to take them . . .your favourite . . .Moher. You know the roads round there better than I do. Mangon and the rest of them have been seen in Quilty. Con Murphy's lads will have every road there by this time blocked off just leaving them the choice of going up the road through Liscannor or sitting where they are; after that it is along past St Brigid's Holy Well and then the entrance to the car-park for the Cliffs of Moher. What I have arranged with the Strawboys is that that will be it. In other words, they will be blocking off the road just round one of the bends. I don't know just how many of the lads are coming along, but you may well be surprised; especially the lady and gentleman from France. I've a score to settle with that Mangon man . . .he shouldn't have done what he did to the Uniackes. No! And he shouldn't have said what he did about Katty. Tomorrow he is going to pay what he owes to Neptune Blood.'

'Do we have any idea that they still may have the Dürer with them?' said Nell.

'Well, not in a manner of direct looking, so to speak Ma'am. But I have a sense that it will be there. What do you say, Mother, is it with them?'

Katty Blood looked around the little group:

'How many of you is believers? Out here in Clare the powers are still ours — many have thrown them away. Don't smile, my lady and gentleman; out here the sight is still a thing. I know it. Neptune my little lad knows it and so does Miss Aideen.' Katty stood still and closed her eyes and took a very deep breath:

'It will be there. For sure is it not in the arms of Mary herself . . . I'll be saying goodnight to you all,' and she left the room and walked across the hall and out into the gathered night.

'You know what,' said Aideen, 'it could be a lovely fine day tomorrow and why don't we have a picnic over at Moher . . . a special picnic. Mary, will you help with it? Now, how are we all going to get there? I propose René and I go with Tim and Nell in their Volvo and take some sandwiches. We should arrive around ten thirty. I think you said someone was picking you up, Neptune. So Mary, can you bring the picnic and all the bits and pieces over in my Peugeot and don't forget Katty else she'd never let you rest. Please ask you mother if she would mind holding the fort for us all. I'll give Batsy Croker a ring later; there's no way that she should be left out.'

*   *   *   *   *   *

Down in Ennis, Chief Superintendent Con Murphy was just giving his last instructions. The concentration of Garda cars was by now so great that there was no chance that the rabbits would be able to break through and run for it. The order of the day was to centre in on the road that led past the Cliffs of Moher. Another contingency was to be covered; Con gave the order for three Ban Gardaí to accompany the main detachment from Ennis — good strong girls they should be. For the outlying Garda cars, the plan was that they should squeeze the Mangon party but at the same time take care that no escape roads were left uncovered. This last stage was going to start with an all-night vigil — one officer at a time in each car to take a bit of sleep. Crisis time, as Con Murphy liked to call it, would be between midday and two o'clock the next day, September 13th. He made sure that the canteen was working on bag rations and thermoses of coffee for all concerned — no mean request, as this was one of the largest operations Clare had witnessed for some time. Chief Superintendent Con Murphy was quite determined about one crucial point — if Albrecht Dürer's painting was still with that bunch it was not going to leave Clare other than under the orders of the rightful owner.

Finally he turned to his second-in-command and the assembled sergeants and special duty men and Sergeant Bridget Kelly of the Ban Gardaí,

'I'll be seeing you all out at Moher and by this time tomorrow we'll be looking for a good night's sleep.'

There was one other detail; as far as possible he wanted the press and TV people out of the way if only for their own safety. He could not be certain how those characters would react when cornered. Likely access roads to the Moher area would have to be closed from eleven in the morning.

* * * * * *

For Neptune this was going to be a great old day. Some of the lads had picked him up around eight and by nine thirty the Strawboys of Clare were all in the positions they had worked out. Maybe it was going to be a bit of a wait, but the sun was warm on the back and not a sign of a promise of rain in the sky at all. As Neptune surveyed the turn out, he turned to Peter O'Dea from Corrofin saying,

'By all that's good Peter, when they see the likes of this lot coming for them they'll be thinking the harvest fields themselves are after them!'

* * * * *

Percy Mangon had roused himself from a muddled and broken sleep at just after seven. Beside him Herta was sitting upright and alert.

'It is good that you wake,' she said, 'Now, Percival we must treat all this with the stern manner of soldiers — there must be no fear — if one is taken we do not pause. Percival, you wear my emblem — do not tarnish it.'

Percy saw that the chameleon Herta had changed again. 'I'll go and see the others,' he replied and getting out walked back along the lane to where Myles and Brigg had parked. Alfie had had the sense the previous evening to scrounge a couple of bottles of cold tea and some beef sandwiches off the cook where they had had the meal in Quilty. It was not a great way to start a day but much better than nothing.

'So we go for the cliff road and then through to Lisdoon-varna — we forget about the Doolin idea,' said Myles.

While Percy was down with the others Herta had been pre-paring for an emergency. From the back of the van she had taken the can of petrol, the milk bottles, old rags and cotton waste and put them behind Mangon's seat. She now had the makings of a deterrent for unwelcome followers if they came too close. Herta was back in her seat when Percy arrived with her share of the breakfast.

'We've decided to stay here for a while — they could be ex-pecting us to make a run for it as early as possible. If we don't move until around eleven it might throw them a bit,' said Percy.

'Ja...Ja, good thoughts,' exclaimed Herta. 'My, how can you drink this cold tea stuff...but we must have liquid. If we thirst we shall be tired — so I drink.'

* * * * * *

It really was a beautiful day, the sun giving an unexpected heat for September. The landscape was rising to the occasion. The turf had the life in it, the yellow-green hart's tongue ferns licking the air as they uncurled towards the warmth. The birds' songs almost had the sound of spring. Two late-born leverets were out there dancing and leaping without a care for tomorrow.

* * * * * *

Shortly after eleven Mangon led the little convoy back on to the road for Lahinch — travelling at a leisurely speed and about fifty yards apart the vans passed through Lahinch and turning left after O'Brien's Bridge made their way through Liscannor. Every-thing was at peace — the old fellas sat on the window-sills chat-ting the day away, the women shopping, talking or just standing with the latest babe slung in their arms. But there was something

missing — Alfie Brigg, more animal alert than the others, picked
it up. There was just no sign at all of the law. Alfie's intuition told
him that the place must be alive with Gardaí. He could feel their
eyes reaching out to him and the others. They drove on past the
O'Brien Monument and St Brigid's Well, and the tension grew.
Brigg wanted to stop and get out and shout at the unseen ones,
'come and get us now, what are you waiting for?'

Mangon's van was coming abreast of the turn off for the
Moher car-park and he slowed slightly for a gentle curve to the
right. At this moment 'Crisis Time' as Con Murphy called it,
struck. There was one great big bang and a cloud of grey smoke
burst out ahead of the scoundrels. Showers of rocks and turf
were flying through the air and clattering down on the roof of
the van, one particularly large chunk smashing the windscreen.
Percy jammed on the brakes and the van skidded to a halt at an
angle across the road.

Before he could get out, the van was surrounded by a seething
mass of weird animated sheaves and bundles of straw. They were
everywhere. Behind, on the road, the other two vans had also
been encircled. Even the stolid Alfie Brigg would remember this
day for years to come. In a darkened room at night he would see
the vision of running, yelling straw-covered figures — what
seemed like whole fields rising and racing towards him with an
evil intent which he could only guess at.

Neptune wrenched the van door open and seized Mangon,
pulling him out and away into the centre of a crowd of Strawboys that were moving off the road and up the hill in the general
direction of O'Brien's Tower which stands near the cliff edge at
the highest point of Moher, seven hundred feet sheer up from
the ever-breaking waves below.

Now the wailing sirens of Con Murphy's cars could be heard.
There was no way out. A loud hailer clicked into action:

'Could you make a way there . . . make way.' The Gardaí had
arrived in considerable force.

Up on the green turf on the cliff top to the left of O'Brien's
Tower, Aideen, René, Tim and Nell sat on a rug. A select audience for a show, the likes of which certainly Tim and Nell had
never seen in their lives before. Standing behind them was the
Honourable Beatrice Croker cheering on the forces of both the
law and the Strawboys so loudly that the seabirds responded
with ever increasing screams and calls as they dived and zoomed.

Brigg and Myles Fyrken weighed up the opposition and then just held out their wrists for the handcuffs. They were led away to a couple of Garda cars where they were kept safe under the eyes of four officers.

Herta still sat in the van. The crowd of Strawboys had withdrawn. She looked in the wing mirror and and saw a group of Gardaí slowly approaching about forty yards down the road. Her moment was coming. Her visions returned. Her Sir Percival must have perished, torn to pieces by the rabble. She turned and removed the top of the can and splashed the petrol over the bundles of wood palings.

Now she got out and stood defiant, her wall-eyes spitting fury at the group of Gardaí which stopped and eyed her uncertainly. She heard a voice shout out,

'It's over to you, Sergeant Kelly.' The front rank of the Gardaí opened out and from behind them came the three Ban Gardaí. Aideen in her excitement had broken away from her friends and had run down to where the mass of the Gardaí were standing in hushed silence as they waited for what might happen next. She felt impelled forward, shouldering her way past the officers.

Herta, sighting the Ban Gardaí, yelled,

'Ah … Ah … Ah … The men have no stomach for it then…. So send in the women.'

The three Ban Gardaí began slowly to advance towards Herta.

'Oh no … Oh no you don't … You stop. I told you no further.'

The loud hailer came on again,

'In your own time Sergeant Kelly, don't rush, we've got all day.'

Bridget Kelly was one of those not short on courage. She spoke to her two companions and told them to hold back a step or two. She looked again into those strange eyes and took another step forward.

Herta's reaction was immediate. She drew her pistol and held it trained right on Sergeant Kelly.

'For the last time, you stop,' cried Herta.

The Sergeant did pause, facing Herta square on.

'It is mine … do you hear Beatrice Croker, it is mine. Your ancestors stole from my Empress. You had had no right for the painting to hang in your castle!' Bridget Kelly was inching forward again.

'Stop! Stop! Do you hear me,' Herta's face was streaming with perspiration, shining under the bright sun. Her lips were drawn back from her teeth as she snarled with the savagery of some jungle beast. She pulled the trigger and Bridget Kelly dropped to the ground with blood spurting from an ugly wound in her right thigh. For a few seconds, as the crack of the Biretta echoed away over the cliffs, everyone stood still, and then came the action. Figures were moving speedily, another shot came, but this time no one fell. As the maddened Austrian started to line up on a fresh target, something shining-bright flashed towards her and the gun dropped from her hand as a knife sank almost hilt-deep into the muscle of her shoulder.

Herta let out a frightful scream, a violent protest of hate, defiance and a challenge to her persecutor to come forward and finish what she had begun.

'You think you are going to have my Dürer, my dear Dürer,' Fraulein Poll was spurring herself onto be worthy of a place with those mystic heroes. Already the pain of the blade was drawing her over to one side:

'You shall not...have it ...it shall go with me.'

With her good arm she managed to take a box of matches from a pocket. Somehow she got the box open and pulled out a bundle of matches. Then unable to hold the box with her other hand she put it between her teeth and rasped the matches across the striking surface. They flared. She took a pace backwards and flung them into the van. Instantly flames roared out.

Above the sound of the inferno Herta's voice could be heard once more:

'Come, come down, strike fire with me! Take me away, Odin's beautiful Valkyries, to my place in Valhalla.'

The wounded figure appeared to shrink and wither as the spirit of Herta Poll for the moment deserted her. The two Ban Gardaí picked up the Austrian and carried her down to the cars. Others were ahead helping Bridget Kelly.

Up by O'Brien's Tower another fragment of the happening was being brought to a climax.

A large group of the Strawboys were tight-packed together and in the centre could be made out one extra tall figure who was being carried shoulder high. It was, it had to be Neptune, for tucked under his chin was a fiddle. The shouting and yelling quietened down as every eye looked up.

Even Con Murphy stood still. What were the crazy fools going to do next? Neptune began to play a wild piece that carried down to the onlookers. The tempo increased and as it did the group of Strawboys opened out and four of them carrying what looked like a body stepped to the edge of Moher and swinging it back and forth three times, let it go and the form, spinning slowly at first, began the long, long, drop.

Con Murphy was horrified, he called to his men to follow him and charged up the path to O'Brien's Tower.

As he reached the Strawboys, he forced his way to where Neptune was still held shoulder high and pulled him to the ground.

'Sergeant, get the bracelets on him. You murderous pagan.'

'What do you mean, Mr. Murphy?' said Neptune as he pulled off his straw mask. 'Who's a murderer?'

'You are, didn't I see it with my own eyes,' cried Con Murphy.

'Did you think we was throwing a body over Moher?' asked Neptune.

'Don't you try to talk your way out of this, Neptune Blood.'

'Con Murphy, on the honour of my own Saint, that was no body . . . it was an Effigee . . . yes an Effigee.' To back up his words the Strawboys pulled a dishevelled figure from their midst. Mr. Percival Mangon standing there in his shirt-tails and Y-Fronts. His best suit had gone over the cliff stuffed with straw. Two Gardaí moved up to him, clamped on the handcuffs and led him away — a miserable and finished figure if ever there was one.

*   *   *   *   *   *

It took several hours for the area to be cleared up and to come back to normal. An ambulance had been radioed for and had taken away the casualties. Garda cars had driven off with Mangon, Myles and Brigg. There had been one small pause as Brigg got into the car. Alfie had turned to the sergeant who was in charge of him and said,

'You know something, the silly cow didn't burn the painting. I switched the loads on her. It is in the van I was driving. Don't forget that. I saved the ruddy Dürer.'

René and Tim opened the back of the van and carefully eased out the bundle of palings. The lashings were removed and there safe and snug inside was something that certainly looked like a panel painting well wrapped up. A small crowd gathered as the wrappings were removed and there was the long forgotten masterpiece by Albrecht Dürer. Batsy wept quite openly, Tim and the others clapped their hands with joy.

Soon there were few left on the scene: Aideen, René, Tim, Nell, Batsy, Neptune and Con Murphy. Aideen looked at her watch,

'Do you know what the time is? Coming up to six and I am famished. Chief Superintendent Con Murphy, will you give us the pleasure of your company at a picnic? I think you've earned it.'

Con looked at her with a kindness in his eyes and replied,

'Aideen Uniacke, I will.'

The little party walked up the slope to where Aideen and friends had been sitting. Up there was a great sight. Mary Dancy and Katty Blood had arrived with the picnic. They had borrowed a trestle-table and benches which they had put on a roof-rack on Aideen's Peugeot and were at that moment putting the finishing touches to a spread, that, out here on Moher, seemed truly magnificent: marinated trout in wine, a large round of spiced beef, a bowl of fresh salad, buttermilk scones, Katty's bog cheese and chocolate cake. They had even brought out a pressure stove and Mary had the biggest teapot from Quin ready to pour.

They insisted that Aideen should be at the head of the table. As she sat down she saw beside her place something wrapped in a piece of newspaper. Curiosity made her open it. Inside was her knife, now clean and shining again and wrapped round it a single sheet of paper that might have come from a Ban Garda's notebook; it just said 'thank you'. Aideen raised her eyes and looked round at her friends but not one of them caught her gaze.

Neptune got up from his seat and came to Aideen and gave her something he said he had picked up. It was the edelweiss pin that Herta had given Percy.

'I think you should have this, Miss Aideen.'

For a moment Aideen paused, and then whispered:

'No, Neptune — please give it to Katty when you both get home.'

René rose,

'Just a moment before we start . . . Come with me, Neptune.' Together they went down to Tim's Volvo where the Dürer had been put. They lifted it out and carried it back up to where the picnickers waited. The sun was already getting well down in the west and was becoming slightly dimmed by a couple of dark clouds. René and Neptune leant the painting against an outcrop of rock where the last of the light would catch it. Dürer had, at his best, something almost magical with the way his brushes could put down not just a physical likeness but could capture the very spirit of his model. In this panel he had indeed brought into being something of the wonder that he must have felt when he painted it and which had been retained in this pure beautiful image of the 'Virgin in Majesty' through the centuries.

Out there at Moher was a picnic but there was never one with such a backcloth before or since.

As the contents of the dishes shrank, the light from the west suddenly began to grow brighter, Katty was the first to notice it. The two clouds were drawing apart and when they were well back the sun came through with a glorious brilliance — the golden light brightening a path across the sea until it fell full and splendid on the Virgin, lighting her face with what could only be seen as a heavenly radiance.

Katty rose and walked over to the picture and for a moment stood still. Then she dropped to her knees . . .

Glossary of Terms associated with Fine Art and Antiques.

Appliqué: With needlework it describes the laying on of figures cut from fabrics and either sewn or glued in place. It can also be used to describe lacquer designs applied to metal.

Arita Ware: Japanese porcelain made in the Huzen district from the early years of the 17th century. It was exported from Imari and so took the name of Imari or Imari-Yaki. Yaki is the Japanese for ware.

Art Assessor: One who will give valuations and who is often found working as a freelance — the term is used more commonly in the United States of America.

Assay Office: A place where in metallurgy, and with gold and silver in particular, the amount of the precious metals in objects or samples can be determined.

Atelier: Studio or workshop of an artist or craftsman.

Axminster: Carpets produced in a factory founded by Thomas Witty. They were hand-knotted on the Turkish pattern in the Court House at Axminster in about 1755. The factory closed in 1835 and the looms were taken to Wilton where production continued.

Bell-boys : A term close in meaning to 'knockers' (see below).

Block Front: A type of front, as with some American chest of drawers or with secrétaires, characterised by a sunken central panel flanked on either side by a raised panel or block. The idea was probably developed by John Goddard of Rhode Island, USA, about 1770.

Bole: A red earth, coloured by oxides, used in preparing an area for gilding. It is painted over the hardened gesso to give a rich ground for the fragile gold-leaf.

Bombé: Forms in furniture which appear puffed-up, blown-out and inflated. Noticeable with the work of the cabinet makers of the time of Louis XV.

Brasses: Ornamental brass plates which in earlier centuries were often let into the floor to mark a burial place. More common usage today is a collective term for small medallions attached for decoration to harness.

Bric-à-brac: An assembly of assorted small objects, curios etc., that are kept because they are ornamental or rare.

Brocade: Rich fabric with a raised design induced during the weaving — generally includes gold and silver threads.

Bulling: Slang term for activities during a sale that can lead to an artificial raising of the price.

Carlton House desk: Large English desk of the latter part of the 18th century. It had a superstructure of small drawers at the back and two sides. Top was panelled with leather; and there would be an adjustable easel rest. Gillows charge book for 1796 mentions it.

Carrickmacross Lace: Earliest examples date from around 1825. There are two types: appliqué, when designs are cut from muslin and, after having had their edges whipped, are sewn to net; and guipure, when the pieces are joined by brides.

Ceramics: (from the Greek *Keramikos*) It is a general term for the study of the art of pottery; in its widest sense it includes all objects fashioned from clay and then hardened by fire.

Cerulean: A compound of cobalt and tin oxides; a light blue with a slight greenish tinge. It was discovered as early as 1805 and was introduced as a pigment by George Rowney about 1870.

Champlevé: A process used by early enamelists in producing plates for the foundation of the work. It consisted of cutting down the copper so that the outline of the ornament formed a band between the enamel colours and it resulted in the plate being hollowed out for their reception.

Châtelaine: Ornamental hook, clasp or pin worn at a woman's waist; to which could be attached various objects such as keys, purse, watch and other trinkets by small chains.

Chippendale, Thomas: (1718–79) Born in Worcestershire the son of a cabinet-maker. He drew inspiration for the Louis XV period and from various aspects of Chinese and Gothic work.

Cloisonné: An enamelling process that dates back at least to the Byzantine period of the 6th century. Small fences of metal, sometimes gold and silver, were soldered edgeways on the base; the interstices thus formed were called *cloisons*; these were filled with the vitrified enamel pastes.

Commode: The term generally applied to a chest of drawers designed in the French manner.

Console Table: One in which the top is carried by one or more brackets or consoles. It would be found fixed against a wall with legs at the Front only.

Deruta: Fine painted majolica, both polychrome and lustre. It was made between 1490 and 1550 at the town in Umbria which gives it its name.

Dish Ring: A decorative silver dish-stand, often elaborately worked with piercing and *repoussé*.

Distressors: Those that work over faked or lesser antique objects to give them a false appearance of age and patina.

Drum Table: Circular top table which rests on a tripod base, it can be revolved and has real or mock drawers. It came into fashion in the latter part of the 18th century.

Ébéniste: A worker in fine cabinetmaking, especially concerned with veneering.

Egg Tempera: A method of painting with which the pigments are mixed or ground with pure egg yolk.

Empire: Styles, ornaments, designs or fashions developed during the French Empire (1804–15).

Enamel: Painting technique in which the colours are vitrified on to a metal, glass or pottery surface.

Epée: The slenderest of all sword blades, once a great favourite for duelling.

Epergne: Elaborate centre piece for a dining table, often in branched form with fanciful and romantic designs.

Famille Verte: Variety of Chinese enamelled porcelain of the K'ang Hsi reign (1662-1722) it was decorated with a rich palette of bright green, red, dark purple, yellow and violet.

Feraghan: Persian rug of fine quality with the warp and weft of cotton and the pile of wool.

Follower of: One that honestly or slavishly apes the manner of a master painter, sculptor or craftsman.

Gesso: A mixture of plaster and a water soluble glue that is applied to furniture or panels which are to receive gold leaf.

Gilding: The laying of gold leaf on a surface that has previously been covered with gesso and bole.

Glair: Egg white that is beaten thoroughly with a little water. It is used to lay gold-leaf.

Hallmark: Mark of authenticity that shows that a piece of silver (or gold) was of a required standard when it was assayed. The marks would include the symbol of the assay office, the makers mark, a date and a letter.

Kakiemon: Japanese potter active around 1650, probably the first to enamel Japanese porcelain.

Knocker: Usually applies to one who goes around knocking on front doors and hoping to make an entrance to see if there is anything of value within. One dodge is to make an over-the-odds offer for some object of no great worth which by so doing may impress the owner who will then show more of the contents of the house. The knocker may then buy another item of greater quality, pay for it with cash, and arrange to come back for the first object and pay for it. The second object which has been paid for is probably worth three or four times what was given. The knocker does not return for the first object.

Laid-in: The first tentative strokes of a composition brushed on the canvas or paper by an artist.

Lambrequin: Ornamental drape to hang from a shelf or to hide curtain fittings in the manner of a pelmet.

Malachite: Native carbonate of copper with a bluish-green tint. It is one of the oldest pigments, although not completely permanent.

Marquetry: Laid work, used in the decoration of furniture of many different periods. Materials used include wood of varying types, ivory, mother of pearl, tortoiseshell and metals.

Meissen Ware: Produced at Meissen on the Elbe about twelve miles from Dresden. Experiments for the making of hard paste porcelain were started there by John Bottger about 1706. The manufactory had almost total supremacy from 1710 to 1756.

Morion: Foot-soldiers helmet without a visor and with a turned up edge.

Needle Lace: Lace made using needles instead of bobbins.

NSV: No Sales Value

Ormolu: Gold that has been ground for use as a pigment on bronzes and basses.

Paddles: Objects rather like table tennis bats on which a bidder's number can be fixed and then shown to the auctioneer when a bid is made.

Phantom Bids: A device sometimes used by auctioneers to try to increase the bids. Pretend bids are seemingly accepted from the back wall, a window, a chandelier, etc.

Pie-Crust Table: Small round table often with a tilt-top on a three-legged base. The name arose from the raised and decoratively carved edge to the top.

Pietre Dure: Also known as Florentine mosaic. Precious materials such as lapis lazuli, agate, cornelian etc, and sometimes minute pieces of gold, silver or diamonds employed to build up small panels of miniature mosaic.

Prie-Dieu: A high-backed chair with a low seat used for kneeling to say prayers. In general use from the early medieval period onwards. The name was not used until about 1600.

Provenance: A document which can state the maker, relevant dates, previous owners and other details helpful to the collector. Provenances however, can often have been tampered with or falsified.

Puffing: (see Bulling) A device to up the bidding — in the worst examples a stooge may be employed on a commission basis to force the pace.

Putti: A small boyish cherub figure used for decoration in stone, plaster or woodwork.

Rose madder: A delicate pink colour obtained from the madder root.

Runner: One who may act for antique dealers to bid on certain lots.

Sheraton, Thomas: (1751-1806) English furniture designer born at Stockton-on-Tees.

Thurible: A vessel for perfumes, generally incense.

Triptych: A painting executed on three panels joined together by hinges, often used on an altar.

Wheel-Lock: A gun-lock in which sparks could be struck from a flint, sometimes a fragment of iron pyrites, by a revolving wheel. The name can also be applied to a gun equipped with such a lock.